I0720646

DREAM WALKER

BLOOD LEGACY SERIES BOOK 1

ELISE HENNESSY

Copyright © 2020 by Elise Hennessy

All rights reserved.

No part of this book may be reproduced in any form or by any electronic or mechanical means, including information storage and retrieval systems, without written permission from the author, except for the use of brief quotations in a book review. This book may not be redistributed to others for commercial or noncommercial purposes.

This novel is entirely a work of fiction. The names, characters and incidents portrayed in it are the work of the author's imagination. Any resemblance to actual persons, living or dead, events or localities is entirely coincidental.

Flutterbye Trail Press
797 Sam Bass Road #2541
Round Rock, TX 78681

First edition

Editing by Red Loop Editing
Cover Design by FrostAlexis Arts
E-book Chapter Art by Real Life Design
Published by Flutterbye Trail Press

ISBN: 978-1-7345137-1-4 (E-book)
ISBN: 978-1-7345137-3-8 (Print)
LCCN: 2020907437

Feedback: Encounter a problem with this book? Let us know at
elisehennessyauthor@gmail.com

Books by Elise Hennessy

Books in the Altare World

GRYPHON RIDER ACADEMY
Second Chance
Chosen
Storm Front
Wild Flight

ROYAL SPY INSTITUTE
The Crown Heist
Five & Chance

Also by Elise Hennessy

BLOOD LEGACY SERIES
Dream Walker
The Winter Key
Queen's Return
Court of Illusions
Shadow Dance
Rule the Night
Dhampir's Wish

Blood Curse
Blood Legacy: The Complete Series

Dream Walker

Blood Legacy Series Book 1

Elise Hennessy

Chapter 1
Alex

Alexander Tamerin Rehnquist, vampire coven master and shapeshifter, was used to escaping tight situations with the grace of his favored animal, a lion. But being stuck in a box and stuck as a lion was the most literal "tight situation" he'd ever faced.

His vision swam, ghostly doubles dancing around what he could spy through ragged holes in his box prison. The two goons who'd been tasked with removing him from New York were having a party up in the front seats. They blared heavy metal tunes on the loudest setting to further disorient him, shaking their car with blown-out, struggling speakers. He couldn't see either of them, as they'd unceremoniously stuffed his bleeding body in a shipping box more suitable to transporting grandma's care packages rather than a living, breathing lion shapeshifter who was even larger than the average animal. Then they'd shoved that box into another which had clicked with metal.

They were Haveners, serving Alex's longtime enemy, but they weren't quite so stupid as to rely on tape and cardboard to keep him contained. Instead, whatever contraption they'd put him in was lined with silver barbs, causing wounds that wouldn't heal easily with every bump and jostle of his cage.

At least it had breathing holes. He took labored breaths as he wrestled with his inner beast, a panicking, feral part of him doing its best "beast at bay" impression. *Escape. Escape!* it called.

Such a genius idea, but panicking didn't help him. He didn't know how long he'd been in this vehicle and was loathed to put his eye to one of the holes torn by his barbed cage for fear of an errant jostle. If he angled his head just right...

There! An interstate sign loomed ahead. *Cincinnati Zoo. One mile.*

He was far from home, and his mouth was parchment dry as his body struggled to heal its wounds. A hot flush came over his pelt as someone rapped their knuckles against his cage. "'Ey, you ready for your new home?" an unfamiliar voice crooned, nearly drowned out by the screaming echoing from the speakers.

There was no way he'd hear Alex, but he tried anyway on a dry cough. His voice was little more than a gruff rumble, fighting the utterance of syllables while in animal form. "Ready to kill you for this," he muttered.

He could barely move, so tightly packed in the cage that he felt silver barbs scraping his side with a turn of the vehicle off the interstate. *Escape!* his inner beast repeated. It thought to claw their way to safety in the blind panic of a caged animal.

Alex grunted with frustration. His inner beast wasn't usually so insistent, instead a hum of instinct whispering at the back of his mind. But ever since he'd been poisoned, it was taking more and more control, full of rash thoughts that wouldn't help him escape with his pelt intact. He tried to ignore it as he studied his enemies' plans.

They'd hit him with a dart full of some unknown drug, trapping him in this form, his magic numb. He could no more be a man than a mouse. So, a lion it was.

Next, they were taking him to a zoo far from the rest of his coven to hamper an easy rescue. But he was driven there by two vampires he'd never met before, likely new recruits who were eager to please the leader of Haven, Bryant Collins, and expendable should things go wrong.

"How many bodies do you think it will take?" one of them asked. Alex strained to hear.

"As many as we can find," the other responded as the vehicle came to a shuddering stop. "Who works late at night at a dump like this?"

Bodies? Alex thought, a thrill of horror passing through his fur. There was only one reason for their discussion. What need did they have to kill innocent people except to frame him for the murder?

His inner beast's mood shifted to a deep fear. It lashed and clawed within the confines of his head, helpless to change anything while stuck in this cage. Despite his age and experience, he was trapped perfectly. A mind that knew him well had designed this setup, manipulating events to this devastating moment.

Collins was one of Alex's oldest enemies. After centuries of fighting between their covens, he'd come to one conclusion.

Collins didn't just want to see him die. He wanted him *humiliated*, and thus this plan had to lead there. What would be more humiliating than to die as a beast instead of a man?

The music blessedly went silent as they prepped to leave. "You take him," one of them insisted.

"Hell no, man. You do it."

"I need my hands free."

"So do I!"

Alex rolled his eyes despite himself as they played rock-paper-scissors over the duty. One of them cursed and punched the dash when he lost while the other laughed at his expense.

Next thing he knew, his cage was being hefted with a labored grunt. Even a vampire's preternatural strength would be taxed lifting a shapeshift lion in a metal box, but that meant an extra unpleasant ride as the cage tipped forward. He hissed as a shard of metal pierced cardboard, scoring a bleeding cut over his forehead.

"C'mon," the other goon hissed. His cage jostled as they hustled him into the zoo. At this time of night, he hoped no one was still around. A sick feeling settled in his stomach as he imagined what lengths these two lackeys would go to to impress their ruthless boss.

Chapter 2
Violet

Violet Reynolds took another sip of burnt coffee and wished she were home instead of waiting in the pitch black of night for an evening delivery that was four hours late. And counting. She checked her phone with a sigh, imagining putting her feet up and watching the news rather than listening to a tinny voice reporting from Stephen's antique of a crank radio.

They awaited the arrival of the zoo's newest resident, a male lion to be socialized with the pride of lionesses before he became an attraction for guests to see. The next days would be labor-intensive for Violet and the rest of the team as they made sure the transition went smoothly.

Violet loved her job and the animals she worked with but longed for the long hours to return to normal. Her bosses had capitalized on the passing of their last lion to engage community interest, though. Who better to be the face of their campaign than the youngest zookeeper on the team?

So, Violet was the one recording advertisements in the new enclosure and inviting kids to vote on the new lion's name. He would be Enzi, meaning "powerful" in Swahili. Young and strong, he was part of an animal swap with a neighboring zoo. Even if things went well with a quarantine period and the introduction to the lionesses, his debut was still weeks away.

She turned a weary look Stephen's way. He was in his late fifties and had exhausted tales of his grandchildren about an hour ago. At some point during her introspection, he'd laid the brim of his ball cap over his eyes. Faint snores drifted from him.

Sipping her coffee again, she debated shaking him awake. They were out here together to ensure Enzi was given an initial inspection before retiring him to quarantine for further testing at a reasonable hour. Between them, Stephen was running the show while she was there to observe and document the animal's behavior and temperament. Deciding he needed to be the better rested one, she instead turned the radio toward her and inched up its volume.

"...recovery efforts continue in the wake of the largest geological event of our lifetimes," a firm male voice narrated over the sounds of buildings toppling, the earth shaking, and water rushing.

"Scientists are scrambling to explain the rise of an entire island from the Pacific Ocean. With us today to review the newest footage from this mysterious island is Dr. Collin Peters."

Violet sat up straighter as the other man introduced himself verbally. Her imagination filled with what they watched and discussed. Hailed as the rising of Atlantis, the island had captured the fancy of many while ruining the lives of many more. Its sudden and violent rise from the ocean a couple of weeks ago had triggered earthquakes, tsunamis, and other major disasters around the world.

Lucky to live in a place that was safe, she was full of wonder for what the island was and how it worked. Unfortunately, it seemed there was some electromagnetic interference for equipment. No camera could capture an image of the island without it getting scrambled to static. For those waiting for news of what was going on, visual depictions were reduced to sketches of a grand, kelp-covered palace with spires that stabbed into the sky. Most hints of civilization were reduced to rubble as the land sloped down to a sandy beach.

"...We've gotten our first shipment of stone from this place," the expert, Dr. Peters, was saying. "This is an exciting time for us because the rocks are a complete unknown. It's like we've been handed an ancient secret to explore."

"Would you say it's possible this is Atlantis?" the news anchor asked.

"I would say anything's possible at this point. We are just scratching the surface of this place..."

Violet turned down the radio, spotting flashlights bouncing down the path. As soon as the voices were silenced, complete quiet surrounded her. The hair on the back of her neck lifted as she heard no warble or hoot from the animals further inside the zoo, nor the singing of night insects.

Rubbing the goosebumps prickling up her arms, she turned to nudge Stephen awake. "Wha—huh?" He snorted at the end of a snore, whipping the cap from his face.

"I think they're here," she whispered, wetting her lips and repeating herself when he turned his ear her way. Why was she whispering anyway? Something about the night was too still, too quiet, as if the world held its breath.

Maybe it was the lion scaring the few animals that would call once the sun set. She got to her feet, hoping this wasn't a false alarm as one of the bat handlers, Margaret, stepped into view on the path, holding the flashlight. A second person, one of the cleaning staff, flanked her, his expression curiously blank. They were a motley crew and not needed for this particular task.

"They didn't call ahead?" Stephen asked, looked as confused as she felt.

Following after them was a pair of men wearing all black. One carried a cage nearly as long as he was tall with obvious effort while the other barked orders to the zoo staff.

"This is quarantine, sir," Margaret said, her voice more monotone than Violet had ever heard from her. Usually quite passionate about her little charges, she bore a face as passive as a granite statue's as she gestured toward the building half-hidden in a display of tropical greenery.

Stephen stepped forward, hand outstretched. "You must have our lion. I'm—"

Holding up his own hand, the stranger took a good look at Stephen. "Open the door," he replied in a voice that allowed for no argument. "You, girl. Help him." He barked at Violet, hooking a thumb toward his partner.

Trepidation growing, she walked toward him and inspected the cage. It listed in the back, as if something heavy was weighing it down. "I could get a dolly," she offered.

Her gaze met his, and she forgot the words the moment they were uttered. "Support the backside," he said, and she did, her mind blank of any other thought. Suddenly, supporting this cage was the most important thing she'd ever done. Wrapping her fingers around the underside, she hefted some of its heavy weight.

Together, they walked to quarantine, Stephen unlocking the building. They'd cleared out the pens for now, wanting nothing getting in the way of Enzi the lion's stay being as fast as possible. Violet remembered that as a stab of pain sliced her thumb.

Glancing down, she nearly dropped the end of the cage as she realized the very tip of a hooked lion claw pierced her skin. "Shhh," came from inside as the claw retreated. She noticed the man carrying the cage glance back at her, but it was a fleeting look.

"Let's do this nice and easy," the other man said, pointing to a corner of the first clean pen. "You, kneel there." Though he hadn't specified Margaret, she moved to do as he said.

Under the cadence of his loud voice, another whispered up toward Violet in a rasp of dry sandpaper. "I need your help. Please." Did that come from the cage? She looked to the man holding it, who just watched his partner with a grin.

This isn't right, she said to herself, unable to fight her unease any longer. These two men were hours late and now came to boss them about. But worse than that, they were going along with it instead of questioning how the lion was transported or why these other zoo employees hadn't called ahead for them to prepare a proper welcome.

And now, inexplicably, she was hearing things. "I need you to open the cage," the whisper continued while Stephen was relocated next.

"You can let the cage go," said the man holding it, giving her a pointed look as she stood there, face creased with confusion. He was lowering it to the ground and gesturing for her to stand next to him. As she looked up, their gazes met, and her worries faded as if they flowed away on a stream of consciousness.

Standing there with a dopey expression, she heard but didn't register what the two men talked about. It was like she existed with no thoughts or feelings of her own. "I brought in the cage. You do the rest."

"Gladly. This is the fun part." The man full of orders drew a hunting knife and grabbed Margaret by the hair. He slit her throat, and she died with barely a burble of air or struggle. "Too easy, my man. You sure you don't want some of this?" He laughed, tossing the knife to the man by Violet's side.

"Yeah, I'll take one," he said, turning to inspect Violet for a moment. "Not this one, though. She's too pretty."

The other man gave an impatient wave. "We'll have fun with her later. Boss wants a setup, so we're not done."

As he moved into the pen, another stab of pain jolted Violet with a gasp, this time feeling like a scratch over her ankle. "If you want to live, open the cage," the same voice whispered. But this time, her good sense caught up with her a moment before the reality of her situation did.

These men where murderers—and she was next if she didn't do something. A cry passed from her lips as she fumbled the cage door open, releasing something that knocked its metal edge into her calf. A blur missed her as she stumbled backward.

The blood-soaked dagger quivered from where it was embedded in the cinderblock wall, tossed at her in haste. A true cry of terror rose from her throat, and she crab-walked backward, away from the sounds of struggle and flesh tearing. "Oh my god, oh my god…"

She needed to call the authorities, zoo personnel—anyone. Maybe a stray soul would hear the gunshots erupting from the pen, quickly silenced.

Or maybe they'd simply hear her scream as the largest lion she'd ever seen limped away from the fight. He looked to have three paws already in the grave, pelt ripped in multiple places and flank soaked with blood. Eyeing the container he'd been carried in, she was shocked he'd been compressed in such a small space and still emerged the apparent victor.

"Don't worry," said the lion. "I won't hurt you."

THE MORTAL WOMAN COWERED A FEW FEET AWAY, STARTING to hyperventilate. A thrill of frustration ran through Alex as he imagined how much easier it would be to comfort her if he were a man rather than stuck as his lion form.

She was in the wrong place at the wrong time, but somehow, that'd led to her saving both of their lives. The two Haven goons had been careless, or simply ignorant of the fact that their mental influence only stayed on a human so long as their thrall didn't experience even a prick of physical pain. He'd been lucky, so lucky, to have this person stand so close to his cage. But now, with her panic and disbelief paralyzing her on the spot, it felt like his luck was running out.

Haven never sent a single team in to do their dirty work just in case something like this happened. They had to clear this crime scene fast, he and this mortal, before more goons finished what the first started. "I need your help," he said, slowly and clearly. From a lion's vocal cords, his voice was strangled and dry. He'd forgone every bit of his charm.

"You—you're talking," she stammered.

"I'm not really a lion," he said, taking a step toward her, which she measured in a backward scoot.

"This is impossible. Is this a dream? Am I dreaming?" The scent of fear drifted from her. He imagined there was no way she could possibly process what was happening, but he needed her to try.

"This isn't a dream, unfortunately. If only we both could wake from it." He lifted a paw in his best approximation of a shrug.

She stood shakily. *Progress*, he thought, backing up so he stood at the stairwell. He meant to block her from trying to run away, but this also opened a path for her to see what'd happened in that small enclosure that reeked heavily of shed blood. It did little good for her panic, but he let her see exactly what was there. "Are they all dead?" she asked, sounding like she spoke from numb lips.

"As dead as we'll be if you don't help me," he replied. She turned toward him, her face pale but fists balled at her side. Shock was setting in.

He had three options. He could leave her here to call the mortal authorities and try slipping away on his own, but he was a lion trying to outrun the preternatural senses of vampires in full control of their faculties. Or he could continue trying to convince her to move instead of lingering at this murder scene. By her expression of glassy shock, he figured he would have more luck trying to drive her car by himself.

So that left the third option, a risky one when he was shapeshifted. It was his only real choice to look her in the eye and compel her just as the two Haven goons had. He felt a headache bloom in the back of his head as he met her gaze and expressed a mental command for her to be calm.

Her muscles relaxed, her expression going neutral as she waited for her next command. Compelling mortals was easy work, something even a newly turned vampire could accomplish with ease. It helped them take the blood they needed to survive and erase the memory, thus keeping their race a shadowy secret.

But the effort to keep this woman from panicking was taxing. His lion shapeshift didn't have the same raw influence as he would as a man, so he needed to make this quick and get them both on the right track. "Take me to your car," he ordered.

She moved forward with the intentionality of a robot,

marching out of the blood-soaked room and into the night, where a myriad of animals had resumed calling and crying to one another. Alex would have ordered her to move faster, but his limping prevented them from making haste. It would have to do.

Every moment that passed was a chance for Haven to tighten the net around them. He imagined the two goons would soon fail to check in, signaling to the other crews that something had gone wrong. By the time they arrived at the zoo to finish the deed, he and this woman needed to be long gone.

Unfortunately, no matter what they did, every scrap of evidence would be altered and bent by Haven Entertainment, a media giant the Haveners took their namesake from. The supernaturals would leave, and the murders would need someone to blame. As the only mortal survivor, the blonde woman leading him to the staff parking lot would be the perfect victim.

She unlocked the doors to a white sedan, opening the back for him to squeeze into. Pain blurred his vision as he pulled himself into the small space, tense muscles spasming. *Escape?* his inner beast whined, not so sure of its impending panic when Alex knew that danger was on the outside of this car.

"Drive. Get us as close to New York as you can," he ordered. As the car jostled over speed bumps, he laid his head down, uttering a groan as his passive control of her turned from a strand of awareness to hot knives in his skull.

"What's in New York?" she asked, her voice uttering as a hazy murmur. Without him compelling her to speak, she shouldn't have asked or thought to wonder. He knew his control over her was slipping, but as long as she wasn't panicking, he wouldn't try to force her back under his complete thrall.

"Safety," he said.

"Safety," she repeated, smiling in the rear-view mirror.

Snarling, his inner beast sank its claws in his already painful headache. The animal was attempting to gain control, something he was weak to without being able to change forms.

It was said that to remain too long in a shapeshifted form would be to doom yourself to become that animal. As Alex fought off the press of animal instincts and emotions, he wondered how long he truly had before he would succumb to being a simple lion.

It would be a slow, excruciating death to be the little voice of reason stuck in the head of an animal. Something told him his longtime enemy had intended for this, too, even seeing it as the true plan, with the zoo being the easy way out by euthanasia.

Alex cleared his throat, fighting off panic to speak to the mortal once more. "Do you have a phone? There's a number I need you to call."

Chapter 4
Violet

Violet returned to coherent thought slowly, like waking from a dream. It gave her the chance to really think about what had happened without the lens of panic, which she would surely return to if she could.

The lion had done something to her, hijacking her body to make it robotically answer to his whims. Thus, they fled the scene of the crime in her old car while he stained her backseat with his gruesomely hurt self. Something was very, *very* wrong here. How was a lion able to talk? And why had those two men taken him to her zoo just to kill innocent people?

She'd had such a close shave with death, or worse, that she could still feel its cold, clammy hand upon her neck. And something told her they weren't done outrunning danger, not with the urgency he'd somehow instilled in her body. At this time of night, the interstate was nearly deserted. She zoomed past any stray cars, hoping to be caught by a policeman so she could communicate her distress...somehow. If anyone would believe she was only doing this because a lion had told her so.

Stealing a glance into the backseat, she saw he had his head down and covered with a massive paw. It was a clear sign of pain, though the worst of his injuries were the cuts lacerating his flank. His fur was matted, covering signs of any open wounds.

"Do you have a phone?" She jumped and used that motion to

snap her gaze forward, as if she hadn't stolen a peek at him. "There's a number I need you to call."

"I have a phone," she said. Whatever he'd done to her made her measure out her words without inflection.

He ordered her to slow down and call a specific number, which she did, dialing an unfamiliar area code. "Is this safe?" she asked.

He seemed to ignore the question. "Put it on speakerphone."

Her thoughts came closer to the surface. A groan came from the lion, sounding pained. "Are we...are we safe?" Because this didn't feel safe. Hurtling down the interstate with a wild animal she'd stolen from the zoo was the opposite of safe already. But she'd gotten the impression that they weren't done with the men who'd seemingly arranged a hit on this talking lion.

The phone rang. One ring, two...

And the lion breathed a sigh of relief as someone picked up the line. "Hello?" a curt, male voice rang over the speaker.

"Sam, good to hear your voice again," he said, relaxing in his seat.

"You're alive!" Sam exclaimed. "Julian said you're far from home."

He nodded. "Ohio. Bit of a situation here."

"When is it ever not?" Sam sighed. "Especially if you're involved."

"That's a man that knows me well." It seemed like the lion was directing this at her. She managed a faint grimace of a smile. "We're traveling your way; I believe this is I-71 North. I need a status report."

"We?" Sam repeated.

"I have a mor... a civilian with me."

"Bloody hell." Sam sounded distinctly British to her at that point. "You know—"

"I know. Status," he demanded, cutting him off before he could say much more.

"Right. Julian is still chasing Cox. He's got a tag on her now, good old Bloodhound he is," he said. "Nicholas is holding the..." he hesitated. "Is your friend listening?"

"Yes," she murmured.

"Hello there," Sam said briskly. "Nicholas is in charge," he added. "I have a team monitoring the news and internet for damage control. Melanie and I are prepping to go on I-71 South now, so we should meet up somewhere in the middle. We'll bring as many enforcers as we can spare right now. Do you have a mile marker or a landmark so we know where you are?"

The lion yawned, seeming to grow disinterested. He circled in the backseat, resting his head on his flank. "Alex? Alex, you with me?" Sam asked after a pause.

Between one blink and the next, Violet shook off the last cobwebs of his control. "He's not," she said, taking a sharp breath as her heart sped to a staccato drumbeat.

"What do you mean, love?" he asked.

"He's... taking a nap," she said, her fingers tightening on the steering wheel. They were twenty-some miles and counting away from the zoo by the mile markers. It wasn't too late for her to turn around, call the authorities, and try to explain what'd happened.

She heard murmuring on the other end of the line as she debated her decision. "It's what we were afraid of," Sam sighed, his tone gentling. "Maybe you can answer a few questions for me. First, what's your name?"

"Violet."

"Violet, hello, I'm Samuel Rainey. I know Alex is not a forthcoming gentleman on the best of days, so you must be very confused. Help me, and I'll try to clear some things up, okay?"

"Okay." It was difficult to force words from her throat, her hands trembling on the wheel. The offer of understanding was too good to resist, though.

"Can you tell me where you are?"

She read a passing mile marker to him. He repeated it to someone else, a feminine murmur in the background.

"Great, thank you. You must be driving."

"Yeah."

"Do you know if Alex used anything that seems like magic to you recently?"

"Yes... he did something to me," she admitted.

"And you're all right?" he asked. The concern in his voice had her throat tightening up.

"Y-yes, I'm fine."

"You sound about as fine as I'd expect," he said, a touch of dry humor there. "Let me tell you what I know. Alex there is a high-priority target for people who hunt...people like him and me."

"What kind of people are you?" she interrupted.

She waited several beats for him to reply. "We're vampires, love."

And that was when she heard an engine revving behind them.

Chapter 5
Alex

Alex struggled with himself, a war waging silently in his head. Fatigue dragged at his frame. The animal in him wanted to rest, and rest it did, wrestling away control of his body.

He still heard Violet and Samuel talking. His deputy and best friend started soothing her in the way only Samuel Rainey could do. As years passed, he remained kind when most of their ilk quickly lost that human edge amongst their feelings of superiority.

Alex did not feel superior right now. In fact, a level of shame passed over him as he pulled himself together just in time to see Violet's look of horror as Sam revealed their biggest secret. The woman was a shade of shocked white that hadn't relented since they'd left the zoo. While he worried for her health, he worried more for their lives.

His ears turned backward, picking up the sound of an engine revving. They'd been found, he thought. "Get down!" he roared. Violet ducked a split second before glass shattered behind them.

Sam cursed over the phone as Violet peeked into the rearview mirror, swerving their car out of the way of their pursuer. An errant bullet struck the center of the windshield, sending up a shockwave of cracks. "I can't see!"

"Stop the car!" Alex yelled. It had been a foolish hope to think she could outrun the military-grade vehicle on their tail in the regular car she drove. But Alex had hoped it anyway since he was not fighting fit. It felt like his body had been through a grinder and back again. But if either of them was to survive this, he would be the beast at bay. He would turn on their pursuers and secure safety for both of them.

The car was rammed sideways, veering toward a guard rail. "Samuel, you will have to find us," he said in a rush.

"Roger," he replied gravely. "Good luck." The line went dead as Violet screamed. A second ram sent them off the road. Alex's heart lurched as the car fell several yards, machinery screeching from a hard impact.

The wheels struggled for purchase against damp clumps of grass and weeds, the car heading downhill at a poor angle. He sank his claws into the upholstery as they rolled. Once. Airbags pummeled his aching body. Twice. Three times. They came to a stop with a groan of protesting metal splashing into water.

He punctured the airbags around him with sharp claws as he felt water rushing over his fur. They were sinking. "Violet?" he called, pushing his paws into the bags surrounding her slight form. No response. He smelled blood, sweet and rich. No, she couldn't die now. He pushed harder, fighting the limp fabric as it became wet.

Violet's head rested back against the seat, her eyes closed. A trickle of blood leaked from her nose, the only hint of the trauma she must've sustained. But he didn't smell death upon her, so he knew there was a chance. His paws fumbled with the seatbelt, releasing and snapping it away from her body. Shards of glass rained upon them as the car went nose-down in the water.

Alex grasped the back of her shirt in his jaws and tugged, using the seat for purchase as he dragged her and tried to keep her head above the water line. She lolled to the side like a limp doll. He waited for the river to pull them further downstream, praying to anyone who was listening that they be washed out of range of the firepower their pursuers were packing. The water level rose steadily until he was barely treading against the current. Violet splashed along under his paddling paws, completely dead weight. They passed through the shot-out back panel, glass shards raking her clothes and his fur. Ruby ribbons trailed from them both, eaten up by the greedy water.

He struck out for the opposite shore, muscles burning in protest. Dark, polluted river water choked his senses as he struggled. He wasn't sure if he had the strength to make it.

It took all of his effort to pull them both to safety. The shallows suckled with thick mud as he dragged Violet through it, laying her on the shore. Filthy, but alive. He wanted to lay down, too, but turned to regard the pair of men on the far bank of the river several yards away. They were heading back to their car.

Alex cursed to himself, knowing they'd soon be close enough to finish him and Violet off. "I'm sorry," he murmured to her unconscious form, pushing her shirt up until he exposed a deep cut from an embedded shard of glass. He worked it free with his mouth and lapped up the blood that pooled in the wound, gagging as it mixed with river water. Warmth and power surged through his body. It was electric and heady, a temporary high that hit him hard, brought low as he was.

He bounded into action, crossing the shore up a grassy hill sloping toward the interstate. The Haveners' SUV came to a stop as he took a running leap, catching the first vampire's neck in his mouth before he could blink and crushing his windpipe with a brutal twist. Fire lashed his side as the other man shot him. The bullet left a stinging trail down to where it tore through his thigh. Alex stumbled, ducking behind the bulk of a tire as his body leaked some of the precious blood he'd just acquired. He had to finish this fast, before he was shot again. His ears perked, listening to the footsteps starting to circle the vehicle.

Flattening himself down, he waited. Gravel crunched underfoot as he saw the muzzle of the gun preceding the man himself. Alex shot up, crunching the hand attached to that gun at the wrist. It clattered to the ground. He whipped his head around with enough force to slam the man into the nose of the vehicle. This second assailant crumbled, hitting the ground unconscious. Alex finished the job by slashing the man's jugular with a swipe of his claws.

He cursed the Havener hard as he dragged himself back to

Violet, safe only for the moment. Human law enforcement and emergency services would be following them, alerted when the second team failed to check in. And looking down at Violet, he wondered if he should let them take her too.

She lay sprawled where he left her, clothes and face muddy. He'd seen enough injuries to guess what was happening in her body. A concussion, swelling of the brain, and then infection setting in her mud-smeared cuts. He shifted on his paws, distinctly uncomfortable with the idea of parting with her. Now that they'd foiled the Havener attack on their tail, he knew his longtime enemy would be releasing damning "evidence" of Violet committing several crimes they themselves had done at the zoo. To let humans take her away would be to condemn her to life in prison if not death from a Havener for helping him so far.

No, he had another option, though it had its consequences. He speared one of his pads with a claw and opened her mouth. Concentrated vampire blood welled before spilling onto her tongue.

He gave her exactly three drops before pulling back and waiting. A shudder worked its way through her body. Vampires were rare, and the mortals who knew of them were even rarer. Exposure to a small amount of his blood would lend preternaturally fast healing, but there was a small chance she would begin to turn. Either way, she would live.

Darkness stole at the sides of his vision. He'd overexerted himself again. But he told himself it was worth it as Violet stirred and opened her eyes. The blue in them was shadowed by pain and confusion. He sighed quietly in relief, nudging her onto her feet. "What happened?" Her slurred voice sounded far away, words distorting to something his inner beast didn't recognize.

His last coherent thought was spoken in a few words. "Let's go. It's not safe here."

Chapter 6
Violet

Violet followed the lion into the trees, her head aching fiercely. It felt like her body was coated generously in bruises and stinging cuts. She wondered how she was on her feet at all, remembering the car crash and then waking up on the muddy bank. The humid summer night kept her wet and miserable.

"Where are we going to go without a car?" she asked him. The world seemed tilted, with her stumbling after him like a newborn duckling. The first time she tripped and fell face-first into the dirt, she wondered if she had it in her to stand. She curled in on herself with a sob, content to lay on the cool grass if it calmed some of her aches.

A massive lion's paw pressed into the dirt by her cheek, his head nudging her shoulder. Their eyes met, but there was no compulsion or control this time. She'd seen the same blank animal expression in the lions she cared for. "You're right. We can't stop," she said, struggling back to her feet.

Something told her that she was on her own here. She reached into her pocket, but her phone was gone. Her forgotten swim in the river would've ruined it anyway. They kept walking, more slowly this time.

He must've saved me, she thought, watching the lion's outline slink in and out of moonlit patches.

Feeling some gratitude for the lion—no, the *vampire*—who'd gotten her into this situation seemed wrong. Especially when there was something clearly wrong with him too, as if he were more animal than anything else. Was he actually a man? She puzzled over it to keep her mind off of herself and the dried clots of dirt falling from her ruined pants.

How quickly she'd accepted that he was a mythical creature, too. Perhaps she'd taken a harder knock to the head than she'd realized. A talking lion with enemies so determined to kill him, actually a vampire. Sure, of course. She wasn't crazy or anything.

Just to check, she pinched her arm, twinging a bruise already there. "Ow," she muttered. It wasn't a dream.

"I'd be more careful, love." The lion's gruff voice drifted back to her. This time, he waited for her to catch up to him, giving her an obvious once-over.

"Are you yourself again?" She didn't meet his eyes, instead resting her gaze upon his flanks. His wounds seemed less severe after a wash in the river.

He said, "Of a sort. You seem...better."

"Not panicking or not dying?"

"Why not both?" There was a touch of humor to the words. "I'm sorry you had to be caught up in all of this."

She opened her mouth to say her usual default. *It's all right.* But was it? Her gaze fell to her mud-spattered boots. With the adrenaline of their flight fading, exhaustion was setting in fast, like lead weights tied to every muscle.

"If we survive this, I'll replace everything you've lost and then some," he continued when she remained silent.

"If," she echoed, rubbing her arms in the wake of a new wave of goosebumps.

"Without a car, we're sitting ducks out here. Let's keep moving," he said, turning to go.

"Why did we run anyway?" She forced herself to follow him, her stiff legs protesting every motion. She hadn't been this tired in her life, and her eyelids threatened to engulf her vision. "We could have called the police. Locked ourselves in quarantine until they arrived."

A sigh echoed back to her. "Mortals are easy to control. Even mortal authorities. Any vampire worth their salt could puppet a group of police to fire at us instead and report that they'd eliminated a hostile threat rather than gunned down a pair of innocents."

"I already hate vampires," she muttered. She'd felt that same compulsion, she realized, both from the lion and one of the thugs who'd planned openly to kill her and...

Stephen, so proud of his grandkids, had been senselessly slaughtered, his body laid out with the other two, and hers meant to join it. She stopped again and grasped her knees, her breath leaving her in short pants. In a way, she was beyond lucky she hadn't joined them. But in another, a painful and sour knot tied itself just below her windpipe.

"Violet. That's your name, right?" The lion nudged her side. "We have to keep moving."

"They shouldn't have died," she said. "I don't...I can't..."

"You can honor their memory by surviving this night." He was gentle as he gave her another push, this time starting her forward momentum again. Instead of letting herself crash to the ground, she took a shaky step and another.

"Try not to think about it. The most important thing you can do is walk. Follow my voice. Think you can do that?" he coaxed, staying only a few steps in front of her now.

"I'll try," she promised. He coached her over tree roots and around thorny bushes grown unchecked in the wilderness.

As they seemed to drift closer to the interstate and the whoosh of the occasional passing car, he said, "This will be a while. Tell me of yourself?"

"Right now?" His question startled her from the precipice of a micro nap that promised to drop her if she let it take over.

"It helps to talk."

"I would much rather know about you then," she said, casting a glance over her shoulder as they moved away from the interstate. If danger were to come for them, it seemed most likely that it would be from that direction.

He hummed to himself. "I wonder how much you would believe."

"Anything. I'm a believer now," she said, perhaps too quickly, as he was quiet except for the rustle of his passage through the underbrush to give her something to follow.

"I'm Alex Rehnquist. I'm a vampire," he said at last.

"Uh huh." She waited for more, recognizing a cagey tone when she heard one.

"And I'm a shapeshifter. It's a vampire thing, to simplify things for you. We have bloodlines, and I'm from the bloodline that shapeshifts."

"So, you're usually not a talking lion? Thank god." She uttered a laugh and then found that she couldn't stop a stream of manic giggles from escaping.

"I'm only a talking lion when I want to be," he said dryly, flashing her a glance. With moonlight reflecting from his eyes, they lit like twin drops of green light. *Very un-lion-like,* she thought. "Except now. I'm stuck, else we wouldn't have a problem right now."

"How do you get stuck as a lion?" She was still giggling, a pair of tears streaming down her cheeks.

"Poison. My enemy has been experimenting with compounds that might cause this. I was poisoned, flung in that box, and taken to your zoo to be set up as a killer and put down tomorrow, I imagine."

She saw that quarantine cell once more, its sand running red with shed blood. Bile struck the back of her throat, and a fit of coughing interrupted her laughter. "Who'd you piss off enough to do that to you?" she croaked.

Alex paused, both to let her catch up and to consider. "You know the company Haven Entertainment?"

"Who doesn't?" she said. Haven Entertainment did it all, hosting television shows, the news, and even had its fingers in some of the most recent blockbusters.

"It was founded before the radio was invented by a man who's wanted me dead for even longer. The name at the head of the company changes, but the man does not. His name is Bryant Collins." His voice was full of heat, as inflexible as his face was in expressing the hatred that flowed between him and this other man.

Violet frowned to herself. A man in charge of a company that huge had to have all the money and resources he could possibly desire. "How old does that make you?" she asked. Older than the radio, apparently.

"Ah-ah. Don't you know it's rude to ask a lion his age?" he said lightly. "It's your turn anyway. Tell me about you."

Mouth already open to follow that dodge, she acknowledged he'd told her more than she'd expected. Yet she was left holding more questions and uncertainties than ever. "I'm Violet Reynolds. I'm married to my job, and it would seem I'm about to get a divorce."

After what she'd seen, she didn't know if she could ever return to her job and fall into the same routine with three person-sized holes missing. Her throat clenched, and she cleared it awkwardly. "I...was quite heavily involved in the PR effort for the male lion's debut. His name was Enzi, and I wonder if your... enemies...if they did something to him too."

"Not that I would know, but I can have my people look into it," he said, a note of sympathy to his voice.

"Thank you," she said, sighing. "I mean, what's there to tell you? I left home at eighteen and never looked back. My dad lost his arm in a freak accident at work and became a mean ol' drunk overnight. My mom got pregnant with another man's baby and ran off with him, leaving me alone with my dad and his parade of girlfriends." A stirring of old resentment hit her belly, but it was better than the exhaustion nipping at her heels.

"Before you worry, don't," she continued. She hadn't told many of her past for the pity that would result. But it was old news, wounds that'd long scarred over with the combination of time and professional help.

"Then I won't worry," he said. "I appreciate your candor. It's refreshing. You strike me as the kind of person who learned early on to appreciate animals' simpler natures."

"If you mean that they're better than people, yeah. Tell me of a scenario where an animal would've done something like this to us," she muttered. She very much felt like a grounded bird being tormented by a bored cat, wondering when and if she were taking this peaceful moment for granted.

"Nature is far more brutal than you give her credit for. But you'll find little out there crueler than Bryant Collins and his men." He shook his head, stopping in a clearing far from the sound of the interstate. "I think we should stop here to rest."

She didn't need him to say it twice, lying down in a patch of overgrown grass with a grateful sigh. There was no thought to what bugs or other things could be sharing the grass with her. She'd deal with them in the morning.

"I'm going to try shifting," Alex said. Cracking her eyes open to watch, she barely mustered the energy to lift her head. She expected something flashy, like a blast of light and the sudden appearance of a man in place of a lion. Instead, his bones popped and crackled as they shifted position. It sounded painful from his groan.

His transformation lasted only a few seconds, but the end result was not what they were hoping for. He shrank dramatically, fur shading darker as he became a black cat, a handsome tom save for the chunks of fur missing along his flank. A smile touched her lips despite herself, and she reached out to try coaxing him to curl up with her for sleep like she would her own cat.

Alex arched his back with a feral hiss, darting off into the underbrush. *There's that animal side to him again,* she thought to herself, offering a tired shrug. *He'll be back.* She closed her eyes.

When dawn was close, she was thrown over a stranger's shoulder like a sack of potatoes. Barely a murmur of protest passed her lips before a cloth smelling of sweet chemicals and copper pennies was pressed to her face. She slept like the dead after that.

Chapter 7
Violet

Violet woke in a haze of disorientation, her head feeling like it'd been cracked open and stuffed with cotton fluff. She wasn't lying on a bed of grass, as she'd expected to find herself, but instead inside a cinderblock-lined bathroom lit by fluorescents. The corners of the room were caked in dirt, and cobwebs had taken up residence on the ceiling. She cringed to be in such an unclean space, making to stand.

She didn't budge. Her hands flexed uselessly behind her, tied to the back of a solid, wooden chair too heavy for her to move. The throbbing in her ears grew in intensity as her heart pattered.

Great, I'm the damsel in distress, she thought, feeling what she could of the rope securing her arms. It was too well-tied to manipulate.

She sagged in the chair, leaning her head back and closing her eyes. What did she remember of her situation? Foggy words from last night seeped into her memories, of Alex the vampire turned lion talking about his longtime enemy, the owner of Haven Entertainment. That man must've arranged her kidnapping, but to what end?

Who would pay ransom for her? She had no family to speak of, having not spoken to her father in a decade and her mother in even longer.

She couldn't count on Alex, who'd run and hid the moment

28

he'd transformed into a housecat. If he were still a lion, he could've fought off whoever had come to grab her in the middle of her rest. Would he even try to save her now? He was probably far safer without her as baggage.

Bowing her head, she acknowledged that if she was to get out of this alive, somehow, she'd have to save herself.

She'd have to tell them of Alex, who'd gotten her in the middle of his mess. She felt a sort of loyalty to him that balked at the thought, even though it was his fault her car was junk. If he were better off alone, as she thought, it made no sense that he would save her and let her slow him down as she stumbled through the night. There was no means to an end there. He was still a stranger, and she couldn't count on him to rescue her again.

Not that anyone gave her the chance to talk her way out of this. Time passed, measured in the drip of a leaky faucet and the fast throb of her heart. There were other people around; she could hear the murmur of their voices, sometimes close. There was no way to kid herself here—anyone who would tie her to a chair in a dirty bathroom wouldn't be a friend to her for an interrogation.

When someone finally came to check on her, he burst into the room with little preamble. Two people followed, setting up a chair for him and wheeling in a cart piled with various tools. He dismissed his assistants with a wave, leaving Violet alone with a man she assumed was a vampire.

There was little different about him that would suggest it despite an attractive face and muscles a gym rat would drool for. He didn't move with any particular kind of otherworldly grace, instead dropping his weight into his chair with a sigh like any man would. When he spoke, there were no long fangs, but his eyes...

Entrancing. A shade of brown close to amber, they were more prominent and noticeable than any man's that she'd met, almost meant to be noticed and stared at. She had already learned that to glance in a vampire's eyes was to become a puppet to their whims, so she kept her gaze on the thick vest he wore instead. It looked like something straight from an action movie, only missing the camouflage and string of bullets looping over one shoulder.

"Hello, Violet," he said. "It's a pleasure to meet you. There seems to be a misunderstanding."

"How do you know my name?" She relied on the smooth humor in his voice to know there was neither pleasure in their meeting nor a misunderstanding.

"Well, you're something of a celebrity. With a little visit from our men, it seems you're a murderer now." It felt like he'd submerged her in cold water, every hair on her body rising with alarm.

"I didn't kill anyone!" she protested, jerking her arms with fists balled.

"Tell the nation that. Your face was on the nightly news," he said. Taking his phone out, he showed her an old photo of her posing with one of the older lionesses. The website headline was obvious even from a distance. She'd made national news, but not in a good way. Her face went slack with a heavy combination of denial and disbelief, choking off any words to her defense.

"That's just good business, Miss Reynolds. We can't go telling the truth, can we?" He grinned, a flash of white at the corner of her eye. She glanced over to see that he did indeed have fangs, the lethal points replacing his upper canines and almost reaching the bottom gum line. "No one would believe the vampires and magic side."

She found her words on a gasp, part outrage and all shock to see that he really *was* a vampire. They existed, and she'd landed smack in the middle of two factions of them overnight. "But they'd believe someone without a motive would kill three random people?" she snapped.

"Like a charm. So, now you know what's at stake." He placed his phone back in his pocket, reclining in his chair like a lounging king. "What if I told you I have the power to run a correction on this and lift the blame from you?"

"People only believe the first thing they read," she said, sounding numb even to her own ears. They'd taken the most important thing from her—her job. Such a sought-after position would be impossible to get back with a cloud of doubt and hatred following her. Over something *she hadn't done*, no less.

"You underestimate Haven. So, you help me, and I'll help you. You can go back to your life with only a few scratches." He sounded like he believed her only a bit roughed up, wearing a self-satisfied air as he waited.

"Depends what kind of help you want from me," she said, resigned to at least hear him out. She'd expected something like this, but agreeing to work with someone was made more difficult when she was already fostering a raging hatred toward him and his smug face.

"You can start by telling me where Alexander Rehnquist is," he said, flipping his hand. "We found you, so we assumed he would be close by. Did that lion abandon you?"

"Not that I know of," she said. So they thought Alex was still a lion. She didn't volunteer his change of form as she glowered in his general direction.

"Hmm. He killed four of our men. Two were in the car that chased you, and you left that car there. Why?" he asked.

There was a car they could've used? She blinked rapidly for a moment, remembering waking up from her impromptu swim. "I was in no shape to drive," she said, imagining how badly she would've weaved in and out of lanes in that state.

"What a shame for you both." He chuckled to himself. "In that case, he wouldn't have abandoned you. Why go through all that trouble to keep you alive?" Leaning back, he called to one of his assistants, who came in and bent down so he could whisper in her ear. She nodded rapidly and rushed from the room, but not before she told him something that made him curse.

"You see, Violet," he continued, shaking his head. "If he feels some emotional attachment toward you, he'll come rushing if he learns where you're held."

"So, I'm bait," she said, lips pressing tightly. She knew he was about to offer a trade—if they got Alex again, they'd let her go free and try to clear her name. But he didn't get the chance to say it before the door was kicked open and a woman sauntered in on mile-high heels.

"Willlllliam," she sang, bending down behind his chair to press her cheek to his, drawing blood-red nails over his vest.

"What are you doing here?" His voice held a scowl as Violet risked a glance at the woman.

She was a beauty, heart-shaped face complimented by a fall of wine-red hair. Straight from the pages of a gothic magazine, she wore a tight, corseted gown that showed ample cleavage from her pose behind him. While she would have assumed the man, William, could've been a human, there was no second guessing that she was a vampire.

"Am I not allowed to be here?" she asked, putting a hand to her chest.

He spoke through gritted teeth. "No, you are. As long as the rumors aren't true. You haven't been tagged, have you?"

"Oh, well, I have." She had a cackle for a laugh as she waved it off.

"Coven Rehnquist is going to follow their Bloodhound straight here. You have to go." He flinched away from her, jumping to his feet with a new shot of urgency.

She sidestepped him, having noticed Violet with a vicious smile crossing her face. "Oh, don't be such a stick in the mud. Look at this cute girl."

"I was handling it—"

"Now I'll handle it." She patted his cheek as if speaking to a child.

"I was making progress, Kim," he protested.

She looked him in the eye, and, to Violet's surprise, he backed down, sitting without another word of complaint when she told him to do so. The hair on the back of her neck rose as the woman approached in a fluid sashay. "Alex's new plaything," she purred.

Grasping Violet's chin, she jerked her head up for them to make eye contact. "Relax," the vampiress ordered. Kim's eyes were a burning red, fangs standing out behind painted lips of black. If she wasn't suddenly frozen, Violet would've thrashed in terror. "William, be a dear and get me a bucket of water."

She stroked Violet's cheek with the edge of her nails, leaving stinging trails behind. Curling her hand around, she licked a few beads of blood from them. "He does have good taste. You seem like you clean up well," she remarked. "Sweet blood, too. Are you a virgin?"

Violet's eyes bugged wide, but she was unable to speak until Kim told her it was all right. "Go to hell," she muttered.

"Oh, what happy happenstance. I'm not going there today, but you will." The vampiress grinned. "My bloodline specializes in it, in fact. I'll show you horrors you didn't know existed." She leaned in so Violet could smell the blood on her breath. "And when it's over, we'll deliver your broken body to Alexander so he knows exactly who he's playing with."

"H-he won't care. I don't even know the guy," she stammered, trembling and pressing herself back into her restraints. She could only squirm as Kim sat astride her.

"Aw, poor thing. It doesn't matter, you see? Innocent blood spilled," she purred. "He'll live with the guilt that he caused your death for the rest of his limited days."

"William was saying you would let me go if I helped you." She was hedging and knew it, but he'd suggested as much.

Kim slapped her thigh with a laugh. "William is still young. He's got a little human left in him." She turned and beckoned when the man in question came back, his expression perfectly blank. Offering her a sloshing wooden bucket, he sat after his task was done. "See how obedient he is? Such a good little boy."

She turned back to Violet, red eyes full of manic energy. Whatever came next would be the promised magic, and she saw clearly that nothing, not even one of her underlings, would stop this woman. Violet decided she wouldn't go out whimpering for mercy she wouldn't find. "Are all vampires freak shows like you, or are you a special case?" she snarked, proud that her voice didn't shake.

"Oh, so brave." Kim laughed, leaning in with an open mouth. She changed course from Violet's jugular, instead pressing a kiss to her forehead. There was a lash of lightning behind her eyes, and she felt herself tumble face-first into an abyss of darkness.

Violet couldn't breathe. Water choked her senses as she gasped for air, just to find none.

Inside her head, Kim showed her snippet after snippet of

horrors, as promised. Every breath of air was punctuated by terror, knowing more scenes of bloodshed and screaming would pile up in her mind's eye. Kim's voice narrated it all, pointing out exactly what evil vampires were capable of. Specifically from Alex and the friends he called his coven.

She had no time to process it all, her head heating with splitting pain that jerked through her body from her agonized brain. Was this what death felt like, the seizing of muscles past their limits, jerking uncontrollably as if to a demon's dance?

Her eyes blinked open, pink froth dripping from her lips as she took another raw gulp of air. The screams continued, and it wasn't until Kim ordered William to investigate that she realized those sounds belonged to reality instead of the nightmares forced into her head.

Black spots winked through her vision as the world swam around her. Kim was on her feet, posing to leap at anything that came through the door.

It flung open with enough force to knock it from its hinges. *Bang!* A body hurtled through, propelled by an unseen force to throw Violet's chair onto its back. She cried out hoarsely as her whole body throbbed in agony from the impact.

"What the—? What *are* you?" Kim's voice drifted to her, followed by a shriek and the rip of flesh.

Violet fought her body to stay conscious, aware that if she closed her eyes, they probably wouldn't open again. She felt herself starting to drift away, too full of nightmares to continue on. Pattering irregularly in her chest, her heart counted down the moments as it struggled to keep her alive.

It slowed as she felt air flow past her cheeks. Someone was righting her chair with surprising care. Her world narrowed down to a tight band as her lids hovered millimeters from closing. "Poor thing," whispered an unfamiliar, female voice belonging to the pale, unfocused figure in her line of sight. A cork popped, followed by a fizz, like a champagne bottle opening.

"Such a victim. Fated to die so senselessly." The woman's voice was smoother than silk. *An angel*, Violet thought, hardly able to understand the words she spoke.

"Take this. Take my blessing, and live. No one shall victimize you again under my protection."

Gentle fingers pulled Violet's lips apart. It wasn't difficult with her lying slack and near gone in her restraints. She coughed and gagged weakly as the first drop touched her tongue.

Coppery blood.

Nasty. Musty. Old.

Her vision sharpened and focused on a white glove and the glass vial it held. Viscous orbs of liquid dropped into her waiting mouth until it was about half full.

"Now rest. I will call for you when it's time."

Darkness embraced her, sweeping away the pain.

Chapter 8
Alex

Alex spent most of the daylight hours napping and fighting his inner beast for control of his own body. The cat wanted its solitude and peace and went far up a tree to achieve these things. It cleaned its fur with distaste at the blood and dirt that had matted it, content with its simple thoughts and wants. They hunted a mouse. A search party combed the forest, passing under the tree bough he'd settled in. He watched them from that vantage, lazing in a small patch of shadow.

As night started to fall, he started to acknowledge that this might be it. He may have permanently lost his mind, just as Bryant Collins had wanted. But instead of spending his immortal existence being shamed in a cage for mortal entertainment, he'd suffer the crushing guilt of what could possibly become of the mortal who'd had the misfortune of meeting him in his final days, whom he'd failed to protect.

It came as little surprise when a different kind of search party started combing the forest, wielding guns and blades instead of tranquilizers. They didn't think to look for anything other than a lion, and he watched them circling from dusk until late at night. He yawned, brooding, when the team put on their silencers and started shooting into the night. An owl thumped to the forest floor, dead. A booted foot crushed a vole as it scurried back to its nest. He watched with a cat's dispassionate stare, but on the inside, he felt the elemental fear of a cornered beast. Someone had figured out that he was no longer a lion.

Alex hissed angrily as a hand shot out of nowhere to grasp him by the scruff. He was hauled from his safe haven by none other than his Italian friend, Julian Fairfax. Julian was the only blood tracker in the whole of Coven Rehnquist, able to sense someone's location after one sip of their blood. Dubbed "Bloodhound" for this uncanny ability, he often used it for situations like this one.

While Alex was relieved to see him, the beast in charge snarled and scratched Julian in an attempt to free himself. "Stop," Julian muttered, shaking him hard enough to rattle his brain. The cat side of him didn't listen, needing to be muffled to stop from yowling a battle cry. He ended up chewing on his hand hard enough to draw blood. Alex was hopeful for a moment at the taste of his friend's blood, but it brought him no extra power or control.

Julian slipped through the trees with silent grace, outwitting the fledgling Haven vampires that had been sent to massacre animals. He dashed to a car idling just off the side of the interstate where Julian's patrol partner, Armando Nizzola, sat looking bored. *Only Armando would look bored at a time like this,* Alex thought, wishing he could roll his eyes. "Go," Julian said, slipping into the back of the vehicle.

"You got a cat, man," Armando noted, looking back at the struggling Alex still gnawing on Julian's hand. He took the pain with a stoic frown.

"It's Alex," he said.

"Seems like the wrong cat." Armando idly stroked his shoulder badge of a lion's head. He and Julian were enforcers, a type of police for immortal covens. Both wore the badge and black clothing of the Blackguard, Alex's elite team of fighters.

The two men were a study of opposites otherwise. Julian was broad with muscle, fair-skinned, his hooded brow shadowing eyes of brilliant blue. His blond hair was cropped military short. By comparison, Armando smiled with bright teeth in a Mediterranean complexion, looking like he'd be more at home on the cover of a magazine with his arm slung over the steering wheel rather than prepared for a fight with the weaponry strapped to his waist.

"I don't make mistakes," Julian replied, as cold as a winter's storm. Alex's fur bristled at the sudden chill.

"I'm just sayin'. I expect some pip pip, cheerio, not animal noises," he said, shrugging. Both Alex and his inner beast growled. "Oh, you in there, boss? Sorry," he added more sheepishly.

Julian sighed, a long-suffering reaction to Armando. "We need you back. I found out a lot about the drug they hit you with." Alex tried to show some flicker of recognition, a twitch, anything but animal growls. But he firmly did not have control of himself. Julian's glacier-hued eyes glimmered with disappointment.

"Do you think you should just... talk to him? Maybe he'll come back to himself," Armando suggested.

Julian nodded slowly. "They hit me with the same stuff. Armando as well. Neither of us lost our blood abilities or any hint of control." He waited, as if expecting some sort of response. "When I caught up to Kim Cox, she dropped the antidote vial right in front of me. It was water." Alex's heart sank immediately. "We followed her to see if she'd take us to Haven headquarters. I figured it would be there, if anywhere. But instead, she led us to a warehouse very close to you. We came to get you instead."

"You're forgetting the part where the Haveners were napping," Armando said.

Julian tapped his knee, considering. "I still don't know what to make of that. Most of the people inside the warehouse were... asleep, I suppose. Laying around."

"They all got up to fight us, though," Armando put in.

"Most of the ranking members used it as a cover to escape. We found your new mortal friend tied up in a bathroom next to the corpse of Will Jaxom. We torched his body and took her to see Melanie, but it's unlikely she will survive the night." He shrugged, distracted by his own thoughts. Alex wanted to reach out and shake him for more details. His friend had been born a vampire just like him and had little care for mortal kind. Alex tried hard to avoid the same jaded outlook.

Either way, he didn't understand their strange testimony. But if it resulted in Will Jaxom, a ranking Haven member, dying, there was a glimmer of hope in this dark night. He just hoped they were taking him to Violet, though he didn't know what he'd be able to do for her.

"But, yeah. We don't have an antidote for you," Armando frowned. "You gotta shake it off on your own, man. It wasn't so bad. I barely noticed it, really. Kinda like a bee sting. You know, a really annoying one..." he kept talking, but Alex tuned it out.

"It seems your theory was right, old friend," Julian murmured, quiet enough just for Alex's ears. They perked, folding back to indicate that he was listening. "But we will do whatever we can to reverse your condition. You'll be right as Rainey again." Alex wanted to groan, even though he knew it was bad if Julian was telling Rainey puns. He may never come back, a prisoner within his own body. He hoped his friends would have the proper mercy upon him and end an existence like that.

"Here we are," Armando said, parking the car at a shabby old motel. Julian hauled Alex's struggling self from the car, rolling his eyes as he set off a fresh chain of yowling. He walked right up to one of the rooms, the door opening before him from an effortless push of mental energy. Samuel and his mate, Melanie, sat together before a muted television, grim-faced. "Look, we found Alex," Armando said with more cheer than any of the other vampires felt.

Sam got to his feet and held out his hands. Alex found himself being shaken vigorously. *Mighty fine to see you too,* Alex thought, going limp and hoping for mercy. Sam held him by the scruff, eye to eye. His hazel eyes were narrowed to catlike slits, his own inner beast close to the surface. Alex bowed his head, immediately cowed by the current stronger predator of the two of them. "Snap out of it."

Alex barely twitched, feeling the weight of his stare and staying hunched to show he was no threat. Sighing, Sam held him to his chest instead, carrying him to Melanie. "Maybe he just needs a push to get his shapeshifting working again," he suggested, handing him off.

Melanie was gentler than the men, which set his inner beast at ease as she inspected him closely. As a Gifted, her vampire ability was healing. He, too, was full of hope as her magic rippled from her fingers, setting his skin to tingling.

Breathing out, he felt control shift within him with a great mental wrench. He turned his head of his own volition, whiskers splaying forward. "Thanks for the save." He spoke to Julian, his voice high and squeaking from a cat's vocal cords.

"Bloody hell," Sam said, sighing tensely.

"I was afraid for a second there!" Armando blurted.

"Now, heal yourself. Shift back." Melanie frowned.

Alex put a paw over his eye, the closest thing he could do to a salute as a cat. "Bloody hell, I missed you all. Truly. I'm glad I can tell you my final wishes, should I lose myself permanently." Armando opened his mouth to say something just to get a sharp jab from Julian. He muttered an apology.

"If I try to shift, I might become a beast again for another full day or longer. These... episodes of me losing control. They're getting worse." He flicked his eyes to Sam, who shook his head in dogged disbelief. "Every time I use my mental influence or try to shift, it sinks its claws in me. So, I want you to know I love every bloody one of you. Please treat Violet like one of us. She saved my life."

"It sounds like you're trying to say goodbye, but I'm not ready for that." Melanie hugged him closer. "Why don't you try shifting back? I'll run some of my Gift through you at the same time to help."

While his friends looked hopeful, Alex doubted this would work. He could already feel that mental block in place, a brick wall of sorts that he would run into if he tried to approach his human form. Waiting for the familiar, warm feeling of her healing, he prepared and pushed all his limited energy into forcing a shift.

Talons of pain seized his skull. *Not yet!* his inner beast screeched, dragging him back from the edge of a shift. He slammed back into Melanie's chest, howling as the bones shifting under his pelt cracked and reestablished a cat's fragile skeleton.

"No?" Sam watched with a wince of sympathy, the only one in the room to understand how painful an aborted shift could be.

"Not yet." Alex echoed the words as Melanie's magic soothed the worst of his aches in a consistent flow.

Well, at least that side of his magic was still talking to him. He didn't feel malice from it holding him back but instead a deep worry. *Something's wrong,* it whispered.

Melanie placed him on the ground as she turned to Sam. "Why don't you shift so I know what part of it he's getting caught on?"

He padded away while they experimented, his paws steering him on that kernel of instinct. The bedroom was saturated with blood scent, stinging his sensitive nose as he hopped up on the bed. Something *was* wrong, that much his eyes told him.

Violet lay across the bed, bound tightly in on herself. He realized why quickly, seeing the bandages around her fingernails and the bloody lines over her exposed skin. She wore a blank, empty stare while she bit down on a belt someone had threaded in her mouth. Her body twitched, caught in the horrors of a daymare.

Hellscape. Alex recognized the stare and the maddened reaction all too well. Violet had met Kim Cox then, whose blood ability was reviled by most immortals. Even the most minute touch from the woman could bring terrible, realistic nightmares that would haunt for years. A mortal mind could not tolerate such things without breaking.

He inhaled the scent of blood and terror, shuddering all the way to the tip of his tail. This was his fault—a message sent directly to him. Anyone who dared to help him would suffer a similar fate by the hands of that sadistic witch.

His paws took him closer, sniffing one of the scratches on her arms. *Something's wrong,* his inner beast repeated urgently.

Her blood had a new quality, something old and bitterly metallic. Tilting an ear back, his friends were still discussing the mechanics of shifting. He unsheathed his claws, pressing the sharp edge to one of her wounds to draw a bead of blood.

It surfaced silver.

Shimmering in the low light, it left a gray trail down her skin as he jumped backward. He meant to turn and call to Melanie, but his every muscle locked.

Hellscape, his beast reminded him.

That's *what we're focusing on?* he grumbled internally, resisting as it pushed their paws into motion. Even his slight weight caused Violet to groan as they stood on her chest, beholding her anguished face.

Sleep, it told him insistently. It prompted with that one word as they watched her wide-awake gaze shift as if in a fever dream.

Alex opened his mouth, taking a deep breath. The inner beast allowed him to speak the command as they looked her in the eye. "Sleep, Violet." And she listened, the tension leaving her body like a dropped doll.

The beast took back its control. It flooded him with a sense of gratitude and curled up quietly against her flank. A soft purr lifted in his throat as his eyes closed. Alex roared with impotent fury to be sleeping *again,* and the beast responded with a sense of peace. Patience. The unwelcome warmth of sleep enveloped him.

Chapter 9
Alex

Through darkness, images started flashing by him, fragmented and broken, made of screams and blood and gore. Gunshots. Burning flesh. He watched this all with the warm detachment of a dream, walking around the shards of thought as if they were polaroid pictures planted in a depthless sea. He padded on four paws, still a cat but at least half in control of himself. The beast was the other half, steering him away from each image, leaping and rolling when they moved to intercept them. *What is this?* he thought.

Dreams. Nightmares, the beast answered.

They stopped before the image of a burning village. Alex hesitated, but his beast did not, plunging in headfirst. The smell of ripening corn mingled with distant smoke. It was straight from one of the worst days of his life, a memory he recoiled from. The beast steered their paws through stalks of corn, weaving around them with the grace of familiarity. They stopped before someone who didn't belong to this memory of ancient times. Violet, whole and hale-looking, was curled up beneath a scarecrow, knees drawn up to her chin, weeping. She wore a zoo uniform, the pristine version of what she'd started this ordeal in. He ventured forward, placing a paw on her shin.

Her watery eyes lifted, and she gasped quietly when she saw him. The beast purred deeply, meowing to her like a common cat wanting attention. She reached forward and tucked him into her chest. "How did you get here?" she murmured.

I have no idea, love, he wanted to reply. Instead, he purred fiercely, nuzzling under her chin. She was smiling, wide and genuine. He reached out and pawed at her cheek, acting just like the cat she thought him to be.

"Aren't you sweet?" she cooed. He meowed. No, the beast did, wiggling free of her hold, trotting into the thicket of corn, and turning back with tail held high as if asking if she were coming. She got to her feet and let him lead her out of the scene. His beast only let her pick him up again when they re-entered the blank space that was filled with jagged shards of nightmares.

The beast held out a paw, drawing on Alex's mental power. The burning village popped into shards of color and light, fading like a handful of confetti. Alex watched in astonishment. He knew what mental order the beast had given, but to see a memory erased right before his eyes was something new. Violet blinked at it, drifting with him idly. He and his beast came to an understanding in that moment, paw extending every time she approached one of those bladed nightmares. Before she could touch one, it burst, erased. "That's not right," Violet murmured in confusion, not seeming to otherwise question this odd dream of hers as she kept walking. Alex could not see anything outside these jagged scenes ahead of them, black mist swirling around Violet's legs.

The path seemed endless. And there were so, so many memories. Alex recognized about a third of them, most badly distorted and false. Kim Cox's work, he realized. His paws swept away scene after scene. Many more lay ahead, beckoning. A soft growl left his throat. He would destroy her for this.

No, the beast replied.

No? he echoed.

Violet's dreaming mind continued on, but he started to feel distant, fading. He passed through her fingers as he woke, shaking out his fur in shock at the sudden change of scenery. His eyes adjusted to the warm colors of peeling wallpaper and the light of dusk filtering through tightly shut blinds.

No. We will, the beast said, fading out. Alex flexed his paws as it retreated to the back of his mind, strength and awareness flooding him. His vampire's senses returned in a rush. He shifted with a pained crack and grunt, falling off the bed in a graceless pile as his body unfolded to that of a man once more.

Naked as a jaybird, he looked up from the claws retracting to fingers as Sam rushed into the room. He knew he was a mess, his hair having grown out of control from an extended time in shapeshift form. "Guess who's back," he said from human vocal cords. Feeling the natural thrum of his voice in his chest was all he needed, jackknifing to his feet and giving Sam a backslapping hug.

"Put some clothes on, you lunatic," Sam laughed, though he hugged Alex with the same bone-crunching fervor.

"Tell me you have clothes. And a razor."

"Clothes, yes. Razor, no."

Alex muttered something uncharitable.

"Of course, I brought a razor," Sam laughed, pushing him into the bathroom and giving him a full set of toiletries. He took his time, waiting for the kiss of nightfall with a predator's patience. If she knew what was good for her, Kim Cox would already have fled far and fast.

He knew his eyes were still slits, his inner beast active and ready to hunt. But he was going to do so clean and trimmed up. He strode out in his Blackguard uniform, lions stitched in a flat yellow on either shoulder. He could barely look at them, much less stomach the idea of ever becoming a lion again.

Melanie wept in the other room between relieved laughs. "Do I hear that someone missed me?" he teased, pausing at the doorway and leaning indolently on the jam. She came over to hug him nearly as hard as her husband had.

"You're back, man." The extra in the room was Armando shifting awkwardly in his boots.

Alex beckoned to him. "Where is Julian?" he asked, good humor fading rapidly. The two Italians were rarely parted for long.

Armando's shifting became more uncomfortable. "I don't

know, boss," he admitted. "He's the tracker. I just hit things." But Julian's absence meant something was bothering him, and he had a feeling it had to do with the mortal girl still sleeping a few yards away.

"I bloody well know your specialties. I must have words with him." Alex sighed. "Give me your phone." He rang up Julian's phone and when he got to voicemail, sang a poor, off-the-cuff number asking where his loyal Bloodhound was. "There, that'll piss him off enough to call," he nodded, offering Armando his phone back.

"Yeah, boss. Great," he said uneasily. He must've seen the battle lust Alex left unconcealed. "He texted, says he's on the roof. Why didn't I check the roof?"

"Because you don't brood, Armando," he said, crossing to Violet's bedside in a few strides. He knew he was brooding too, watching the mortal shift restlessly, still dreaming. "Mel..."

She seemed to read his mind, making shooing motions. "I'll take care of her. Go do what you have to."

He sighed and left the motel room, scaling to the roof once he found the fire escape. Julian sat in the shadows, watching the stars wink into sight. Crickets sang as humidity caressed their skin. The other man didn't turn as Alex sat beside him. "You're back," he said, speaking Italian. A chill breeze blew around the two of them, preternaturally swirling.

"I'm back," Alex agreed, waiting.

Julian seemed to weigh his words carefully. A man of few of them, he preferred action over talk. Alex had always found it a shame since his friend was so skilled with weapons, having even honed his body into the sharpest one of all. A little diplomatic skill, and he would be even more deadly. "Why did you let the girl slow you down?"

"She was dying," he said, remembering her waterlogged and lacerated body lying on the shore, how he could've let the greedy river sweep her away and continued on his own. But there was something else, a kernel of emotion that went past duty. He couldn't personally allow Violet to drown. He liked her too much.

"She could've gotten you killed." There was a thread of

betrayal there, even in his expression. *You would have left me,* that expression said.

Alex shook his head. "My friend, you are too cold. How do you expect to find your lifemate when you encase your heart in ice?"

"Why bring that up now?"

"Let's face it. You've searched the whole world for her. If she were a vampire, you would have already found her. She is probably mortal. What would you do then? Would you hate her for her imperfections? For the untainted blood in her veins?" A tic throbbed in Julian's temple, and his jaw clenched tightly as he stared down his coven master with those cold eyes. "If she lay dying from your actions, would you give your own life to save her?"

"You speak unfairly," Julian murmured. "This girl is not your lifemate. Nor did your actions deliver her to Cox's hands."

"Didn't they?" He shook his head. "I want you to meet her. There is something different about her." The beast rumbled uneasily in the back of his mind, where it belonged. It ruled the uncomfortable prickling at the back of his neck as he thought of that silver drop of blood welling in her wound.

"So, she lives."

"Yes."

"How?"

Alex had been waiting for the question, though he had little idea of how to answer it. "It would seem I learned a new trick," he said, explaining his dream as best he could.

"Huh," Julian said once he was done.

"All that just for a 'huh.' I feel so accomplished to earn your sage advice," Alex said dryly.

Julian started to smile. Alex knew forgiveness when he saw it and breathed a soft sigh of relief. "Well, if you're going to be an ass, I won't share what I know," Julian said. Alex mimed zipping up his lips and throwing away the key. "You don't know this one? It's dream walking."

"Bloody difficult to put a name to it when you don't know

what's going on. Dream walking. That's..." he drifted off, troubled. "Underwhelming."

"Perhaps the first time I've seen someone underwhelmed to ascend," Julian snorted. "Congratulations... Elder Rehnquist."

"You well know it's not the blood power I wanted," he grumbled. Blood powers followed age hand-in-hand. At two hundred years of age, most vampires developed a single ability. They were considered Master vampires at that point. Five hundred years brought on the second ability, an age Alex was close enough to kiss. The third, and final, came at eight hundred. He had a while to survive to become an Ancient.

Julian considered. "I will likely gain my father's ability to speak mentally across great distances as an Elder. How underwhelming it will seem in two hundred years. Power ebbs and flows. Our first ones are strong, so the second must be weak. And if we live to be Ancient, the third will be devastating."

Alex nodded, watching the moon rise. The cold aura around his friend was lifting. Alex had always found it curious that the force of his mind manifested as cold, giving chills and freezing gales. Every other vampire he'd met gave off auras that manifested hot, a pins and needles sensation that grew more unpleasant as they aged. One could judge a vampire's age simply off the power of their mind. While Alex kept his on a tight rein, some vampires like Julian always had a little leaking like a natural barometer. "So, about the girl. How do you plan to return her to a mortal life?"

"I'm not sure yet," he admitted.

"Did you want to have her as a new fledgling then?"

He worried his lip. "That would be the wisest path for her. To wait out what Haven will do to her good name. To disappear." He didn't mention the silver blood, figuring that was a topic for their resident doctor, Melanie.

"You know, I came up here to ask you a question," he continued to distract himself from that thought. Julian tipped his hand, waiting. "Where is she?"

"Downstairs," he said, deadpan.

"No. Cox."

He closed his eyes, concentrating. "Northeast. Approximately eighty miles. On the move away from us."

"Let's catch up before she can burrow underground again," he said, getting to his feet. "Oh, and Bloodhound, as useless as my Elder skill is..." he drifted off, and Julian nodded in understanding. He wouldn't say a word to anyone. Alex had won his loyalty long ago, in an abandoned French barn. Now, they shared the same enemies. And one was about to see the full brunt of Coven Rehnquist's wrath brought down upon her.

<h1 style="text-align:center">Chapter 10
Violet</h1>

REALITY AND DREAMS MET, MIXING TOGETHER IN A SLURRY of screaming and silence punctuated by the gentle touch of a stranger upon her face. "I've never seen anything like it." A woman's voice.

"What do you think it means?" Another voice, a man's, seemed so familiar as it ebbed in and out of Violet's awareness.

"It's too early for me to say. It could be a rare disease or..." firm fingertips pried her eye open. Violet screamed, instantly awake from her drifting. The woman did too, dropping a tool as she jumped from surprise.

Clutching an armful of covers—when did she get on a bed?—Violet pressed herself to a headboard, taking in her surroundings as she covered up the flimsy nightgown she'd been changed into. Her hands were tied together by a length of satin. So, she was still a captive, just in a different place. By the looks of it, it was a cheap hotel room, where no one would ask questions if someone disappeared.

Her chest rose and fell rapidly as she took in the two people, no, vampires, that were also in the room. Their faces were like faded memories, shown to her in the nightmares she could barely remember. The woman was tall and thin, her dark hair up in a bun that did nothing to soften the sharp lines of her cheekbone and jaw. She stared at Violet as if she'd grown a horn, her mouth half-open.

"Sleeping Beauty awakens," the other person in the room said, the man. He stood at the foot of the bed, hands in his pockets as he affected a casual air.

"W-who are you? What do you want?" Violet rasped, her lips and mouth as dry as if she'd eaten pure salt.

He offered a smile. "You don't recognize me, love?"

She really didn't. Nothing about him was familiar, from his accent, to the vampire-handsome face, to his generous lips shadowed by a mustache and goatee the same black as the tousled waves of hair on his head that had been cut messily, as if in a hurry. *Throw in some eyeliner, and he could be an eighties rocker,* she thought, taking in his dark outfit.

But if he were even asking...that made the answer obvious. "You're Alex. You shifted back?" she asked.

"That's right. Pleasure to meet you," he said. A faint smile touched her lips, glad that their struggle hadn't been in vain. "And this is Melanie Rainey, a doctor and Gifted vampire healer. We bound your hands up for your protection."

"What? Why?" Despite herself, she'd looked into his eyes and was fixed on them. He had eyes like a spring forest, a clear and depthless green. Like the other vampires she'd met, they were his best and most noticeable feature, doing their job to distract and transfix her.

She wrenched her attention from him with effort when Melanie leaned in, untying her wrists and the bandages over her fingers. "You were hurting yourself," she said, gently turning over her arm to display an array of scabbed cuts. They looked days old, ready to start flaking off.

"How long have I been asleep?" she murmured, her head full of questions. These people saved her somehow, and yet her nightmares left her with a slimy feeling, a dread that something bad was yet to creep up on her. Alex, Melanie, and others starred in half-remembered scenes of blood and torture, yet that wasn't the version of them she saw here.

"About a day. You're healing remarkably well." Melanie

offered a tentative smile. "The sun is setting soon. We were about to move you to a more secure location."

"That won't be necessary," she blurted, shifting her legs. Though she felt like she was tethered to several iron weights, she could still move. If she could move, she could go home instead of trusting any strangers with her care.

Melanie turned to Alex with a meaningful look. He puts his hands up as he drifted out of the room, leaving her to help Violet to her feet. "I don't want you to think we're holding you captive," the vampiress said. "But it would be for the best if you came with us to New York until we figure a few things out."

Following her lead to the full-length mirror in the bathroom, Violet said, "They didn't really broadcast me as a murderer, did they?" Her train of thought derailed as she checked herself in the mirror.

She rubbed her eyes, doing a double-take at what she was seeing. The veins that spider webbed around her collarbone were the wrong color, staining gray lines right underneath the skin. It gave her a sickly, unnatural pallor. But the most noticeable change was her eyes, made more prominent and shading away from blue into the same sort of gray as her veins.

Recoiling from herself with a curse, her back ran into Melanie's front. She startled away, her breath coming in short pants. "It'll be okay, Violet. We're going to figure this out," she said, speaking gently.

"Am I a *vampire*?" Her voice cracked with terror. She hadn't known of their shadowy world mere days ago, and no part of her wanted to join them. Not with half-remembered nightmares of bloodshed and sadism resting behind her eyes every time she blinked.

Melanie brought her wrist to her mouth, popping her skin with twin fangs. Wordlessly, she held the bleeding wound out to Violet, who watched two rivulets of blood run down her arm with revulsion.

"No, I don't think you are," she said, wiping away the blood with a rough hotel towel as the punctures closed and healed on their own. "If you were a fledgling vampire, you wouldn't be able to resist the smell of my blood. Our very youngest are always thirsty until their fangs grow in."

"Well, I am thirsty." Violet looked at her toes, where even the veins over her feet were that strange gray.

Taking a glass of water from her bedside, Melanie pressed its cool edge to Violet's lips. At first, she was indignant about being fed water like an invalid, except she knew the moment she took the first few sips, she would've drained the glass and more in desperation to chase away her dry throat. "I don't know what's going on with you yet. But I will find out," she promised. "I need you to think back for me. What happened after you parted ways with Alex in that forest? Did anyone feed you anything against your will?"

Violet closed her eyes and tried to think back. She remembered Kim as a red-eyed demon, pushing away the deal she was cultivating with another vampire named William to instead torture her with evil magic. Those visions of death and gore hit her as she focused, drawing tears as she trembled. She looked around desperately, reminding herself that she was in a motel, not in those nightmares.

"I-I don't know." Melanie held her as she wept, murmuring soothing encouragements.

"No worries. Let's get you cleaned up."

Violet was quite eager for a shower, turning the water up extra hot to scrub away the oily, dread-like feeling still clinging to her. She was reasonably sure that these people wanted to help her, especially Alex. The chilling touch of nightmares must be leading her astray, but she still had no intentions of abandoning her old life.

That was, until she saw the news report. Alex, Melanie, and one other familiar-yet-not vampire sat in the cramped front room once she emerged from her shower, clean and changed into a set of Melanie's clothes. They were more suited to her tall frame rather than Violet's petite one, but they were better than a nightgown.

She stood to the side, all the blood draining from her face as she realized the broadcast was about her. Her unflattering employee ID photo was on screen, showing her thirty pounds heavier and with exhausted bags under her eyes. For that alone, she could go crawl under a bed in mortification. But the contents of the news were worse, so much worse.

Just as William had promised, she'd been framed for the murder of her coworkers. She shook her head in quiet denial, feeling like she was stuck in yet another nightmare. "This can't be happening," she said, backing away from the damning images on screen. The news didn't show bodies, only the pen where they'd been found.

Alex switched to another channel, standing. "Violet—"

"No! I just...I need some air," she said, backing away when he started approaching her. She undid the lock on the door and flung it open, running into the early-evening sunlight. She had to get away, she had to—stop.

Every exposed inch of her skin screamed. The smell of burned flesh surrounded her as the merciless sun scorched down. She turned around in time to see Alex reach her, his skin smoking. He hefted her off her feet and back into the motel room with haste. Her face tingled unpleasantly, and she saw her arms were a lobster red as the burns set in.

"Oh my god," she said. Alex had splotches of pink over his skin, fading as she watched.

"Seems you are a vampire too." He supplied what she wouldn't, couldn't, say about herself. Melanie interrupted them with packs of ice quickly wrapped in towels. She pressed one to Violet's cheek while Alex held two more to her arms.

Her face burned further with shame as they spoke in low tones, coordinating like this was a routine injury they saw. At odds to their serious expressions was the other vampire, who watched from the couch and offered Violet a kind look. He was subtly handsome, more boyish than the others she'd met, being overweight and clean-shaven. He wore casual clothes and a halo of brown curls. "Hello there. We've spoken before. I'm Sam," he said when he noticed her attention drifting away from the emergency intervention going on.

"Yes. I...remember you," she said. They'd spoken before her car was crashed. It was one of the only whole memories she had of that night's ordeal. She'd knocked her head hard right afterward.

"First rule of being a vampire, the sun's not your friend. Takes some getting used to, I know." His British accent was more pronounced than Alex's, enunciating each syllable precisely. He had a voice for the radio, she thought, starting to relax as her burns were soothed as much as possible.

"I don't know how this is possible," she said, glancing to Melanie. "Didn't you just say you didn't think I was..." she couldn't bear to say it.

"Seems I was mistaken," she sighed, placing a hand on her shoulder. "You have to come with us. Life is brutal for a vampiress on her own. We can teach you everything you need to know of your new life."

She set her jaw, discomfort prickling her skin like the pins-and-needles pain of the burn settling in. "I have a life I'm leaving behind then. A job and..." she drifted off, gazing to the television, which was playing a sitcom instead of the news. Despite herself, she knew that old life was over. She was married to that job, pouring her time and effort into it rather than friends or hobbies. "...and a cat. I have a cat."

"We can send someone to get the cat for you," Alex promised. "I, for one, will not be shapeshifting for a long time. A real cat will be the only cat you see. Is there anyone you want to send a message to? Or that could shelter you for a while?"

Violet thought to her old roommates and the scattering of friends she had. "I don't think they'd ever believe what happened," she admitted slowly. It came as a reality check for herself, too. She'd experienced something so extraordinary, no one but actual vampires would understand.

"You've been through something truly traumatic. Please, let us take care of you for a while. We'll get you back on your feet and to a stable, new life." Alex rested a hand on her unburnt shoulder.

There didn't seem to be any other attractive options. She couldn't go backward, so instead, she decided to step into the unknown. "Yes, all right. I'll go with you."

Chapter 11
Violet

Violet felt she'd made the right decision, mulling over it as she watched the world scroll by in the passenger's side of a quiet car. Alex and Sam were in a separate car, leaving her and Melanie alone. Melanie winked as she explained she'd talked them into it, wanting some girl time. Violet had laughed uneasily.

She half-remembered Melanie, that recollection growing sharper the longer she was alone with the sharp-featured woman. Vague memories of her taking down men twice her size danced behind her eyelids, showing them seizing their chests and dying on the spot with barely a glance from Melanie.

"So, what did they show you about me?" Melanie asked as the miles flew by.

"Hmm?"

"I'm taking a guess from your silence that you think you know something about me. Is that true?" she asked, glancing at Violet out of the corner of her eye.

"No. I just don't want to talk," she murmured.

"You are a poor liar, my dear." Melanie offered a smile, which softened her features and made her look almost normal, if uncommonly beautiful.

"I don't want to talk about it," she said again.

"I understand. I just... I hope you know they lied to you.

About us," she said. "We're not bad people. There's nothing to fear from any of us, but you are afraid. I just want to help."

"It's not your fault," Violet said to her window, finding it hard to look over at her. The reality of her situation pushed in. "I don't want to be a vampire. I don't know *how* that happened. My head's full of half-truths."

"I was mortal-born too and none too pleased at first to be turned," Melanie said, sounding distant. Though Violet's interest was piqued, she changed the subject quickly. "Alex has never been saved by an outsider like this. This situation is new to us too."

"I imagine," she murmured. He seemed so much larger than life to need the help of someone else.

"I can answer any questions you have."

Violet considered quietly for long enough that she didn't think she would answer at all. One question was nagging at her enough to ask. There was a dam of questions she worried would break the moment she started asking them. She started with an offhanded comment from Alex about Melanie. "What is the Gift? It sounds important."

"It certainly is. It's the manifestation of a gentle soul, some would say," Melanie said. "It's the only blood ability I'll ever have, but it is very powerful to make up for that. It's used to quickly heal other vampires from life-threatening injuries. I am the coven's strongest healer."

"Can it be used to harm?"

The vampiress paused for a moment. "Only in the direst of circumstances. The Gift will leave forever if you abuse it too often."

"Have you done it before?" Her gorge rose as she saw it again, men dying with barely any effort exerted on Melanie's part.

"Only once, love. Collins and his Haven flunkies overran our headquarters in Massachusetts. I defended our wounded in the only way I could, blade and Gift alike." Violet felt the daymare vision close in, the horror of the moment rippling under her skin. Bodies piling up, clutching their chests as their organs betrayed them. She made a sound like she was choking, finding it hard to make her lungs work.

When she regained her senses, they were parked by the side of the road. Melanie was shining a flashlight into one of her eyes. "All good there? Can you tell me what happened?" Her face was creased with concern.

"I... I saw you. Killing them," she murmured, trembling hard. She took great gasps of breath, trying to calm her racing heart.

"Oh. I'm sorry," she said. She nodded in slow understanding and clasped Violet's hand. "I would never do such a thing to you. I am a doctor and sworn to do no harm. Whatever Cox showed you, that isn't me. I would venture everything you were shown is all distortions of the truth."

"You can't prove it," Violet said, finding it difficult to turn from Melanie's earnest face. She believed it all the same, and that scared her. She didn't know what was real anymore, not when a vampire could apparently reach inside her mind and plant memories like a foul gardener.

"I sure can." Melanie pulled out her phone and offering it over. "Search my name. Melanie Rainey. Read that first result."

Violet did as requested while Melanie drove them back onto the interstate. She read and reread the first result multiple times and then paged to the next. And the next. "You're a surgeon. For humans?" she said.

"And proud of it," she smiled.

"And you have a scholarship in your name. And Sam's." Her eyebrows raised from how long they'd funded it.

"We like to see young minds joining the medical field," she nodded.

"And," Violet added, reading it directly from the page, "you've never made a mistake in any of your surgeries. No manipulation?"

"Not a drop."

"How were you going to hide how you won't be living a normal person's lifespan?" Someone would notice eventually that the flawless surgeon wasn't aging or changing as the years passed.

"The same thing we always do when the time comes. Change

names, locations. There are so many hospitals in need of qualified people," she said.

Violet made an impressed sound, wondering how many times they'd had to do that.

"Well? Do I still seem so bad?" she smiled.

"I... I don't know."

"Bit of cognitive dissonance then," Melanie said. "You know, we could erase the whole ordeal you experienced and start your new life without that trauma."

"No!" Violet blurted. "I mean... that's okay. I would rather remember everything. I... I like knowing my memories haven't been tampered with. More than they already have."

"I understand. Better than you think, I would wager. Such things leave a hole in your memories. It usually doesn't smooth out evenly." Violet felt goosebumps at the idea of having something like that. She would never trust it. "Can you promise me something then?"

"What?" she murmured uneasily.

"You'll give us all a chance to show you our real stripes," Melanie said. "I would hate for you to think me a murderer when I'm quite the opposite. I imagine my blood family would feel the same way about what the Haveners showed you about them."

"I'll try," she said, though she hesitated. That oily dread was back, coating her throat and chest with uneasy ripples.

"Any other questions?" Melanie offered.

So many, she thought, and her uneasiness spurred her toward the most uncomfortable of them. "When will I need to drink blood?"

Tapping her finger on the steering wheel, Melanie considered her answer. "The answer to that should've been right away. But you aren't showing any signs of being a hungry fledgling, which, trust me, you would notice. The only thing giving you away as a vampire is your photosensitive skin."

"So, what's wrong with me?" She frowned, looking down at the gray veins crisscrossing at her wrist.

"Nothing's wrong with you." Melanie was firm rather than

gentle about it, her serious expression saying she would shoot down any contradiction.

She found herself appreciating that bit of bedside manner, searching for something else to talk about that didn't have her skin crawling. She settled for something else readily apparent. "I hope this isn't a personal question, but are you British too?"

Melanie chuckled. "I was, yes. I practiced an American accent with Alex, and usually, I do better at keeping it. It helps that most of my patients are American."

"So, you've been a group for a while."

The other woman said, "If you call three hundred years 'a while,' then yes, we've known each other a while." She glanced over to see Violet gaping and smiled wide enough to show fangs. "There are older vamps out there. We're nothing too special."

"Like, how old?" she asked. Three hundred years was boggling to her. To think there were others who were even older...

"One Ancient lives in New York, and she's about... nine hundred. The years get fuzzy when you get that high," Melanie said, chuckling as she took in Violet's incredulous reaction from the corner of her eye. "To be fair, there's only a handful of Ancients around. It's hard to survive the attention of being the strongest around."

She explained the ranks of vampire-hood, Master, Elder, and Ancient, and how they related to blood abilities. Violet listened with fascination, finding it straightforward if surreal that all this information was completely secret. There were approximately eight bloodlines, with specific abilities inherited from sire to fledgling that developed over time.

"Of course, there are some quirks to this. If a vampire is born from parents of two different bloodlines, their abilities mix or swap around, and that's what gets passed on. So, almost no one can accurately predict what abilities they'll manifest."

"Hold on, what? Vampires can be born that way?" Violet asked, putting her palms up. She thought of vampires as undead, unchanging, allergic to garlic, and unable to see their reflections in a mirror.

Melanie offered a shrug. "It might seem weird, but we're basically humans that have been infected with a blood borne disease. It gives enhanced strength and reflexes, immortality, and a taste for blood, among other things. To simplify things for you, we lose no human functions. Vampire children are a hundred percent human until they come of age, which is when they turn."

"That's crazy. So, I might've met a vampire child and not even known it?" She had a new appreciation for the quirky personalities she'd met in high school.

"Possibly," she said with a smile. "Alex was born a vampire, just so you know. He's our coven master as the eldest and strongest of our group. Since you're joining us, even for a little while, you should know how that works."

She shifted uncomfortably at the reminder that it was an *us* now. For all this talk of bloodlines, she had no idea who'd turned her into a vampire and thus no hints as to what abilities she was to inherit. "All right," she sighed.

"There are twelve covens that share New York City. The more mortals in one place, the higher a population of vampires it can support. I estimate that's about ten thousand vampires concentrated in one city, which tends to cause conflict regardless of resources."

"But why?" Violet interrupted.

"You know how mortals get competitive over money? Vampires are that way with power. Everyone wants to be top dog, especially the coven masters. That means coven warfare and assassinations at their very worst." Violet made a sound of distress, and Melanie frowned. "Sorry, touchy subject. Just know that you're in a stable coven. We have allies and enemies, but Alex can tell you more later."

To Violet's relief, they steered the conversation away from talk of bloodshed. Melanie kept her talking all the way to the city, and she found herself grateful to have found a friend to relate to in the mess her life had become. She watched the city's skyline on the horizon, amazed at the scope of the buildings. She'd never been anywhere so big and sprawling before. But now, for a time, it would be home.

Chapter 12
Alex

Kim Cox and the Haveners were long in their underground burrows by the time Alex and his friends had their boots on the ground in New York. Even vampires of their advanced age knew they wouldn't win if they entered Haven's warren of death traps hidden in abandoned subway tunnels.

Alex returned to his mansion home frustrated and brooding and called a meeting with his most trusted. Samuel and Melanie, his deputy and chief healer. Julian, head enforcer. Luke Tsosie, a feral-eyed American Indian man who had long declared Alex his brother and served as his faithful shadow. Nicholas Ochembu, head of security and former coven master, a true ally and friend. And Petra Jolovic with her lifemate and husband, Frederic. She served as head provider while he supported her and kept her safe.

Alex glanced around at the seven of them, his inner circle when times were rough in Coven Rehnquist. "As you all know, I got into a firefight on my own and ended up drugged and stuck in the form of a lion," he began, sipping from a glass of wine. How easy it was to resume his place at the head of the table, relaxing in the wing-backed leather chair. They all nodded. "You fought to release me, but you didn't get me back."

"Not for a lack of trying, brother," Luke remarked.

"I know. Now for the part you all got secondhand. I was transported by Haveners to the Cincinnati Zoo, where I was to be framed as a man-killer, either to be euthanized or to live out my days as a wild animal, being pointed at like some carnival sideshow. That was where I met Violet Reynolds. She was the only survivor, and we took her vehicle to safety."

"Then the car went into the river, you two got lost in the forest, she got captured by Haveners, and now you are back?" Petra said, her words difficult to make out through a thick Russian accent.

"Yes. I was going to tell you more, but that's my story there. Meeting adjourned," he joked, getting a few chuckles. "But to add to that quick timeline: she's captured by Haveners, given a hellscape via Kim Cox, and I discover a new power saving her from it." Now he could hear a pin drop. Only Julian seemed disengaged, cleaning under his nails with a blade. "My friends, I have ascended. I can now walk in dreams." He explained the dream he'd had and journeying with Violet to destroy many memories that weren't hers before they overwhelmed her waking mind.

"So... can you do it again?" Nicholas asked. "Without the beast?"

"I don't know, my good man," he admitted. "All I know is that I want to keep this as secret as possible. Perhaps with some control, I will walk the dreams of our enemies. Spreading influence and misdirection or even stealing memories." They nodded in approval at that. "While I wish it were daywalking, I can see why my father's claim to fame would be last." Daywalking was a coveted vampire ability, which allowed a vampire to experience sunshine in all its deadly glory without being hurt.

"This seems like it would be more useful if you can do all that with it," Sam remarked.

"Indeed. Time will tell," he nodded. "There is another thing I would have us discuss before we turn to the matters of the coven. Violet is in the process of transforming into a vampiress. Her blood, however, is silver, and she exhibits none of a fledgling's usual bloodlust."

He chewed on his guilt for a moment before revealing that he'd given her a few drops of his blood to survive the car crash.

Ever since she'd burned herself running into the late-evening sunshine, he'd blamed a combination of his blood and Cox's torture for her odd transformation. But when he presented these facts to his friends to see their opinion, he earned only confused glances and murmurs.

"I'm going to consult my Gifted friends and see if they've seen anything like it," Melanie promised once he was finished.

Julian looked up from his blade, licking dry lips. "My father used to speak of a silver-eyed woman."

"Well, your father didn't have all his marbles," Alex said, though he made an encouraging gesture. Julian so rarely mentioned his father, an infamous Ancient by the name of Marcus the Fair. Some of the things Marcus had done defied belief in the level of his cruelty and megalomania.

The murderer of that tyrant sat close by, reluctantly speaking of an old memory. "Regardless, he knew of one. She was one of the women who ruined his view of relationships." He shrugged, speaking to his dagger. "So, at least we know that someone like that used to exist. No one else has silver eyes naturally, not like what you're talking about."

"I see. Well, I'm keeping Violet with us until we can figure out what's going on with her transformation." Alex flashed him a concerned glance. He knew Julian would brood now that he'd brought up his past.

"Any objections?" He glanced around the room.

"A question. When do I get to meet her?" Petra asked, smiling broadly. "Sounds like a girl in need of a makeover."

"I'll leave that to your expert care," he said.

When no one else spoke up, he let the council sweep him into talk of the coven and what he'd missed. With most of Haven mobilized to dispose of him before he could be rescued, it had been quiet at home. He was thankful for that as they planned their counterattack.

He found he was rather distracted by the time he adjourned the meeting and went to bed early. He laid down to rest in his mansion's master suite, alone, hoping to walk in Violet's dreams again. Tentatively reaching out to his inner beast, he baited it to awareness with the idea of dream walking. It yawned and stretched out tendrils of mental influence as sleep took him.

THIS TIME, HE WAS HIMSELF, THOUGH HE WOULD'VE wandered aimlessly in the dark if it weren't for his inner beast. He didn't know how it worked. All he knew was that he followed Violet's dreaming self like a shadow, shattering shards of hellscape before she could enter them. This went on for a couple of memories until she came up to one that resisted erasing. She disappeared into it while Alex muttered a curse.

Following her, he realized it was the same nightmare he'd first found her in as a cat. *I thought we erased this.*

His inner beast responded with a surge of animal fear. On the surface, a field of corn and a fire in the distance was not scary...to Violet.

Cox couldn't have predicted that he'd see this nightmare personally, but she'd conjured up a night that still haunted him.

"Alex?"

He startled. Violet had spotted him there, her dreaming self's brow scrunched in confusion. Here, she appeared mortal, her eyes a natural shade of blue and her veins blessedly normal where they pulsed at her neck. She smiled, carefree in the scape of her own mind. There was no way for her to know he was real, and he kept that information to himself as he offered a tentative smile back.

"Do you know what this place is?" she asked, looking him over. "And why are you wearing that?"

Glancing down, he realized he was wearing a native's leather clothing. His hair was longer and clicked with beads. "Just remembering," he replied. Almost as if on cue, his old hunting group appeared out of the corner of his eye, laden with the evening catch for the mortals who lived in their village.

Laughing with one of the men was a younger Luke Tsosie, whose own carefree way died this night. Alex realized that his own memories were tainting this nightmare, adding definition and reality to the horrors they were about to walk into.

"I don't think you need to see this," he said to Violet, closing his eyes and blocking out how real this moment felt. He didn't hear Luke joking around or his other friends spotting the smoke billowing on the horizon.

No, he focused on a different night, coming home to his peaceful old village, where he, Sam, Melanie, and Julian were amongst the only white folk living in a generous settlement of Native Americans. He opened his eyes to find Violet next to him, her dreamy smile still fixed in place. "Where are we?" she asked.

Figuring she would never remember this as a dream, he told her what was on his heart. "My first home in America. This is the early seventeen hundreds, Massachusetts. My little coven and I moved to the New World seeking safety from the likes of Bryant Collins and his crusade after he'd massacred the rest of my family." She walked by his side as he took in the old sight of his home. Most were asleep while the vampires roamed, but those still awake and active went about their routine as if he and Violet were ghosts. "There were four vampires in my coven at the time, myself included. We were little more than a small band of rogues, fitting in where we could. I met my lifemate here, in this village."

"What is a lifemate?" she said.

"A one and only. The other half of your soul. A soulmate. A vampire's perfect partner." His heart hurt as he saw her memory, waiting for him to return from his evening hunt.

He spoke to Violet like the other half of his heart wasn't there, for while Violet lived, the other woman was only a memory now. "Mary Ann."

Mary Ann was a pretty native woman, tall and strong and dark as her people. Alex looked down at her wistfully as she stroked her belly idly, revealing a swell hiding underneath the generous dress she wore. "Collins found us," he told Violet. "He took the entire town from me. Only Mary Ann's brother survives to this day."

After a hesitant last glance toward Mary Ann, he walked through the village with his hands in his pockets. Once more, he was his modern self, wandering his old home like a tourist might. He took a purple flower from a florist's shop, offering it to Violet with a bowing flourish. "I'm sorry for your loss," she said, her dreaming smile fading at last.

The dream fell apart around them, leaving them in the misty darkness of her sleeping mind. Only the flower remained, pinned behind her ear. But her gaze sharpened, turning silver and keen as a subtle *pop* filled the air. He glanced over her shoulder to see the last of the hellscape shards loosening, weakened enough to fade from her subconscious mind.

He breathed out his tension, glad for a job well done even if his chest hurt with heartsickness. For a few long moments, it was just him and the vampiress version of Violet. Perhaps she was finished with her transformation already, gaining a hint of the otherworldly beauty that came so easily to most vampires. She was petite, but her strong features belied an inner strength he couldn't help but admire.

She was...

Gorgeous, he admitted.

If she hadn't been through a hellscape and back in the last two days, he might've complimented that very thing. No one recovered from what she'd experienced immediately, especially if they'd nearly died from the experience. He'd been around long enough to know when to approach a woman, and in the middle of a dream when they both nursed their own private wounds wasn't the time.

He didn't know how long they drifted there together before her expression contorted with fear. His inner beast raised its hackles as they heard a woman's voice. *"Poor thing."*

"Who is that, Violet?" Alex asked, taking her by the shoulders as she twitched, seeming to stare through him.

"Such a victim. Fated to die so senselessly."

Alex woke with a bitter taste in his mouth.

Chapter 13
Violet

Violet woke clawing at her covers, covered in cold sweat. That woman's voice was enough to make her skin crawl. She associated it with the bitter taste of death, which had had her in its grasp.

Shrugging off the clammy sheets, she went to check herself in the bathroom mirror. *"Poor thing,"* whispered that woman's voice, smooth and terrible.

She inspected herself in the mirror, shocked by how clear and shiny her eyes seemed after a rest. The color of newly minted nickels, they tracked perfectly in her face, as alien as they seemed. Her visible veins had faded, leaving her skin flawless and smooth like a doll's. It was so different from how she'd appeared mere days ago, and she found herself wanting that normalcy back.

"What happened? Why is this happening to me?" she whispered.

This time, it felt like the voice from her dreams was talking directly to her. *"I made you strong. You are a victim no longer."*

Violet shook herself. "Okay, creepy dream voice," she muttered, splashing her face with water to wake fully from the foggy tendrils still coiled up in her waking thoughts. She'd just had the most lucid of dreams, experiencing a brief taste of the past with Alex, who'd opened up for her like a book.

Just a dream, she thought to herself. Someone old and

powerful like him wouldn't be so forthcoming, especially to a troubled near-stranger such as herself. She showered off the memories, focusing on what she could control. It would be her luck that someone would recognize her, vampire looks or not. It seemed she wasn't the only one thinking of that, as she heard a visitor knock at her door once she was finished and dried off.

Petra Jolovic, a red-lipped beauty with a thick Slavic accent, took in her measure at the door, clicking her tongue. Violet was dressed in another of Melanie's borrowed outfits and distinctly aware of every wrinkle and overlong sleeve. "This will not do!" the vampiress announced after a brief introduction.

"Are you going to take me shopping?" Violet asked hopefully before remembering that, despite being in a mansion somewhere in the suburbs of New York City, she had no money to her name.

"No, sorry," Petra answered. "I'll buy you clothes and give you a makeover. You need to avoid the police. And..." she looked Violet pointedly in the eyes.

"They are strange, aren't they?" she admitted.

Petra came into the room, various tools clattering at her belt. She took out a measuring tape and shook her head. "Your eyes are *beautiful*. We ladies understate ourselves. Hold still!" Violet sputtered with surprise, a flattered blush rising to her cheeks.

Wielding that measuring tape with expert precision, Petra murmured to herself as she took down several specific measurements. "Did Alex send you to do this?" Violet asked.

"It's my job," Petra said. "Providing for new coven members is big part of what I do. Are you hungry?"

On cue, Violet's belly groused. Fed on little but air and rest stop snacks, hungry was an understatement. "Just food. Regular food. No blood, please," she said politely.

Petra considered her with a frown. "Have you actually tried blood? Melanie said you have no interest."

"I really don't. Look, I'll make breakfast myself—"

"No, dear! I'll get it for you," she promised, backing toward the door. "Hang tight!"

Violet had the suspicion that she'd try sneaking blood somewhere into her meal and wretched at the thought. She followed

Petra down a flight of stairs to make sure, taking in glimpses of a brick fireplace and antique, carved chairs in a sitting room before they were in a kitchen big enough for commercial use. She checked the cabinets, rummaging for cereal but coming up empty.

Literally. The kitchen was almost empty.

"You vampires don't eat, huh," she remarked. She recalled Melanie stating that they could, but most didn't. It was hell of a diet, too, leaving most vampires svelte. Apparently, one could tell if a vampire ate mortal food or not depending on their weight. Which meant Sam must have snacks somewhere, she thought.

"Not usually," Petra answered cheerfully. She set aside some staples from the fridge and let Violet take control of things with a smile. "I'll be back with your new wardrobe. And contacts."

"Thanks," Violet said, offering a genuine smile for a moment. She wouldn't forget the generosity, biting her lip on asking that she buy groceries too. Violet could make do with eggs and Poptarts, for that's what she found in the kitchen. Still, she breathed a sigh of relief when Petra left, glad she didn't need to watch food prep like a hawk for any contamination.

She hid herself in the breakfast nook, watching stars speckle to life and a breeze shake through a garden muted by twilight's grace. There were some perks to vampirism, she admitted, realizing that there was no ambient light beyond what nature provided. She waited for that oily dread to reappear as it had yesterday at every inopportune moment.

But she felt no fear over planning for the future, just a gaping uncertainty. How had she really become a vampiress? And what would she do now that she was one? Her old job was ruined, as was her name. She would need a whole new start.

Maybe there was some vampire-related task she could do. She'd have to ask Alex. But she couldn't rely on his charity forever. As much as he may think he owed her, she hated relying on another's goodwill. There was no way of telling when that generosity would evaporate.

"Don't tell me you're brooding." Alex's real voice was a surprise. She startled, glancing up, expecting for a moment to see a lion instead of the man dressed in black having a seat next to her so he too could admire the garden outside.

"And if I were?"

Humor was tugging at his lips as if this were some inside joke to him. "You'd be in good company. It's a fine pastime for some of us," he said, eyeing her breakfast. "Still not feeling blood, hmm?"

She wrinkled her nose. "Not at all."

"Hmm." Now she could feel his gaze on her. "I think you've finished transforming at least. That's pretty typical. It takes a few days for the change to settle."

"But I should be craving blood."

"The most dangerous time for a vampire is when they first start," he said, frowning to himself. "The bloodlust is that bad. And if it's not sated, they die."

"Brutal," she said, shuddering.

"Indeed. But nothing like that for you. You don't remember being fed any blood by a Havener? Nothing like that?"

She remembered the voice. *"I made you strong."*

"No, nothing like that," she said, swallowing past a sudden lump in her throat. She looked into his troubled expression.

His dream face had been so crisp, so perfect. It'd mimicked what she'd seen of him yesterday. But this version of him had the shadow of an unshaved jaw and frown lines. His face wasn't perfectly symmetrical, like any normal person.

"You look different," she said before she could think better of it.

He raised a brow. "What do you mean, love?"

A mortified blush rose to her cheeks. She couldn't believe she'd uttered that thought aloud. "Do, uh, vampires have some magic? For their appearance?"

"Yes, actually. We call it a glamor," he said, offering a casual shrug as liquid as the prowl of a big cat. "The older a vampire is, the more attractive they are until it's nearly impossible to look at them. It's part of the mental abilities we gain as we age. You may have noticed there's no unattractive vampire."

"Pretty quickly," she said dryly.

"Underneath the glamor, most of us are normal people. In

addition to this, there's also the aura, which tells you exactly how old a vampire is. Someone will need to teach you to keep yours under wraps when it develops fully. It's rude to run around broadcasting how old you are." He offered a lopsided smile. It was more charming than any perfect one he'd flashed before, she thought.

"How does that work?" she asked curiously.

"So glad you asked! I'm going to unleash mine on you briefly," he said, a tone of warning there. She realized why a few moments later as every hair on her body stood on end. Heat and mild pain prickled at her skin, like a second burn overtop the first she was still raw from. "Not fun, right? The older a vampire gets, the less pleasant it is to be close to them."

"Could you, maybe, turn that off?" she asked, rubbing her arms, which felt hot to the touch. He nodded, the heat of his aura retreating until she could relax again.

"The only vampire I've met with a different aura is my friend, Julian. His is bitter cold. Maybe he'll show you sometime."

"Is your glamor up right now?" she asked, nodding to that. She figured he had a lot of friends she could meet, but it really depended on how long she was staying here.

"Yes, always."

"Oh, all right." It felt lame to leave it off at that, and she recognized the curious look that earned.

"Why do you ask? Is it not working?"

"I'm not sure." She could feel the heat return to her cheeks. "You're not, like, flawless right now. You look like a normal person."

"You see me as a normal person?" He frowned thoughtfully. "That should only be possible if you're an older vamp than me."

"Yes. I don't know," she said, feeling like she was about to put her foot in her mouth.

Especially as he slanted her a sly look. "Like what you see?"

"Uh, sure. You have a nice smile. A little off center. It's charming," she babbled.

He flashed a wink, kicking up her pulse. "So you can see what I look like. It can be our secret." His soft voice twisted up her insides effortlessly as he leaned in. For a moment, she thought he'd steal a kiss, but he took her plate instead and stood, putting some distance between them.

Her heart calmed after a deep breath, and she gave herself a little shake. *Stop imagining things,* she told herself.

"Petra said she's getting you some clothes and possibly giving you a full makeover," he said, crossing to the sink and running water over the plate. His movements were stilted.

"That's right," she said with a nod.

"I imagine she'll sort all of that out with you by daybreak," he said. "Nicholas...you'll meet him later. He says I have a visitor."

"Yeah?" She didn't see a phone on him. It seemed he came up with this out of nowhere.

"Yeah. She's a dangerous vampiress. I need you to go back to your room for now. We have Netflix," he said, flicking water from his fingertips.

She raised a suspicious brow, feeling like he was suddenly trying to ditch her. "Sure. I can babysit myself."

"What's that tone for?" He sounded distracted, checking his pockets.

"Oh, I dunno, just you getting word of a visitor out of nowhere."

He paused, glancing up to meet her eye. *"Another vampire perk. Mental communication."* His voice was in her head, his lips unmoving.

"How did you...?"

"Later." He made an impatient gesture. "I know this is strange, but I need you to hide out in your room. I don't want my visitor to know I have a new fledgling around."

"Just vampire things, huh?" she asked with a nervous chuckle. She parted ways with him, going back to her room. His quick dismissal didn't bother her as much as it appeared.

It was just the mental communication part. How similar his voice in her head felt compared to the woman's voice from her dreams. The one who had, supposedly, made Violet strong.

Chapter 14
Alex

Alex rushed to his office where Cossette Deveaux would be waiting for him. His mansion's location was hardly a secret; however, vampire society was based on a hierarchy of rules. Coven members could come and go from his home as they pleased, but it was different for members of rival covens. They were trespassing on his territory.

Vampires were heavily territorial creatures despite their mostly human appearance. So, when his head of security said Cossette had arrived and demanded to speak to him, he was on high alert.

She was an exception to the rules, a girl who could go where she pleased. Cossette sat in his office chair, which gave him pause for a moment before he realized his computer was locked and on a screensaver. The girl smiled like she was about to share some giddy secret. "Hi, Mister Rehnquist. I'm glad you're back," she said, giggling sweetly. She spoke in French, her mother tongue.

Cossette was no normal girl. She was the Ancient who lived in New York, a neighbor to Coven Rehnquist with a mega-sized following she'd acquired over the years. One of the eldest and strongest of their kind. Despite that, she had the body of an eight-year-old girl, with an albino's pale skin and pinkish-red eyes. She kept her white hair tied back in pigtails, her ribbons a sky blue today to match the ruffled dress she wore.

"I'm glad I'm back too. To what do I owe the pleasure of your visit?" he answered in French.

"I missed you! You weren't around when the island rose from the sea. I've so been wanting to talk to someone about it," she said, crossing her arms.

He masked a sigh of relief as a cough, seating himself in one of the chairs he saved for visitors. Her visits were like a box of chocolates, usually pleasant, but he always steeled himself for that one gooey chocolate that made a mess. "To be honest, I haven't given it much thought."

"That just won't do. I've seen you there." She spoke with solemn surety, a sober reminder of the Ancient power pulsing within her fragile frame.

He frowned. "You have? When?"

"Oh, a couple of days ago when you were in mortal danger with your new friend," she said, switching to cheerful and giggly in a blink.

It took him a moment to realize his mistake. He had meant when would he visit the new island, but she'd answered him far more literally with when this vision of the future had struck her. "Watched the news lately, have you?"

"Oh no, I saw the whole thing," she said, still smiling.

He raised a brow. "Did you see what happened to Violet?" So much for keeping her a secret from the Ancient's attention, which meant she would speak of it to others. But if she could shed some light on her abnormal transformation, it would be worth it.

Cossette smiled wider. "I can't say."

"All right. I'll bargain for it." Now he did sigh aloud. "What are your terms?"

"I mean, there's something else you were going to bargain for. It might've been even more important than this." The keen side of her was back, knowing exactly what he was thinking.

"I'm not sure anymore." He threw up a hand. It was likely she wouldn't answer either of his desires directly. "But you're right. I was going to ask for an exception to the Accords."

One of the benefits, and drawbacks, to an Ancient neighbor was the power her coven wielded over its neighbors, the eleven covens that'd cut out and parceled the city's territory. There was a twelfth—Haven—which operated in the shadows and underground but kept an appropriate deference to Cossette. Following her master's example, she'd created the Deveaux Accords and destroyed, drove off, or assimilated any covens not willing to follow her edicts.

It was easy to look at a little girl and think she didn't mean business, but she did. Every time. He'd seen it happen enough that he spoke to the nine-hundred-year-old for permission every time his coven approached a scuffle with the Accords. "Are you sure what you're planning is wise?" Cossette asked now, any hint of childish mirth gone from her face.

"No. But I need revenge. If not for my sake, for Violet. Collins is going to hide his wife's sorry self in his headquarters or tower, and there's not a damn thing I can do about it." He clenched his fist, checking a slam on his chair arm that would've destroyed the thin wood.

"If I allow you to attack his most vulnerable people, he in turn would have permission to attack your mansion and business. And it sets a precedent that I allow all-out war and possible exposure to mortals. You know I allow safe zones for every coven so we can co-exist without murdering mortal employees or innocent vampire children." She spread her hands in a helpless gesture.

"If Collins and Cox never leave their safe zones, it's a manipulation of the spirit of your rules." He shook his head, clutching at his temples.

"Yet they have agreed to the rules as well. You sleep peacefully in your mansion. You can keep your friend here knowing they'll never be able to steal her away and torture her again as long as she doesn't step foot outside the fence."

"So you know about the torture. You know what happened to her," he said, seeing his request as a lost cause. His enemies would continue to hide in their strongholds, hardly venturing out unless there was little chance for reprisal.

He seethed with the need to put an end to both of them, Collins for his constant harassment and Cox for her blatant sadism, but if he acted against the Accords, Cossette's coven would fall upon his own and destroy it like it'd done with count-less others.

Nothing changed. Both sides hid like turtles, plotting.

He figured it could be worse. He could live in Massachusetts again, where there were no Accords or protections from a huge coven like Cossette's. His home could go up in flames on the regular, his coven left to ashes.

If they'd settled in New York, maybe his lifemate would still be alive.

"I know what happened to her." For a moment, he thought she was talking about Mary Ann. A bit of dream walking and the scab over that old wound was off.

But no, she was talking about Violet, clearly the person he'd asked about. He gave himself a mental shake. "You'll appreciate your restraint soon enough. Maybe not today or tomorrow, but someday, you can proudly say you've never broken the Accords."

Cossette hopped to her feet, flashing him a smile. "You'll also figure out everything about Violet. All the best mysteries come together in pieces. I'll see you later, Mister Rehnquist."

He saw her out without another word, returning to his desk to sit heavily in the chair she'd vacated. To distract himself, he typed out every word of their conversation. Sometimes she dropped hints, even when it seemed she left him emptyhanded.

It was a good distraction, keeping his mind on the right track. He narrowed in on one phrase in particular. "You'll appreciate your restraint," he said aloud.

He could think of several reasons why. He'd appreciate having his men rested and ready for another threat. Or maybe he'd like not losing his coven, the men and women he'd worked so hard to support and knit together as a community.

His last thought was that maybe he wouldn't want to set a precedent for another group to come in and attack him. An unknown threat loomed on the horizon, as mysterious as the rising of the island mortals were calling Atlantis or the silver in Violet's blood.

Don't overanalyze, he told himself, pushing away from those words and the unease they brought with them.

Chapter 15
Violet

Petra returned while she was mid-episode of a binge watch, bringing her out of the drama on screen to her reality. Violet appreciated the woman who went shopping for her. It was necessary to change her appearance and lie low for a while, but she still resented Haven for putting her in this position.

As she let the other vampiress into her room, laden with bags from boutiques open late, she decided to shake off those memories and enjoy the moment. *Girls love makeovers*, she told herself, helping Petra find places to leave the bags.

"I brought you everything you'll need," Petra said with a smile and a wink as if they shared the same joke.

She wasn't kidding either. Violet felt uneasy in a different sense as she pushed the tissue paper aside in one bag and came up with a lacy bra. "This is too much. What do I owe you for all of this?" She checked other bags, seeing the essentials were covered and so much more. For someone who went through life wearing baggy shirts and jeans, she saw many items she wouldn't buy for herself.

"Nothing." Petra caught her hands when she moved to protest. "Not. One. Thing. You're in my coven now, and I provide for you. No strings attached."

"But—"

"No buts! Try this on." She pushed a couple items toward Violet. "I bought nice things for you. Show me they fit."

She ended up showing several outfits, all fitting perfectly to her frame. "This one," Petra said, nodding in approval of her in a summer ensemble of khaki pants and a sky-blue blouse with a ruffled collar that opened in a vee slightly lower than Violet was used to. "You'll wear this after we're done."

Lined up on the sink were several different bottles of store-brand hair dye and costume contacts. Petra let her choose, and they worked together to give her a new style so she wasn't obviously the Violet Reynolds broadcasted as a murderer for the world to see. She was glad to move on from that, wanting to forget it'd ever happened.

She was in the midst of learning how to apply contacts when there was a knock at the door. "I'll get it. Keep trying," Petra urged, bustling away.

Violet cringed as she observed the wet plastic disc on her fingertip. The worst time in applying them was apparently the first time, and she hadn't successfully placed one on her eye yet. She gladly placed the contact back into its solution when she heard Petra cry out.

"What are you doing? We don't have pets here," Petra exclaimed. An unfamiliar man stood at the threshold, hardly looking chastened as he tried to step past her. In his arms was a comfortably plump orange tabby.

"Gus!" Violet exclaimed, rushing forward to take her cat and snuggle him close. She blamed her teary eyes on the contacts as she turned a grateful look up at the person who'd brought him. Another vampire, but clearly a friend if he went to get her cat.

He actually seemed familiar on second glance. Ruddy-skinned, with a long, serious face and pin-straight black hair held back in a leather strap. He was clearly Native American, the first she'd ever met in person.

But how did she know him? He wore all black, lion symbols stitched at the shoulders. And his gaze was unmistakable, amber and keen like a wolf's. With eyes like that, she imagined he had to be a shapeshifter.

"Thank you, sir," she said. "I didn't expect to see him again, and so soon!"

"It was no bother." He offered the hint of a smile. "He was being fostered, so I adopted him out." *Completely legal,* she thought, watching him put down a few bags laden with supplies to care for him.

"Are we really keeping this animal here?" Petra muttered to him.

He offered a shrug. "Alex is fine with it."

"Gus isn't just an animal. He's my fur baby," Violet cooed, bouncing him gently until he started to squirm and meow in complaint.

"You're getting fur on your new clothes," Petra fretted, picking individual bits from her blouse once she set Gus down.

"Sorry." Violet grinned, hardly unrepentant. But she remembered her manners, sticking her hand out to the man. "I'm Violet, by the way."

He shook her hand. "Luke Tsosie. Unofficial third-in-command in the coven."

"Oh, I didn't expect someone so important to get my cat," she said, feeling heat lick her cheeks from how informal this introduction was.

"Please. My place is to do the odd jobs. And this was one of the more pleasant tasks Alex has given me." He had that hint of a smile again. "You ladies have fun." With that, he excused himself, and Violet went back to the sink where the contacts were waiting for her.

"Wash your hands. Cat hair, worst thing to get caught in your eyes," Petra said as soon as Violet reached for the basin where the little torture devices rested.

Rolling her eyes, she did and started trying to force one of the discs on her eye before her lids closed instinctively.

It wasn't until early morning that Violet realized Petra didn't live in the mansion. She left to go back to her husband while Violet wandered downstairs in search of something to eat. Primped and newly made-up, her thoughts looped, guilt crashing into several reassurances from Petra that this was how coven life worked.

The strong and stable helped the new assimilate and thrive. She sighed as she rummaged in the kitchen, reminded of how bare it was. "Eggs again, I guess," she said to herself, realizing, for all their goodwill, the vampires were assuming she was exactly like them, not needing this sort of sustenance.

"That seems lame." She nearly dropped the carton as she looked over at Alex lounging against the countertop behind her. Now she was sure she could see through his glamor; she saw that his hair and clothes were tousled.

"Must've been a hell of a meeting," she remarked. "Why does it seem like your place is empty except for a few visitors?"

"Most people don't like living with their boss." He eyed her sparse setup for dinner. "I know of a takeout place open morning, day, and night."

And that's how she ended up getting Chinese takeout with a vampire coven master, who shared that about twenty other vampires shared the mansion with him. "It's a protected area, according to the Deveaux Accords. So, any sick or wounded come and go as well," he added. She watched him in fascination as he wielded a pair of chopsticks with ease.

"Have you any interest in vampire law and politics?" he asked.

"Maybe when my head isn't exploding with all the other vampire facts I'm still trying to remember." She felt the edge of a headache coming on.

"A different topic then. Perhaps I can take you to see the city properly tomorrow? I couldn't help but admire Petra's handiwork." His gaze drifted over her.

She felt a blush start to settle on her cheeks. "Do you think anyone would see me and think of the news?" she asked.

"I seriously doubt it. So, is it a date?"

She paused a beat too long, wondering if he meant *date* like...

well, an actual date. Just the two of them. Did she know him well enough?

Isn't that the point of a date? she thought.

"It's okay if you don't want to. Just an offer," he said as she sat there paralyzed by the offer and her own indecision.

"No...I mean, yes, I'd like to go with you," she stammered. *Oh yes, silky smooth. Really impressing this guy.*

Regardless, Alex beamed. "Tomorrow then. You won't regret it."

Chapter 16
Alex

Alex realized the next night that two successful nights of dream walking lulled him into a false sense of his own abilities. He didn't hook into anyone's dreams in particular and woke with the scent of burning corn in his nostrils. As he shook off the cobwebs, he wasn't sure if he'd stepped foot in another's dreams or just experienced his own nightmare, spurred on by seeing Mary Ann's face again after all these years.

He was being paranoid. Violet, Cossette, Atlantis. Strange times were throwing him off his game.

Violet likely wasn't awake yet, so he settled in the front foyer to wait with a steaming mug of tea. Though he'd taken care of any pressing needs with his coven and investment business, early evening was when most new problems were dropped at his lap. Instead, his favorite Italian duo arrived, Julian and Armando. They were both dressed in black and concealing their weapons, perfect for shadowing him and Violet tonight.

"Hey boss!" Armando sat across from him while Julian remained standing, cracking his neck. "It's nice to see you. I mean, like, you, not a lion or a cat or something."

"Nice to see you too," he chuckled.

"So what are you two gonna do? Are you really laying the charm thick on the missus or...?"

"I'm not sure yet." He took another sip, aware of Julian's

frown over the rim of his mug. Following his date tonight was really a waste of resources when it came to his head enforcer, but Alex wanted to give him an easy night's work. Julian so rarely took time off for himself, even when he needed it most.

"You hardly know this girl," Julian said.

"Isn't that the point of a date, man? Get to know someone, see if you're compatible. See if it goes somewhere else." Armando waggled his brow.

Julian's forehead wrinkled. "Never do that again."

Alex bit down on his lip to keep a laugh from escaping. "Sorry, man. I'll just be uptight about everything," Armando replied, sticking his nose in the air. "I'll tell women my uncle prohibits any fun."

"That's not true." Julian rolled his eyes. "You have enough fun for the both of us."

"Can I get you lads some tea while we wait?" Alex spoke up when Armando opened his mouth, knowing they could go on like this for hours.

"When is this supposed to get started?" Julian asked, glancing at his watch.

"I didn't set a time. Figured we were all patient men. It takes women an eternity to get ready after all." But as if his words jinxed it, he heard footsteps on the stairs. They all turned to watch her descent.

While Petra had made her over, Violet's natural beauty made her new look work. Her hair was a light platinum, layers cut to frame her face and soften her features. She wore a dove gray skirt that billowed to mid-calf, complimenting a button-up lavender blouse and strappy sandals of the same hue.

Stopping short when she spotted Julian, she audibly swallowed. Alex got to his feet quickly to put an arm around her. "You look lovely this evening," he said. "These two are some of my closest friends. This is Julian, or Bloodhound, depending on who you ask."

"That's, um, quite a nickname," she remarked, her dainty hand swallowed up by Julian's meaty palm. Alex could see why he was intimidating, being nearly six and a half feet of muscle with the no-nonsense expression of a solider.

"Just call me Julian." He softened his usually cool tone. "A pleasure to meet you at last. You've made quite the splash amongst the coven."

Armando offered his hand next with a big smile. "Hi, pretty lady. I'm Armando. No nicknames here unless you want to give me one."

"This dynamic duo will be shadowing us tonight. For your protection," he said, seeing her brief smile to Armando fade with concern.

"Will something happen that I need protecting from?" she asked.

"No, just another vampire thing. I would rather focus on you instead of always looking over my shoulder. Shall we go?" He offered his arm.

"I...yes. Let's go," she said, letting him escort her outside with a thoughtful twist to her lips. He took her past the gate of his manor, symbolically leaving the protected zone for his coven and taking a wary look around.

He knew how it must look to her—that she was unsafe. She seemed tense as she mirrored him, seeing only the evening and a pair of cars waiting for them. He led her to the first while Julian and Armando got into the second, ready to follow. The tension left her shoulders as they were alone again.

"Is it really necessary to have two of your men follow us? I feel like a teenager on her first date again," she remarked.

"Think of them less as an escort because they're not here to be our purity police." He snickered at the thought since Armando would encourage them while Julian would do the exact opposite. "I really just want to give you my full attention."

She blushed a lovely gray shade, reminiscent of her clothing. Though her contacts now hid the otherworldly eyes and made them appear a shiny blue, small things like that gave away her true nature. "Okay. I'll trust the process," she said. "What are we doing, by the way?"

"Well, you've never been to New York City before, right?"

He smiled when she shook her head. "Luckily for us, the city never sleeps. Or so they say. I wanted to show you some of my favorite haunts. Maybe get to know you better."

"That sounds like fun." She smiled over at him, though her nose was mostly pointed toward the windshield, gawking as they entered the traffic of the city proper. "No vampy stuff today, okay?"

"No vampy stuff," he agreed.

"Will you tell me more about you?" she asked, turning a curious glance his way.

"I thought you said no vampy stuff."

She let out an unladylike snort of amusement. "Okay, in moderation."

"In moderation, hmm..." He'd lived such a long life that he was at a loss for what she'd actually find interesting. "Well, I'm almost five hundred. You lose track of time except for about three notable birthdays, and five hundred is one of them."

Completely serious, she turned to him and said, "You're younger than I thought."

Taken off guard, he sputtered a laugh. "I'll take that as a compliment, thank you. Everyone wants to be younger than they look."

"Don't say that to someone who had a baby face through college," she said.

"I've had a baby face since I was past forty." For the first time since they met, she laughed clearly. *Progress,* he thought.

Again, said his inner beast, purring at the back of his mind like a content cat. It stirred and yawned. He'd thought it in a coma, having not heard its simple input since their first night dream walking together. But it liked Violet, which was also good.

Nothing canned a possible partner faster than that little bud of instincts and id at the back of his mind screaming or hissing in dislike. Those women were invariably incompatible in several ways. He didn't know how the inner beast could tell, but sometimes, it was smarter than him, born of his shapeshifting magic.

"Anyway, I figure I should start at the beginning, and you tell me if I'm boring you," he said. "I'm from England. A pseudo-noble, so to speak. Neither of my parents were nobility, but they put on the airs and had the money from my father's various business ventures. He taught me how to survive in our dark world. I got into investments a little later in my life. When you have nothing but time, it pays off big dividends eventually."

"Thus the mansion?"

He nodded. "I try not to bring attention to myself or the coven, so I don't throw money around. But I'm a dragon atop a hoard compared to most people, even most vampires. So, if I spoil you a bit, that's where it comes from." He caught the sparkle of understanding in her eyes.

"You actually paid for my clothes, huh?"

"And gladly, too. Petra did well by you." He winked.

She glanced down at her blouse, rubbing one of its little buttons. "Well, thank you. I'm not used to owning something like this. If there's anything I can do to pay you back..."

"You saved my life," he said, reaching over to give her hand a brief squeeze. "*I* still owe *you*." If they were getting more into the "vampy stuff," as she called it, he would explain that no sane vampire outside of his coven would've lifted a finger to help him. That she, as a mortal, was able to do so and endure Kim Cox because of him meant a lot more than he could express.

She seemed at a loss for a few moments. "So, your parents. Are they still around?"

"Ah, no. They're long gone," he said, shrugging when she started to give him a look of sympathy. "When you're immortal, it's inevitable. My father's coven fell the night he died. I ended up traveling Europe with my two dearest friends, Sam and Melanie, and picked up Julian along the way before we all came to America. The New World."

He smiled wistfully for those days, when their little group was simple. "We settled in Massachusetts before coming to New York, growing all the while."

"When did you meet Luke?" she asked, gazing at him keenly.

"We first fit in with a village of Native Americans when we came to America. Luke was my lifemate's brother." Despite how fresh Mary Ann's face was in his mind's eye, hundreds of years had passed since he'd last held her.

"Your one and only? The other half of your soul?" She echoed his first explanation from their dream together. He considered her words for a moment, wondering if her unconscious mind remembered their conversation. Glancing at her out of the corner of his eye, he realized she was simply smiling wistfully for the romantic ideal of a perfect soulmate.

"A sweet woman. But long gone." He'd already done his mourning, except in those long moments between sleep and wakefulness, missing the warmth of another by his side. Two hundred years had passed since he lost her, and he'd been with other women since. No one was quite as perfect, but such was life.

He parked his car, spotting Julian circling around to give them lead time. Putting an arm around her casually, he walked her to the line for the first place she needed to see and watched her look around and then up.

"Is that the Empire State Building?" she asked. As a landmark, it was no coven's territory, thus free for them to visit without him playing any politics.

"Did you know it's open late for night owls such as ourselves? One can't visit the city without stopping here."

A giddy little smile crossed her face. "What a cool idea."

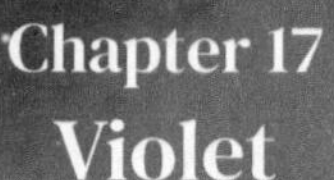

Chapter 17
Violet

She understood his desire to have someone watching their backs as soon as they were in the observatory overlooking New York City's lights. Alex murmured for her ears only, narrating how this skyline had changed over time.

It was amazing to her that he'd been around since before the city had a skyline. He wore his years with the grace of a well-traveled statesman. She appreciated this side of him so much more than the vampire coven master trying to teach her a great deal of insider knowledge within a couple days.

They window shopped together afterward, each enjoying a hotdog from a street vendor. How she'd laughed when he got a smear of mustard at the corner of his mouth.

He wasn't perfect, just like her. She couldn't explain how a bit of mustard had put her so much more at ease. "You ever go to Broadway?" she asked as they blended with the crowd, naming the other attraction she was dying to see now that she was here.

"Dancing cats or something?" he teased.

"Two kinds of people." She tisked as she shook her head.

"In that case, yes, I love Broadway. *Hamilton* was particularly delightful." He smiled just wide enough not to show fangs. "I wasn't so interested in those events when they actually happened, but I enjoyed seeing them play out like a rap battle."

Her mouth dropped open. "You've seen it live?"

"You haven't? Sounds like I know where to take you on a later date."

She quizzed his Broadway knowledge to see if he was pulling her leg, and it sounded like he'd really been to the plays she wanted to see. "I'm really going to take you, I promise," he said, holding his hands up with a laugh as she asked about the minutiae she could remember.

"Well, if you promise." She felt ready to glow with the idea, hoping it was soon.

That was the moment the voice came back, the one from her dreams. *"He's wonderful."*

Violet sucked in a breath, taking a glance around for anyone who could've spoken. She nearly bumped into a stranger as she wiped clammy palms on her skirt. "All good there?" Alex asked, putting a steadying arm around her.

"Just, uh, excited," she blurted.

How exactly was she to explain it otherwise—some creepy voice had just complimented him in her head, as if someone were watching her. Maybe she *should* mention it, but it didn't seem like a good idea while Alex was smiling down at her with such warm regard.

First date rule: don't imply that you might be hearing voices.

Still, she asked, "How do you talk to someone else in their head?"

He glanced around at the crowd. "It's called telepathy. It is an important skill. I suppose we could practice for a bit." He drew her over to an unclaimed bench. As their gazes met, his voice filled her head. *"The first time is always the hardest. You project your thoughts outward, like you're speaking, but in your head. It's easiest to do when you're making eye contact with your recipient."*

"Like this?" she sent back, pretending she was speaking the words aloud.

His face went slack with astonishment. *"Yes...just like that."* Shaking his head, he added out loud, "Showoff. That took me weeks to figure out."

He coaxed her back to window shopping. *"The harder trick is talking to someone across any distance longer than a room or while not looking at them,"* he added. *"I swear, you're a better vampire than me if you get this on the first try."*

She spent several minutes studiously not looking at him, but that did not come as naturally. "I guess it's easier to look at you because I know where I'm sending my words?" she remarked, giving up with the beginnings of a headache pressing at her forehead.

"Exactly," he said, smiling over at her. "There's tricks to it. I'll teach you later, maybe over dinner?"

"That's a good idea." Her belly was on the verge of rumbling in complaint.

"I know just the place," he said, leading her in a new direction. Perfectly willing to let him pick the place, she still stopped short as she spotted a sign outside a quaint diner that was open late.

"'Not eating here would be a missed steak,'" she read aloud, nudging Alex with a grin.

He glanced from the sign to her. "Yes, that's what it says."

"Get it? *Missed steak,*" she giggled. "We have to eat here."

He covered his face with a hand. "Oh no. You're a punster."

"Only when others enjoy it. Mostly, I get your reaction." She gestured to him with a smile. "Finding someone with my sense of humor is a painful pun-dertaking."

"Right, so we're eating here?" he asked, muffling a groan with his palm.

"Yup!"

The restaurant was a traditional greasy spoon with cracked upholstery booths and checkerboard tablecloths. It was the type of place to specialize in burgers...but she got the steak.

While they waited, he taught her more tricks for telepathy without eye contact, showing off with mental speech while studying the ingredient list of ketchup. He handed her the bottle for her own practice. *"Eugh, there's a lot of sugar in this,"* she remarked.

"Second round, first try. I'm really impressed," he replied, though when she looked up at him, his expression was pinched

with a troubled frown. *"Too easy. Further proof that you're a vampiress without a taste for blood."*

"Hey, I'm not looking a gift horse in the mouth." Now, at least, she was ready if that voice from her dreams returned. *If* it wasn't a person setting out to mess with her.

While she had a full dinner, he picked at a small meal. Knowing he didn't need food like her was a strange feeling when combined with the social guilt of eating while the other party abstains. "It's all right. I just need a different type of meal," he said, noticing her eyeing his plate.

"Oh, of course. Your special diet."

"I get cravings every couple of days."

"Anything I can do to help?"

She felt his gaze fall to her neck and the pulse ticking there. "Not right now."

She shrugged to herself, figuring he knew how best to solve that for himself. *"Though I must confess, I wonder how your silver blood would taste."* From the trace of heat to his tone, she surmised that taking another person's blood wasn't nearly what she thought. It felt like the diner's overall atmosphere cranked up several degrees.

"Maybe I'll give you a little taste." She made the offer hearing exactly where it might take them.

He cleared his throat aloud. "And maybe I'll take you up on that."

Once they left the diner, he led her back to where he'd parked his car. They'd spent the better chunk of the night together. But they were close to the summer solstice and the longest day of the year, cutting their time short with agreed-upon haste not to be caught by the sunrise.

"Thank you for the date," she said halfway there when they'd fallen into companionable silence. She tentatively cupped his free hand as he maneuvered the early-morning traffic with the other upon the wheel.

Glancing down, he laced his fingers with hers. "It was my pleasure."

She had the same butterfly thrill as if he were her first boyfriend, holding hands secretly at the back of a classroom.

This just might work out, she thought, a shy little smile crossing her face. A glimmering kernel of hope blossomed within her for the future possibilities in her new life.

He parked right outside his manor, a sigh of relief leaving his lips as soon as they passed its gate. In the middle of the path, away from prying eyes, he turned to her. Her heart pattered as he tilted her chin up.

"This is all right?" he asked quietly. He leaned in once she nodded, kissing her for a fraction of a second. They recoiled mutually from a vicious shock of static.

She laughed while he covered his lips, his brow pinching. "Must be the weather. Maybe it's a good omen?"

"Maybe it is," he murmured. "About your offer earlier. Is that still on the table?"

"For my blood? I mean, if you don't hurt me or anything." She wondered why his expression had gone purely neutral, though, when the invitation earlier had had a particular heat.

"It doesn't hurt or last long. It feels unique...you might like it." He offered a noncommittal shrug.

She would try anything once. So, she swept her bleached hair from her shoulders, taking a deep breath to relax. *This is old hat. He does this all the time,* she reminded herself, her pulse still going wild in her chest.

When he pulled her closer around the waist and tilted her head gently, it did little to calm her heart. He blew cool air over her neck. "Relax," he whispered in her ear.

"I can't help it when you hold me like this, it's very intim— ahh." She'd relaxed mid-sentence, the perfect time for him to sink those fangs into her. *Clever,* she thought. But she wasn't prepared for the sudden pleasure his bite brought her. Heat pooled low in her belly.

He took only a few swallows of her blood, done within seconds. But he left her out of breath and leaning into his embrace. "You might like it, he says," she said, laughing giddily.

"I didn't want to oversell the euphoria in case you're one of the folks who don't experience it." He winked, helping her walk toward the mansion as it started to wear off. "Thank you, by the way."

"Did I taste good? Does blood even taste differently by person?" she asked.

"Honestly?" He drew out the moment, letting her lean in. "Everyone tastes mostly the same unless they're drunk, sick, or high. I try to avoid all three of those things."

"Well, that's disappointing," she huffed.

"You, however, are not." He parted from her side at the foyer, nodding to a woman dusting and studiously pretending not to listen to them.

She drifted toward the stairs, and he backed toward his office suite on the ground floor. She was halfway up the staircase when he called her name.

"I've been trying to come up with one for hours and I think I got it. What time does an early bird vampire wake up?"

Violet considered for a long few moments before brightening. "Bite and early! Good one!"

Chapter 18
Alex

ALEX KEPT TOUCHING HIS LIPS THE NEXT COUPLE OF DAYS, pondering the impossibility of the moment they'd kissed. What was a static shock for her was as subtle as a punch to the gut to him.

Mine, the inner beast whispered. It didn't care about the intricacies. It didn't care that they'd had a lifemate before. It scratched and whined like a caged puppy, wanting her.

He couldn't ignore the truth of their kiss, much as it threw him on his ear. Vampires knew their lifemates from a kiss, and that's exactly what he'd felt once before with Mary Ann. But it was "one and only" for a reason. He'd never met anyone fortunate enough to have *two* lifemates.

So, he purposely spent two days working, mulling over that moment and how his imagination could play such a dirty trick on him. And, yearning, his inner beast dragged him nightly into every one of her dreams.

Her *nightmares.*

Over and over again, the same scene. His inner beast made him watch instead of influencing or joining her. It started as voices in the dark, curses, screaming, and items breaking, always ending with Kim Cox shouting, *"What are you?"*

He woke in a cold sweat, just like he imagined she did several rooms away.

"Fine, you win," he muttered to himself. She needed him, and badly. Because if only she could see this dream through, maybe they'd understand what'd influenced her transformation.

He dream walked to her next nightmare, the same scene once again. In the darkness, he started to speak over the noise. "Violet. What's happening here? When did this happen?"

"Alex?" She was in here somewhere, sounding terrified.

The hellscape was gone from her mind. He'd made sure of that personally. The inner beast was the side of him that was convinced what they were seeing had actually happened. *Open your eyes*, it urged.

"Open your eyes," he repeated.

The sudden onrush of light was blinding. Something—a body —sailed by her head. Kim Cox screamed.

Alex woke up, heart rushing. He didn't wait for either of them to fall asleep again, knowing exactly what would be waiting for them.

He knocked on her door despite it being midday and the shutters tightly closed around the mansion. She answered in her pajamas, hair disheveled and breathing quickly from the same post-nightmare rush he was experiencing. "Good day. I have a confession," he said.

At the same time, she blurted, "I have to tell you something."

They shared a chuckle, her stepping aside so he could come in. "I'll go first," he said, figuring she wanted to share something of her dreams. "I, ah, gained a new ability recently. I can walk in dreams and keep finding myself in yours."

"I..." She recoiled in surprise. "Really? You mean...that's been you?" He shifted, mirroring the discomfort he saw crossing her face. "Like, when you were talking about your lifemate? And... just now?"

"Yes, that was me," he said.

A gray flush passed over her cheeks and neck. "Could you, like, ask permission next time? Or something?"

He put his hands up with a sigh. "I would if I could, love. It's very new, and I have almost no idea how it works." His inner beast purred, pleased with itself.

"I mean, it's all right. If you can't control it and all. I just dream embarrassing stuff." She scratched behind her head self-consciously.

"So do I," he said. "Anyway, I saw your nightmare tonight. Was that what you were going to tell me about?"

"Sort of. Did you hear the voice?" she asked. She fidgeted nervously with a lock of hair, coiling it around her finger. Frowning, he shook his head. "There's always a woman's voice at the end. All 'you poor thing' and 'I'll make your strong again' and...I hear her when I'm awake, too. I'm not, like, crazy or anything. She's not telling me what to do. I just sometimes—"

"Violet."

"—get this voice in the back of my head that has something to say about what I'm doing or thinking. And she just—"

"It's all right."

She blinked at him owlishly. "What?"

"It's all right," he repeated. "You're not crazy. It sounds like a vampiress is toying with you. It's not unheard of."

His inner beast had its hackles raised. It knew more than him. Maybe he'd forgotten the voice, if he'd ever heard it himself.

"How do I get her to leave me alone?" she asked, her shoulders hunching.

"A show of force, love." Flexing his hands, he knew this one might be a fight. "If she's a part of the nightmare you keep having, she may be the reason you're a vampiress. But it's hard to tell because it seems your dream keeps cutting itself off."

"Can you and your dream powers help me see it through?" she asked. He couldn't stand the tremble in her voice and beckoned her close as he stood. Following suit, she sank into his embrace with a sigh.

"I'm going to do everything in my power to scare her off. We'll get through this together," he promised.

This time, she drew him into a kiss. *Mine,* whispered his inner beast.

He blocked out the feral side of him, savoring the moment. She fit perfectly in his arms. "Will you stay?" she whispered as he lingered there, his forehead pressed to hers. They breathed the same air.

He knew what she needed, the grounding support and touch of another. "I can. If that's what you want," he murmured. The last thing he wanted was for her to regret it in the evening.

Violet pulled back, catching his hands. An encouraging tug was all he needed.

ARMED WITH HIM BY HER DREAMING SIDE, THE NIGHTMARE did not return. Nor did the woman's whispers, hopefully for good. Alex accepted the uneasy peace that followed for what it was: a gift.

He had the time to lavish Violet with attention. His inner beast was quelled by her touch and presence, mollified he was considering that maybe they'd found a partner to wash away the ennui of long age.

Trouble came two weeks in when Nicholas tracked him down to offer an envelope addressed to him. "From Coven Deveaux," he said. In addition to ensuring the safety of his coven members, Nicholas occasionally intercepted messages such as this.

"Who was the messenger? Anyone I know?" Alex asked, slitting it immediately to read its contents.

"Her second." Nicholas frowned, waiting. Alex passed him the message, a simple invitation written in a formal hand. He cursed under his breath. "You think she's invited Collins?"

"He technically counts," Alex said, sighing through his nose. For the note proclaimed a full coven master meeting later that evening. In a show of faith, every coven master was to bring their second. It was typical—everyone's territory was equally vulnerable during a meeting of this nature.

He contacted Julian first, calling him from patrol. With the two of them looking after the estate and Nicholas increasing security at their borders, the coven should be fine in his and Sam's absence. Violet should be fine as well. He found her lounging in his room, watching Netflix with a bowl of popcorn in her lap.

"Good show?" he asked. She'd introduced him to the idea of shows playing as background music, but she seemed to actually watch them while he was distracted by her.

"Sure. Is something wrong?" She eyed the taut line of his body.

"Unexpected meeting. All twelve coven masters and their seconds. I got the kind of summons I can't ignore." He crossed to his closet, where he started changing into one of his best suits.

"From that Ancient you told me about?" she asked, pausing her show to help him with his tie.

"The oldest little girl around. Yes. I wonder what she's seen in the future this time," he said with a sigh. Most of her *urgent* meetings where the whim of her future sight. Yet no one would dare miss an all-coven meeting unless they could not physically make it there in time. It expressed the kind of weakness other covens would exploit.

"Well, tell me when you know, okay? I wonder what the rush is," she said.

"I'll keep you posted." He sealed his promise with a kiss.

Chapter 19
Alex

Alex gazed out at the faces of the other coven leaders and the empty chairs around the antique table. The places to Cossette's left and right were empty from her spot at the head of the table. They were seated in order of power and size of territory, with seconds standing symbolically behind their coven masters.

The personalities in the room fascinated him, so rarely seen outside of their territories. New York was a massive city with enough mortals to support covens that seemed obscenely large to an immigrant such as himself. Yet even with so many resources, he and his fellow leaders still fought for scraps of land and jobs and people.

Elder Rockefeller sat across from him, primped and puffed as if posing for an old painting. She had her nose lifted with airs of superiority that she felt none could touch. She'd married into her fortune, leaving when the goings got rough for her adopted mortal family. Alex had lost his respect for her after it came to light, but she'd always been a step ahead of him in age and strength, commanding his coven to heel with force if not with grace. He knew that even now, she thought she was the only Elder in the room, not realizing Alex had ascended to that status as well. Without him flaunting his aura, no one in this room would know for a long time.

The power of blood flowed weaker after he looked past her. With two Elders close to the head of the table, only four of the remaining eight vampires had reached Master age, and their seconds were younger still.

Coven Master Taylor plucked at her suit's cuff, the former politician clearly uncomfortable next to the trinity of Coven Masters Rosas, De Leon, and Washington, all dressed in their very best and leaning over her from their positions at the end of the table to talk to Alex and Elder Rockefeller directly. The three of them were organized crime, the hard men the police could never touch. Alex found their existence rather odious, yet he still played the game. He couldn't afford to touch them without costly war, especially when new, less friendly faces would replace them.

Between these two factions, Masters Ivashov and Weber, both Germanic immigrants, smoked their pipes and spoke together mentally. He liked the men, even if Ivashov often tried pilfering houses from around the outskirts of Coven Rehnquist's territory. If it weren't for that, he might've considered an alliance with them, as they were united in their dislike for Haven's lurking.

And then there were Masters Smith and Wagner, who sat across from each other and shared venomous glares as some of the most vicious off and on friends he'd ever met. Today, it seemed, they were not friends.

"We have an important guest today," Cossette said when it looked like Bryant Collins and his second wouldn't be showing.

"And here he is!" Any good spirits left in Alex left as, fashionably late, Collins drifted in the room with a showman's smile. Master Weber clapped slowly, shooting an irritated look his way.

"A pleasure to see you all, as always." Collins eyed the seating arrangement, choosing the one next to Elder Rockefeller. He was within punching range, and Alex was sorely tempted as Collins flashed a look his way. He'd brought Kim Cox, his wife, to stand behind him as his second. She, too, looked his way when she felt his hostile gaze upon her, a slow smile stretching her face.

Collins never released his aura amongst polite company but was often ranked between Rockefeller and Cossette in meetings of this nature, making him a strong Elder or early Ancient. He also wore no glamor, making it that much harder to mark his power. To everyone, he was a doughy-faced Irishman who indulged in mortal food a little too often, with short-cropped red hair and skin marked with countless freckles.

He often claimed he'd been around for the Crusades, a fact he didn't let slip by as he wore a tie emblazoned with crosses. Just the sight of him was odious to Alex, made more so that the only time he *did* see Collins outside of his protected zones was on neutral ground such as this, where he could be badly punished for attacking the master of a rival coven.

"As I was saying," Cossette said, clearing her throat. She tilted her head. "I've had a special visitor here for a while, but she's only now ready to talk to you all. I think you'll like her."

The pressure in the room shifted. Closest to the door, the youngest coven masters seemed the most uncomfortable, but that sensation passed over them all as one last person entered the room. Dressed in an elegant silver gown, her figure was unmistakably feminine, even if she wore a veil to hide her face. Situated atop the veil was a crown of moonstones. She seemed to float with even, graceful strides.

Alex realized she was heading straight for the chair next to him, except Cossette was relinquishing her place at the head of the table for this person.

She *had* to be an Ancient of sorts, her aura creeping over him with power as hot as the unforgiving sun. Coven seconds pressed their backs to the wall as if physically pushed by her presence. She made the process as slow as possible, letting everyone soak in the sheer power coming from her.

A collective sigh of relief came as she masked her aura, veil panning as she observed all of the faces in the room. There was pure silence, even from Collins and Cossette, knowing now who was the most powerful in the room. "Hello, my people. Where once my entrance was announced with horns and men at attention, now you all have no idea who I am."

She paused for dramatic effect while Alex's inner beast emerged from its frightened cower, projecting feelings of unease.

He agreed with it quietly. Best case, this person was a visitor coming to flex her muscles.

Worst case, she was here to unseat Cossette as the eldest vampire and sought territory for her coven. Alex thought that a lot more likely, even though, for someone to be older than Cossette...

He should know who this person was. And as she'd said, he had no idea.

"My name is Lucia, Queen of Vampires." She held her palm aloft, where a curious object appeared and hovered. It appeared to be an opaque, glass sphere set within a silver-plated sundial carved with several tiny symbols. "The only Sorceress of vampire kind."

Several tiny bolts of lightning connected her fingertips to the orb, which spun even at rest. Alex looked to Cossette, who smiled up at him and gestured as if saying "isn't this cool?"

He raised a brow, skeptical. This woman could be an elaborate fraud, except he knew a vampire's aura when he felt it.

"I'm grateful for the opportunity to speak with you all. Thank you for coming with such haste," Lucia continued. "Listen closely, for I shall not repeat myself. Long ago, I was crowned queen of our people. Back when we were stronger but less numerous. Observe my illusions." She gestured to the table, nudging aside cups and decanters of wine with just a whim.

Light swirled in a little tornado, particles separating and becoming a moving, three-dimensional image of an island as seen from above. One third was taken up by a palace with impossibly tall spires of white stone. Alex recognized it as the island that'd recently come up from the ocean, but nothing was as pristine as the image Lucia provided them. "Behold Nyixa. For centuries, I have slumbered, and it slumbered with me. It was once a paradise for vampires. Until I was betrayed."

"Queen Lucia, I think you should tell them everything you told me," Cossette suggested. "I didn't know any of it, and everyone in this room is younger than me."

"A complicated history lesson, condensed for your pleasure." Lucia inclined her veiled head Cossette's way. With a gesture, she changed the image of the island to a creature that stirred disgust amongst those in the room.

"What *is* that thing?" Coven Master Washington said, nearly falling out of his chair as he reared backward.

On instinct, Alex's gaze flashed to Kim Cox, who was rubbing her neck with an uneasy expression on her face. She'd asked those very words not too long ago but showed no recognition of this creature.

It was humanoid but hard to mistaken for anything but a monster. With overdeveloped legs for leaping and clawed hands braced on the table, it sat back on its haunches with a waiting expression. It had a Cheshire grin of pure fangs, sharp triangles neatly closing together with no overlaps. More chillingly, its eyes resembled black pools of ink, bottomless pits ringed in black veins.

"That is a Fell," Lucia said, letting them all get their fill of the monster. "Before your forefathers could even dream of a place called America, these creatures roamed our world, indiscriminately killing and consuming any living things they encountered down to bones. There was no reasoning with them. They were their hunger, sparing no man, woman, or child. They destroyed their world in their great hunger, so they came to our lands via portals to do the same to us."

"Never seen that in a history book," Sam commented to him.

"Maybe in a horror movie?" Alex suggested. They shared an uneasy mental laugh.

"Early vampires were not willing converts. They were fighters, the type of warriors that survived fighting creatures like this just to have Fell blood burn into their veins like acid. From this horror emerged the first generation of vampires, blessed with the strength and resilience to fight these creatures but cursed with their bloodlust."

Lucia dismissed the image of the Fell with a flick of her fingers, replacing it with something even more gruesome. Mangled bodies, Fell and vampire alike, coated a battlefield stained red with blood. The only pristine thing was a massive version of Lucia's magical object stabbing toward a pitch-black sky. The glass orb's surface seemed to sparkle with its own radiance.

"Of the war, all you need to know is that we won at great cost. Of our army of thousands, only eight survived and became our nobility. They also started our bloodlines, such as they seem to be." Her voice was layered with scorn.

She changed the image to one showing several strangers in formal wear lined up for a portrait. Tall and muscular men, with the exception of a burly, redheaded woman. In the center, a bearded man with piercing black eyes stood with his arm around a lithe woman in silver, reminiscent of Lucia, except without the veil. She was, apparently, a gorgeous brunette with a mysterious half-smile and eyes the color of polished silver.

"Are you seeing this?" he asked Sam. *"Her eyes."*

"Might be the bogeywoman Julian's dad talked about," he said.

"She might have something to do with Violet!"

"How? She take a side-trip to Ohio or something?"

Alex sighed to himself. *"It's our best lead right now."*

"For a time, we had peace. We rebuilt and prospered on the island the Fell left behind. But you see, we had an advisor who schemed against vampire kind. On the day I finally took a husband, she saw fit to poison us all." Lucia showed a moving image now, straight from the movie of her mind. Those same strong men drank wine, just to fall over, asleep, paralyzed, or dead moments later. Lucia herself collapsed, looking into the face of an older woman as she loomed over her.

"That poison sent me into a coma for many years. And with my sleep, Nyixa sank, drowning thousands of vampires and plunging our kind into an age of darkness. All because of my rogue advisor, Gwendolyn Firetree, who, to this day, waits to stir chaos. I believe it's because of her that you have forgotten our past." She waved her hand before slamming her fist into the table, knocking a glass into Master Wagner, who fumbled and nearly dropped it in her distraction.

Alex had never seen New York City's motley crew of coven leadership so enraptured. If anyone spoke, they did as he had with his deputy, keeping it to mental conversation. "Do you know what I see in modern vampire kind? We have become a weak people, scattered, afraid, and outnumbered by the people who should serve us. Mortals. The world crawls with them now."

Trepidation crawled up Alex's neck. Anytime an older vampire moved to expose their kind to mortals, the rest invariably turned against them. But they'd never had such an old and powerful Ancient calling for it. Uneasy looks were exchanged as Lucia paused for effect.

"And what happens to our kind while mortals thrive? We fight. We kill each other for resources and land, dividing like little countries. We separate into groups based off ideology and ambition." She gestured to Collins, who nodded in agreement. "Or what country we came from before arriving here." Now, she indicated Alex, Cossette, and several others with immigrant roots.

"My people did not have warring covens. We had purpose as a nation. My heart aches that you have not seen or experienced this." She touched a hand to her chest, sighing in reverence for her memories. "I wish to rebuild this. No coven boundaries, no coven war. A world where we are all free to live, love, and exist as one nation with one unifying purpose."

And that purpose is enslaving humankind, he thought. But she didn't say it, merely gestured grandly and created a hole in the air. "This is a portal. I came with gifts for you all for hearing me out and considering my proposition. Are you all willing to work together and accept me as your queen? Consider it. I have chosen to grace New York City as my new seat of power."

From the portal floated letters and boxes. One of each settled in front of every coven master. Alex eyed his like she'd placed a venomous snake before him. "I recommend you open your gifts in private. Unless you have questions for me, you may go. I look forward to meeting you all more personally in the coming days."

Alex didn't move, watching who flinched first. It was Coven Master Taylor, adjusting her power suit as she said her pleasantries and quickly left. Lucia sat and cradled a cup of wine, not taking any sips from it.

"Your gift may require some explanation, Elder Rehnquist," Lucia said to him privately as she spoke casually with Elder Rock-

efeller and Collins. *"The letter is for your lifemate. But the potion, it is for you."*

"A potion?" he replied. She'd already displayed an understanding of their names and titles, but his inner beast hissed the moment "lifemate" was mentioned.

"Another lost art, I'm afraid. It is the gift of age, my new friend. You drink it, it makes you more powerful. I only had half a vial left...but who better to give it to than someone who needs a leg up on a religious fanatic?"

He picked up the letter, realizing it was much heftier than a couple sheets of paper. *"Well, thank you. That sounds too good to be true,"* he said, biting his lip as he went to mention something she'd shown of herself earlier. Better to ask, he reasoned. *"You and Violet have the same eyes. They're very unique, even amongst our kind."*

"Quite lovely. I look forward to meeting her," she said with vapid pleasantness.

"Do you know why she turned that way?" he asked.

Her veil turned. For a moment, her attention burned into his side. *"I can't help you there. Just a quirk of our biology. But perhaps you should return home to her, hmm? The newly mated are so needy."*

He didn't correct her, keeping his face completely placid while she was watching. While he had felt the promise of a lifemate in Violet, they were not serious enough to be mates yet. Vampires taking mates was a sacred rite more permanent and influential than marriage. Mates shared everything, including thoughts and emotions, and could only break the bond if one of them died. He was willing to take the dismissal instead, saying his goodbyes and leaving with Sam.

"She knows far too much about us. I don't trust this," he confided to Sam privately. *"Actually, I think that's shaving the bloody iceberg. I want her gone from New York."*

His deputy and best friend glanced up from his phone, his skin blanching. *"I agree and all, but we need to get home. Another Ancient is in the mansion right now."*

Chapter 20
Violet

As if his presence truly scared the voice off, it returned moments after Alex left the mansion. *"It's almost time. At last."*

Violet froze mid-hello to the men who'd come to keep coven life running smoothly. Armando and stony-faced Julian were the only two that didn't hasten to work somewhere else in the residence. They were, she assumed, there to guard her.

"Cat got your tongue, *amica*?" Armando said. The two men exchanged a glance.

"No, it's fine." She sounded distracted even to her own ears. "Are you here to watch me or something?"

"More the estate," Julian said. "Strange things happen during all-coven meetings. A rogue group breaking the Accords for their coven's benefit is not unheard of."

"Why don't you sit with us, though?" Armando offered. He ventured into the kitchen to brew coffee while Julian settled in the front sitting room, crossing ankle over knee casually as he fiddled with what looked like a remote. Above the dining table was a flat-screen television, which turned on with the black-and-white view of several cameras around the property. The only motion was greenery waving to a light breeze.

Violet closed her eyes, focusing on that voice and how it'd felt in her mind. *"Hello?"* she projected blindly.

There was no response. She startled when Armando slid a cup in front of her. "Whoa." He laughed, slapping her on the back. "It really is okay. No need for the jitters. Think you should have this? It's good Italian coffee. Brewed with care. *Bellissimo.*" He put his fingertips to his lips, blowing a kiss.

Across from her, Julian took a sip from a similar cup without a hint of creamer. His lips pinched. "Alex's coffee maker is still broken."

Armando's face fell as he tried his. "Damn. I guess he doesn't drink coffee."

"Usually it's tea," Violet ventured. She tried what he laid before her and grimaced at the burnt flavor.

"Where we're from, tea is medicine," Armando said, shrugging and drinking his coffee anyway.

"So, what do you two do to pass the time?" Violet asked, her shoulders tense as she waited if the voice would return or reply. "Cards? Board games? TV's taken."

"Poker. We tried something new a few years ago and that went poorly." Julian took a weathered deck of cards out of one of his pockets.

"It was Cards Against Humanity," Armando whispered to her.

She muffled a snort as she imagined Julian reacting to some of the cards found in that game. Judging by his description of events, he hadn't enjoyed it. "You couldn't start off easy with Apples to Apples or something?" she snickered.

"Why not go out in a blaze of glory instead?" Armando had a thumbs up and a confident grin. He took the deck and began dealing them all a hand.

"Fair enough. Is this a good hand?" she asked, showing them both her cards.

"It was," Julian said, shaking his head. "Have you not played this before?"

Whoops, she thought. She jumped at the opportunity when he offered to teach her.

Over the course of the next hour or so, Violet saw a different version of Julian. He opened up as a teacher, smiling and encouraging where it was needed, even sharing a compliment here and there. It was nice to see that he wasn't always frigid and distant.

Armando's attention wavered quickly. He wandered off to go fiddle with the coffee machine. "You two are family, right?" she asked, peering at Julian over her cards.

"He's my nephew," he said with a sigh.

She narrowed in on that reaction, frowning behind the thin barrier of her hand. "It's probably not my business, but are things between you all right?"

His expression shuttered as he considered her question. There was serious calculation and consideration behind his eyes, every word measured. "There's something you must understand if you ever get to be as old as me." He set his cards aside for a moment, palms open. "You can love someone and also be sick of them."

"Oof," she said under her breath. He certainly didn't mince words.

"That's about where he and I are at. He would tell you the same thing," he continued. "We're family but two very different people. And we've been in the same coven, working the same job in the same place for nearly two centuries now."

Well, when he put it that way, it took the sting away. She could see exactly how their personalities would clash over such a long time. "So, if we seem frustrated with each other, you know why," he said.

"Yeah, I get you. Have you considered a break from each other?" she suggested.

"That would imply taking time off from work, and I can rest when I'm dead." He glanced up at the video feed, and she followed his gaze, seeing nothing amiss. "I recently got a taste of Kim Cox's blood. You know that means I can track where she is. Armando and I plan to put in many hours trying to catch her leaving a safe zone."

"Alex told me Haven's strongest just exploit safe zones," she remarked, shifting uncomfortably when reminded that Kim Cox was still at large, completely unpunished for what she'd done to her. She held onto a kernel of gratitude that Julian and Armando would try to bring her to justice.

"They do. But the Accords are amazing otherwise. The fact that they exist and are heavily enforced make us near civilized and stable. The type of things mortals take for granted...I hope you don't see the other side of immortality any time soon. Be glad you live in a place governed by any sort of laws."

"I will." They shared a smile. She was glad she'd tried venturing past his steely façade to see the man Alex told tall tales about.

The moment was interrupted by a polite knock on the door.

Julian turned, blue eyes colder than ice. "Identify yourself."

The newcomer had somehow bypassed every security camera, arriving without a hail of alarm from all the vampires keeping watch elsewhere in the mansion. Violet was not worried at first when she saw an older woman in the doorway, leaning on a fine lacquered cane as she observed them both through half-moon spectacles. She carried herself with grace despite her physical age, which Violet guessed to be somewhere in her seventies by the many lines marking stern features.

"There's no need for posturing, young man." Her voice was refined, holding a hint of an implacable accent. As she stepped forward, the door closed behind her on its own.

Julian was on his feet the next instant, his aura unfurling like a frigid wind. He placed his bulk between her and Violet, palpable danger in the coil of his power. "You are trespassing in a safe zone and will be removed by force."

"You couldn't even if you tried, Julian Marcuson." Her aura spread out from herself. It was far more unpleasant than the brush Violet remembered of Alex's power, bringing with it the sensation of her skin on fire. Thankfully, she kept it to a brief burst, enough to make Violet's insides twist up in terror.

"How...? You're an Ancient." He and the stranger sized each other up like a pair of feral dogs. The air grew warm again as he pulled in his aura too, no match to her flame of power. His muscles were tense against his form.

"And a friend. If I weren't, you'd both be dead already. Have a seat, young man. I must speak with your companion." She spoke matter-of-factly as she held out a hand, a chair skidding into her grip.

Violet's heart stuttered, but she forced out the words. "I think she's right, Julian. Let's hear her out." She put away her cell phone, which she'd used to text Alex and Sam about this Ancient vampiress. If their meeting was as useless as Alex assumed, they could come running to help.

With obvious reluctance, Julian took up his former seat, staring at the newcomer with unblinking hostility. She settled her skirt and placed her walking cane over her knees before turning Violet's way. "Are you wearing contacts, my dear? Are your eyes silver?"

Part of her said to lie, but after feeling the Ancient's aura, she decided against irritating her. "Yes."

"Do you remember how you were turned?" Violet shook her head. "Hmm. Despite that, I can smell the magic upon you." She leaned back in the chair, eyes darting back and forth as she considered.

"Do you know something about me?" she asked hopefully. "Why I'm different? A vampire...but not?"

The Ancient's attention turned to Julian, to her disappointment, considering him instead. He raised a brow, full of chilly aggression on a short leash. "I have displayed poor manners. Let me introduce myself. You may know me as the Curator. We have met before."

Violet didn't understand the connotations of the name, but it'd obviously woken something in him. His expression shaded, fists unclenching on the table. "I find it hard to trust someone claiming the title of an urban legend," he scoffed, but underneath the bravado, Violet saw the fear making his hands shake.

And if he was afraid, she realized this chance meeting was far more frightening than it appeared. "Why? I've helped you in the past, and I will help you again," she said.

"Who is the Curator?" Violet asked him privately.

Without so much as a blink to indicate he'd heard her, he said, *"The Boogeyman for vampires. Like I said, an urban legend. It's said if you are a truly wicked, evil vampire, the Curator will come and quietly remove your existence. Alex claims he's seen her once."*

"But then she comes only for evil vampires. And we're not evil," she pointed out.

His hand twitched in a cutting gesture. *"Be that as it may, she's a legend for a reason. She doesn't just come have conversations with random vampires in their safe zones."*

Violet nodded to herself with that logic. If this woman was who she said she was, she was a bad omen. "Remind me of the time you helped me. I'm getting old," Julian said aloud.

The Ancient's lips turned up at the corners, just a hint of humor. "You think you are, but you have no idea. I was once close friends with your father before he turned his back on everything he stood for."

"You are certainly not endearing yourself to me," he said, colder than his aura.

She held up a hand. "You did not know him as I did. He was infected with a darkness that drove him from honor into depravity. And when I decided he'd fallen too far, a challenger arrived who'd come to the same conclusion."

His lips tightened. "Me?"

Violet glanced between them, a sinking feeling in her chest. "Julian, did you—"

"Don't judge him, young lady. It was for the best, and he had help," she said, patting her hand as she took in Violet's distress. "Namely, myself. I helped stack the deck in his favor."

"How?" Julian slammed his palm on the table. "What did you do?"

"You may recall being given water as a symbolic gesture before the fight. An elderly nun delivered it—that was me. I gave you a little something for speed and strength, a gift from those who deal in potions and magic." His breathing grew heavier as she spoke. "So, you see, young man, we are on the same side of things. I need your trust now."

He shook his head in denial. "All this time—I thought I'd beaten him on my own merit."

"That's not how our society works. As a vampire your senior, he would always be stronger than you without some help. But you did the world a favor."

"Excuse me, but maybe I'm missing something," Violet said, almost timid to interrupt as Julian sat back, pinching the bridge of his nose. "What was his dad doing?"

"Trying to conquer the known world," she answered. "Murdering. Whoring."

"So, you took him out. Because that's what you do, as Curator." Violet summarized it aloud for her own sake, earning a nod from the older woman. She felt a twinge of pity for Julian, telling herself that she'd speak to him privately about this later. "So why are you here now?"

"Because you're in grave danger, my dear," she sighed. "I don't know why or how, but you've attracted the attention of the most malicious being in this world and the next."

Alarm thrilled up her arms in a wake of goosebumps. "W-what?"

"You are unique. Your blood and eyes, silver. No blood hunger to speak of, right?" Violet nodded reluctantly. "Seemingly weak and slow for a fledgling vampire. Without any of the reflexes or instincts inherent in the vampires around you."

"That's right," she murmured. Alex had described her as a kitten when testing these very things, her reactions not as fast as he expected.

"That's because you are a Sorceress, my dear. Your strength lies in controlling magic, not in physical prowess. Only one person could've done this to you, and what we have to discover is the how and why."

Though the Ancient was serious, Violet sputtered a nervous laugh. "Magic? Me?"

Somewhere in the mansion, she heard a door slam. Was someone finally noticing that they had an intruder? Surely Julian raised the alarm about it. "Mimic me and see for yourself," the Ancient said, holding up her hands. She overlapped the back of her hands, fanning out all her fingers and stating two words that sounded like Latin.

Violet thought it looked silly, but something thrilled up her spine, something like anticipation as she repeated the foreign words to herself. She repeated the hand gesture and the words, her skin tingling despite nothing happening.

The Ancient smiled to herself, correcting her pronunciation. Violet echoed her, screaming as flames jumped to life on her fingertips as if they were candlesticks.

Alex rushed into the room within the next moment, lips drawn back in a furious snarl. He stopped short, his gaze transfixed on Violet's fingertips.

"Meet the Curator," Julian said, drawing a seat for him.

Chapter 21
Alex

"Bloody hell," Alex muttered. His heart was still beating its way out of his chest from Violet's scream.

"Did you just say *the Curator*?" Sam asked behind him.

Violet blew on her fingertips, putting the flames out one at a time. Alex went to her first, laying a hand on her shoulder and a kiss upon her cheek. "Are you all right?" he murmured.

"I think so," she whispered back. He stood behind her as Sam disappeared to gather the others that, to Alex's fury, were not in the room. "I have to tell you something."

Judging by what he'd walked into, he had no doubt. "Tell me after this," he said.

"Impeccable timing," said the Ancient Julian had indicated, her prim voice laced with a hint of amusement. Some part of her was memorable, an itch he searched the confines of his mind to scratch.

Alex had a vague memory two centuries in the past of a man who had deserved the tender mercy of disappearing and never coming back. His name had been Jacques Laurent, Cossette's vampire sire, the one who'd permanently crippled her body to make her a permanent child in appearance for his own pleasures. The night he'd disappeared under mysterious circumstances, Alex had celebrated the Ancient's fall and became a permanent believer that the Curator was a real, breathing person.

He wasn't sure if he'd really met the Curator or not in the past. His recollection of the woman before him was far more recent. "I've blocked mental communication outside of this room," the Curator said, gesturing to Violet. "What passes between us needs to be secret for your own sake."

"That explains a lot," Julian sighed. The first person to rush in was Armando, smelling distinctly of coffee. Alex waited with barely leashed patience as Sam came in with Nicholas and Luke, both looking chagrined when they saw the uninvited visitor. He was of half a mind to chew them out, but at the same time, they were dealing with someone who had power beyond their understanding.

He loomed over Violet's shoulder like a protective shadow. "I just left the most enlightening meeting with another surprise Ancient."

"Yes. Lucia." She spoke her name with a bitter twist of her lips. "I imagine you were fed a kernel of truth amongst a whole batch of lies."

"Undoubtedly," he remarked dryly. "And now you're going to tell me your version of events that doesn't include you drowning a whole nation of vampires?"

To her credit, she hardly blinked. Yes, he'd pegged her face. She was the same Gwendolyn Firetree that Lucia had shown a glimpse of right before the sinking of the island of Nyixa. "That part is included in my tale as well. It is perhaps the most unflattering of the deeds Lucia could share with you after all."

"So, you're a murderer." He focused squarely on her, aware that everyone but Sam was sharing looks and murmurs of alarm at how quickly he was escalating an issue like this with an Ancient.

Gwendolyn seemed to sag with her age, both inward and not. Violet laced her hand through his, catching his attention for the split second he took over the atmosphere in the room. "She knows what I am, Alex. I *really* think we should hear her out."

He raised an eyebrow. "Well, are you going to leave me hanging?"

She crossed her hands a safe distance away from herself and uttered a Latin-sounding phrase. Her fingertips erupted into flames, each little fire dancing inches from her skin without any sign of pain from her. "I'm a Sorceress."

Lucia had claimed to be the only Sorceress, flaunting the power to bring a whole room of coven leaders to heel. His brow crinkled, helping her blow out these little flames as his friends looked on her with awe. "Congratulations. That's incredible," he said without much conviction, hesitating to meet Gwendolyn's waiting gaze.

There was obvious agenda here, and he didn't like it. Had Violet discovered this on her own, he'd have thrown a whole-coven party in celebration. But add two unpredictable Ancients to the mix, and all he felt was a hollow fear for the woman he was fond of. *"We have to hear her out,"* he said to Sam.

The curly-haired man flashed him a wary look. *"She's Lucia's enemy. We can't trust a word she says."*

"Like we could trust Lucia?" They chuckled unhappily at that insight.

Violet was still looking back at him, disappointment starting to shade her gaze. He spoke to her privately next. *"It's not that I'm not excited for you, love. We're in the middle of political hot water. I'll explain later."*

She nodded, her lips twisting as she turned her attention back to Gwendolyn. Alex took a deep breath. "You have my lady's trust and are obviously here for a reason. What do you want to share?"

"As I was telling Violet, she is in grave danger, and that means we all are. Allow me to properly introduce myself and explain what Nyixa's rising truly means for the world. Have you ever wondered where vampirism really came from?"

Once Gwendolyn introduced herself by name, she launched into a tale similar to what Lucia had told him and Sam earlier. Without the magic to summon images, she described the same Fell monsters with her words instead, drawing nervous shudders from those listening. But at the end of this war of the past, she changed the course of her narration.

"Lucia was our apothecary and a mortal, older than I appear. We thought she would be content with her mortal life when she struck a pact with the Fell Emperor. He gave her magic in return for his safety before he knew there would be no returning to the Fell Lands. One does not break a pact with a Fell, else they suffer a terrible curse. She wears a veil to hide what it's done to her."

Alex had barely given a second thought to the veil, thinking it a quirk of being an Ancient. But he nodded slowly, taking all this new information with a grain of salt. Lucia had painted Gwendolyn as a bad person. Now, it would be her turn to do the same. "At first, things were great. My daughter married Adrius, and they became our first royal couple. Lucia and I served as advisors."

"This is very different," Sam commented. *"Which one do you believe more?"*

He chewed on the question as she went on, detailing the council who'd guided the nation of Nyixa, which was the royal couple, advisors, and Blood Princes, whom she named. *"I'm not sure yet. However...she is rambling. Lucia planned out every word of her speech."*

"Lucia plotted the perfect takeover for months, biding her time. You see, she's blessed with future sight, and with enough time, she can see every angle of an event. She managed to make it look like the royal couple both died within hours of each other and ascended the throne while framing me for the whole thing," Gwendolyn continued. "I lived in exile for years while she turned Nyixa into a modern nation by encouraging the spread of vampirism to everyone interested in immortality who would also bend their knees before her. I'm talking a population boom of thousands from a handful, making our modern bloodlines what they are."

Alex thought of Cossette, the only other person he knew who possessed the ability to glimpse the future. He frowned to himself. No wonder Lucia had known who he was and given him something tailor-made to what he wanted most. The box and letter were still tucked into the crook of his arm. He placed them on the table as the Ancient spoke.

"This turned out to be catastrophic. We all inherited something less desirable from the Fell than their strength and immortal life. The moment a mortal becomes a vampire, they actually become a little bit Fell." She paused there, glancing around them all in turn.

"*Is this true?*" Violet asked, glancing up at him. She looked pale, her eyes wide in their sockets.

"*I haven't heard of Fell before today,*" he answered honestly, rubbing her shoulders to offer some comfort. "*You would think we would know all of this if it were true.*"

"Besides Violet, you all are old enough to answer this. Think of the cruelest, most inhuman vampire you've met." Gwendolyn gave them a moment. Alex thought of Jacques Laurent and how grateful he was that he was gone before he could hurt anyone else. "Did you think of an Ancient?"

Nods and murmurs of ascent followed from the group. "As a vampire grows older, that bit of Fell within them grows like a tumor, sucking out everything good in them. They develop a hunger that grows out of control. For women. For children. For the flesh of babes. I've seen it all." Her lips took on a grim twist as Violet gasped aloud.

"It happens over time and disguises itself as power. What vampire doesn't yearn to be a Master, an Elder, an Ancient? Now imagine that concentration of power being passed on in more pure forms by those who'd drank from Fell veins directly. The Blood Princes. The start of the bloodline."

"Were those people turned as stronger vampires?" It was Julian who interrupted, his cool gaze keen on her. He seemed enraptured by her tale, leaning in.

"Yes. Early vampires did not have their power measured by years as you have it now."

Alex struggled to think of a world like that, where everyone was an Elder or Ancient upon setting into their power. *When everyone's special, no one is,* he thought with a dry chuckle.

"But they were also more quickly falling into their hungers. The Blood Princes and their earliest fledglings were all displaying signs of it within twenty years or so." Now she frowned, troubled thoughts dancing behind a calm façade. "Lucia herself struggled with her curse, growing stronger. She invited me back to Nyixa to end my banishment in the hopes I could cure the depravity our race was quickly tipping towards."

Gwendolyn shook her head slowly. "I'm not proud of it, but I had no true fix, just a heart full of revenge. So yes, I did plunge Nyixa into the sea. Every courtier and high-level vampire was amassed for a wedding. I put them to sleep, as I did for Lucia and the Blood Princes."

"You put them to sleep?" Alex interrupted. "How?"

"That is a more complicated question than you think. I will simply say I was friends with someone with the magic to do such a thing," she said. He chewed his lip, finding her answer unsatisfying. "It was a potent sleep spell, meant to be a final mercy. The only one I did not give mercy to was Lucia. I meant for her to stay aware in her rest so she could feel herself drown."

Alex's inner beast chose that moment to wake up. *Yikes,* it projected. It was otherwise calm, which surprised him compared to how it'd received Lucia.

Yikes, indeed, he thought. Gwendolyn was lost in her past now, her fist raised and trembling in fury. "It was what she deserved for everything she did. More than I can simply recount. But I also didn't want to kill her myself—which was a mistake. She used her awareness to cast one last spell, keeping herself and the rest of the vampire royalty alive in an airtight room until she recently woke. I presume she's been aware this whole time, plotting every facet of the future where she was once again awake.

"I only apologize for the necessity of so much death. Because of the sacrifice that night, vampire kind was not overrun with evil. My actions forced us to live in the shadows, where creatures of the night belong." Alex winced at that dose of bitter truth, delivered without so much as a sprinkle of sugar. "Any questions?"

"So, you really are the Curator?" Sam remarked. "You kill the old vampires who've lost their way."

She smiled to herself. "Something like that."

He combed a hand through his shaggy curls, blowing out a low breath. "That's a hard job. I respect that."

"I echo that sentiment. Many would shy away from the necessity of your decisions." Luke spoke up next, rewarding the elderly woman with a rare half-smile.

"However, you have only shared backstory. I believe Violet might explode if you don't come to modern day," Alex remarked, feeling the tension in her shoulders, especially upon being named.

Gwendolyn drew in a long breath, squaring her shoulders as if coming face-to-face with a new, vicious foe. "Modern day, yes. Lucia still lives, as do the other vampire royalty. Nyixa rising is a ticking time bomb. The time of hiding may be over. Vampires and their magic may be outed to mortals at any moment. If handled poorly, it will be war. And Lucia, aware all this time under the waves, is at least thirty moves ahead on the chessboard." She shook her head slowly. "Modern day is a mess."

"Yes, but..." Violet said, gesturing to herself.

"Sorry, dear. Getting ahead of myself." She reached over, laying a hand over hers. "You've either been turned by exposure to Lucia's blood or a remnant of the old Fell Emperor's. Both of these things are under the complete control of Lucia. I am willing to teach you how to control and hone your new power. I can't tell you why she's changed you, but I must watch you very closely for any signs of corruption."

"I understand." She sighed, her fear at the possibility palpable.

"When I say she's ahead of us, all I know is that there's an end game in mind. Lucia has a plan for you, and she does not have a track record of benevolence for others."

"No kidding," Violet muttered. "She doesn't sound like the type that likes sharing."

Gwendolyn nodded in agreement, her stern features drawing tighter. "There's a lot about you that I do not understand in reference to her plans. I suspect we will only know what she intends when it's too late. Because of that, I would like to extend an offer of protection. I can get you to Nyixa, where the presence of King Adrius and the Blood Princes, Lucia's most dire enemies, will give her serious pause in pursuit. It would be a temporary arrangement, about six days."

"That's a very specific amount of time." Alex eyed her suspiciously. The risen island was quite far away—and this would put Violet directly in the type of viper pit he'd hurt himself to avoid. He would do anything to make Gwendolyn and Lucia just disappear and take their drama with them.

"You could go with her," Gwendolyn offered. "I can relocate you in a flash." She gestured, cutting a hole midair, as if cleaving the very fabric of reality. He'd seen Lucia do the same when conjuring gifts, but to see it again really sank the message home.

This woman was Ancient beyond measure and possessed magic he hadn't seen or heard of past his wildest fantasies. He swallowed uneasily as he watched her gesture again, closing that hole. "Portal magic. Say the word, and you can be gone."

"We will need some time to discuss this," he said, his gaze landing on Armando, who'd been uncharacteristically quiet.

He called his name. "Yes, boss!" Armando jumped to attention in a split second.

"Will you please escort Ancient Firetree to our sitting room? See that her needs are met. We may be a while," he said. Armando was around long enough to know he was being dismissed to an important duty—watching someone as powerful and deadly as Gwendolyn.

"Just Gwendolyn will do in the future. Thank you," she said. Armando helped her from her chair, escorting her out on his arm with as much care as if she were his grandmother.

Alex acknowledged that with a nod, dropping into the chair she'd vacated with a heavy sigh. He gazed over the faces of those assembled, all the while prodding his inner beast. *Who do we trust?* That little bundle of instincts told him he already knew the answer.

"Who do we trust?" he asked aloud.

"You've heard both sides of this, yes?" Nicholas asked. He rubbed his dark chin with a troubled frown.

Sam nodded, saying, "Lucia told us her version of the same story. She was veiled and...mighty. I've never felt an aura like hers."

"I would rather not be involved in any of this," Luke said

quietly. "Is that not how we've survived so long? Keeping our heads down?"

"Would if I could, brother. But this concerns a coven member." Alex's gaze rested on Violet, who was passing a tiny flame over her fingertips with fascination at her newfound power. A part of him was relieved to see that she'd found understanding.

Protect, whispered his inner beast.

Things would've fallen together too easily for them if it weren't for this. The truth about his attraction to her was lingering on his tongue, waiting for an eager moment to tell her that they were meant to be together in the future as full mates.

"What's in the box?" Julian asked, taking him out of those thoughts. He indicated the items he'd left next to Violet, who passed them up the table.

"Lucia gave everyone a gift to consider her by. I haven't opened mine yet," he said, doing so as the five of them looked on. Inside the box, a deceptively small glass vial was nestled in a bed of velvet. For its weight, he'd expected something bigger than this vial, which was the width of his palm and half full once he picked it up and gave it a testing flick.

The liquid within flowed slower than molasses, glimmering as if stuffed with silver flake. "She said this was for me, to give me a leg up on Collins," he said, thinking it looked no more useful for that task than if it were water and glitter. "And the letter is for Violet. You don't mind if I look at it first, do you?"

"Please do," she said. She grew very still as he uncorked the vial.

A mouthwatering scent drifted through the air as the silvery liquid smoked upon exposure to the air. His fangs unsheathed so fast that they nicked the sensitive skin inside his lip.

"I...I've smelled that before." Violet grew paler.

Chapter 22
Violet

THE VIAL'S SMELL WAS UNMISTAKABLE, OLD AND MUSTY, something straight from her nightmares. She covered up a gag while Alex breathed in the plume of silvery smoke originating from it. Within a blink, he had it capped, shaking his head as if waking from a trance.

"How about we look at the letter?" he said, setting the vial in its box and pushing it aside. He slit the envelope using his shapeshifter magic to sharpen a fingernail into a claw, withdrawing a stack of loose pages that'd shriveled down to withered and brittle husks from age. "This may not surprise anyone, but Lucia lied to me earlier about knowing nothing about Violet's magic," he remarked after flipping through a few pages, passing them to her.

Upon them were diagrams and descriptions written in fading ink. She spotted the gesture that'd summoned her fire and realized these were instructions. "I can't read this," she said. The words were in another language.

Alex frowned as he scanned page after page, laying them in a pile before her that she was afraid to touch lest the pages crumble to dust before she understood what was on them. He paused to scan the very last one, unfolding a pristine sheet of lined paper with the same handwriting. "A personal note to you, Violet. It's instructions on how to cast your first spell."

"Guess her future sight missed the fire," she said, rubbing clammy hands on her jeans.

"Yes, well, if her magic is anything like Cossette's, it doesn't see everything. She's already gotten a detail about my life wrong." He sounded distracted, his eyes darting over the page and lips moving over every word. Imagining he was combing the letter for nuance, she turned to Julian and Sam.

"It sounds like Lucia's had plenty of time to see what's about to happen," she said.

Sam shrugged to himself. "We can't be sure of *how* accurate what she's seen is. The only person we know with that magic is Cossette, and she's an expert at leaving you emptyhanded if you ask about the future. I think she's covering for just how little she actually knows of what's to come."

"It's better for prophecy," Julian said, his eyes hooded.

"Might as well tell her yours, mate." Sam elbowed him.

From how his brooding deepened, she imagined it wasn't anything good. But he told her the prophecy nonetheless. "Of my lifemate: 'In the midst of your darkest hour, she will save you.' You must understand, I've turned the world over looking for my lifemate. I went to Cossette for a hint or a location or even a date, and that's all she would say."

She caught Alex glancing up at him and grimacing, looking guilty. Tucking that away to ask about later, she considered Julian's unhappiness and wondered if it stemmed from the idea that he, a Master vampire and seasoned fighter, would need saving by someone he'd sought for so hard in some mysterious future scenario. "Well, there's a bright side at least," she offered. "She's going to save you. Which means you'll meet her."

With a grunt, he drew out a knife secreted somewhere on his person, flipping it through his fingers. "All right, I figured out what she's saying," Alex said, leaning over and placing the note between them. "There's some fluff and faff, but the meat of it is here. She's detailing how to cast a spell over yourself to understand any language, spoken or written. So, theoretically, you can understand the rest of this."

He pointed out the paragraph where the instructions started. "Do you think it's safe?" she asked.

"Oh, not at all," he said cheerfully. "How about you wait on it? We've gotten sorely off track here."

"Yes, sure," she blurted, folding the note up and placing it atop the pile of ancient pages. She would get back to all of this when she was more prepared.

"So Lucia's given us powerful gifts, and at least one verifiable lie," Alex said. "While Gwendolyn has a track record of being judge, jury, and executioner on any vamp past their prime. Who do we trust?"

"Brother, you have not shared of your meeting. We cannot make an informed decision without that information," Luke said.

Alex brushed a hand through his hair. "Right, the meeting," he said briskly. He and Sam summarized what they'd seen and experienced, leaving the room in a pall of grim silence.

Violet was stricken at how many of the other vampire leaders apparently seemed to agree that humans should be some sort of slaves or second-class citizens. The thought made her physically ill with the implications. "They stand on completely different sides," Luke said once Alex was done. "And we've always kept to the honorable path. I would put my trust in the Curator."

"She helped with my father," Julian said. "I, too, would trust Gwendolyn."

Nicholas and Sam echoed that agreement. When Alex's gaze turned to Violet, she swallowed past a hard lump. "I would be shocked if the voice in my head and the reason for my nightmares is *not* Lucia," she said. "She's grooming me for something, and I won't let it happen."

"Then we're in agreement. You have to go into hiding." He rested a hand over hers, leaning in. The coven master gave way to the lover she'd gotten to know, tenderness stealing away his frown. "It's too dangerous for you to go alone. Who knows what dangers you'll be exposed to in Nyixa."

"Come with me," she breathed for his ears only.

The rational part of her knew he had a coven to protect, but she yearned for him to take up the matter of her safety personally.

There was no one else she'd rather stake her life on. She saw the strife in his expression, the desire to be with her. "Sam." He turned to his deputy, and her heart leapt with hope. "Do you think you can manage the coven for six or so days?"

"Yes. Do what you have to." He got to his feet, as did the rest of the men in the room. "I'm going to put the coven on lockdown."

"Bloody good idea," Alex said, gathering up Lucia's gifts and offering Violet a hand up.

"Lockdown?" she asked, following him into the sitting room, where Gwendolyn and Armando were seated across from each other.

He was mid-story when he paused, seeing everyone going their own way except for Alex and Violet. With a jerk of Alex's chin, Armando left, calling out for Julian to wait for him. "Did you all come to a decision?" Gwendolyn asked, sipping from a mug of tea as if it were dainty china.

"We're coming with you," Alex said, placing Lucia's gifts before her. "Can you tell me what these are?"

She tilted the vial, observing its slow flow with a frown as she set her tea aside. "Where did you get this? No, no need to answer that. This is Lucia's handwriting. She tore pages out of her journal." Scanning the note that'd accompanied the pages, she clucked her tongue.

Violet leaned into Alex's side as she set the note aside, shaking her head. "The vial is very dangerous, and the spell she posed to Violet is far too advanced for a beginner. This,"—she held up the vial—"explains Violet's condition. It is preserved blood from the Fell Emperor, containing his magic. I thought it was all destroyed, but...here we are."

"Why did she give it to me and suggest it'd make me stronger?" Alex asked.

Gwendolyn's lips twisted as she passed the vial between her fingers, observing its casual radiance. "Because it will. It's liquid Fell, Alexander. Each sip will enhance your dark powers. Drink this whole thing, and in a blink, you'll have an Ancient's power at your command."

"You had it destroyed, didn't you?" Violet said, picking up the distaste in her manner, the way her fingers tensed as if about to smash the vial.

"What I could find of it. I had no idea it could create more silver-blooded vampires, though." Gwendolyn offered it back to him with great reluctance. "If you are wise, you would destroy this, too."

Alex took it, placing it in his pocket. "I will consider it."

"It is in every vampire's nature to hold onto power. I don't expect you to do anything but drink that blood." She sighed, her weathered hands sorting and placing Lucia's notes back in their envelope to give to Violet, note included. "Pack enough to clothe yourself for a week, and bring camping equipment. The palace has no modern amenities or furniture. There are a handful of mortals, but it would be smart to bring your own food."

"Right, okay," she said, moving to leave, only to be stopped by Alex's arm holding her firm around the waist.

"What happens in six days?" he asked. "I presume there's a plan past going into hiding."

"Why, the summer solstice. The shortest night of the year." She sipped her tea as if unconcerned by his presence looming over her, eyes narrowing. Violet was simply puzzled as to how that affected anything. The day was usually just a novelty on the calendar, if she even noticed it at all.

"And?" he prompted.

She drew herself up, using the cane to find her balance. Her gaze was shadowed full of secrets terrible and ancient. They squared up as the animal in Alex rose to the challenge of her stare. "There are more secrets in this world than you could hope to understand in an evening, Alexander. You trust me enough to accept my help and a portal into the unknown. Everything else will be explained in time."

A low growl rose from his throat. "Alex, c'mon, let's pack," Violet said, laying a hand over his chest. He'd already had a long day, and she suspected he'd been top dog long enough to chafe at being told to wait.

"Fine," he said, breathing out a sigh. "We'll be ready as soon as possible."

Chapter 23
Violet

Stepping through a portal was as dizzying and nauseating an experience as she'd expected. She was glad she hadn't eaten a big breakfast, else it'd be painting the white stone they landed on.

Violet turned to get a lay of the land, her shoes splashing in a deep puddle that soaked water into her socks. Perfect darkness shrouded the island, not a star or cloud in sight, just inky velvet as far as her eyes could track. It was eerie and unnatural, drawing a prickle of unease over her arms. Or perhaps that was the oppressive humidity that immediately stuck her hair to her neck.

They were at the top of a massive rise of stairs, the pristine white of the palace marred by clumps of seaweed, puddles, and the stinking bodies of unfortunate fish. Before them was an opening where she imagined a pair of intricately carved wooden doors, long since eaten away to rusted hinges. The stone portions extended upward to spiked peaks she'd get a crick in her neck to study, studded with empty holes where glass windows should be. "Welcome to the glorious island nation of the vampires," Gwendolyn said without inflection, heading into the palace with her head bowed.

"Thanks, I guess," Alex said dryly. He carried most of their gear and brought up the rear, his gaze roaming for danger.

"You should be aware that this is unlikely to go well," Gwendolyn continued. Violet kept pace with her, shooting her a concerned look. "Not for you, for me. But I will be around to train your magic and keep you abreast of things."

She thought of her ease with portals and nodded to herself. If the Ancient wanted to sneak around, she would. "Why would it go badly for you?" she asked as they passed through a blank foyer. The empty area echoed with their voices and footsteps all the way up a pair of identical stairs curling around to higher levels. There were hallways branching to the left and right as well, but Gwendolyn went straight ahead.

"I can't imagine the other people who survived this island sinking are fond of her, love," Alex remarked.

"That's right. But they're honorable people. They'll take you in." Her voice hitched for a moment. "Even if they don't forgive me, the moment you mention Lucia's unwanted interest in you, you will have allies and protection."

Violet bit her lip, unsure how to best comfort her or even if the stern woman would accept it. "Tell me about who we're meeting?" she suggested instead. They passed deeper into the darkness of the palace, where the dripping stone kept the temperature down to chill the sweat clinging to her skin.

Her vampire sight was working overtime, the world cast in grayscale between white stone and dark shadows. Anyone could be lurking around a corner, even though she knew only a handful of people still inhabited this space besides the explorers sent from around the world to investigate Nyixa's rising.

"I'm hoping Adrius will be on his throne. He's the King of Vampires." Shrouded in shadows, she sounded wistful, lost in some memories of her own. "He's a giant viking of a man and the strongest vampire you'll encounter, save for Lucia. A long sleep means he has the power but none of the wisdom of age."

"That's a dangerous combination," Alex chuckled from somewhere behind her.

"It can be. Hopefully, you will find it easier to connect with him," she said. Wind began to whistle around them as she led them out of a corridor and into an oval-shaped room with tiered seating. It smelled vaguely of cleaning fluid, a welcome change from the sickly-sweet scent of decay that haloed the palace. Gwendolyn squared her shoulders as she led them through an aisle around an empty pit that appeared to be at least a fifteen-foot drop. It looked like a gladiator pit of old, Violet thought.

The room could seat thousands, but instead, she saw it only seated one. A dark figure even amongst the shadows watched their progress from a vaulted throne. No one said a word until the three of them lined up at the foot of that throne. Violet swallowed her nerves as they looked up at the man cloaked in night from his seat of power. Now, she wished for a flashlight, if only to make out his features amongst the gloom.

"Gwendolyn. Explain." He spoke first, his voice deep and smooth, the kind she heard on the radio. It occurred to Violet that he spoke in unaccented English, something that should be impossible for a person who'd slept through it becoming a dominant language.

He didn't sound angry, simply bored. She wondered what such a mighty person was doing, sitting alone in the dark when a whole new world was waiting for him outside his moldering palace. "I bring this young couple to you for sanctuary," Gwendolyn said. "This is Alexander Rehnquist, a shapeshifter from Sirius's bloodline. And Violet Reynolds, a new Sorceress."

Adrius stood, descending the steps to his throne to loom over them. The shadows seemed to follow, clinging to his form as he went straight to Violet. She guessed him to be somewhere above six and a half feet tall, with the same muscular bulk as Julian. Alex tensed out of the corner of her eye as she met Adrius's dark gaze. Per Gwendolyn's instructions, she'd taken out her contacts to show her true nature at first glance.

"Sanctuary. Here?" His laugh was like a roll of thunder, deep and foreboding. "Where shall I put them? Shall they sleep in the stands, Gwendolyn?"

Violet quailed away from him as she caught a hint of gleaming fang in the midst of a snarling, bearded face. He turned toward the other Ancient in the room as Alex put his arm around her, drawing her a few steps away. "Should we say something?" she whispered.

"No. This is not our fight," he murmured back.

Adrius loomed over Gwendolyn now. He didn't shout, but fury underscored every sharp word. "How do I provide anyone sanctuary? My loyal men are *dead*. There's no trace of thousands of people in this palace except the corpses of the fish that fed on their marrow. How dare you come here asking anything of me."

"I'm sorry." She slipped it in while he paused, breathing like bull about to charge. "Fell madness—"

"Did you ever consider the hell you nearly condemned me to?" The shadows around him coiled in tighter.

"Every day. You have no idea—"

"Save it," he muttered bitterly. "And go." He turned his back, shielding her from the barely leashed violence storming around him.

"You can't sit here forever," she said to his profile. "Lucia plots in your absence."

"So? I'm sure you have some brilliant, self-sacrificing plan to thwart her."

This response, not his anger, seemed to deflate her. "I can't do it alone."

A sigh drifted from his shadows. "Go away, Gwendolyn. How many times do I have to say it? There's nothing for you here. No more blood to squeeze from this stone."

"You've given up." She shook her head, inspecting her boots.

From how Adrius's shadows slouched, Violet wondered if he was doing the same thing. "And whose fault is that?" She felt his attention on her and Alex, as if only remembering that they were there. "You may stay here. Modern mortals crawl over the city like ants. What's two more people?"

She winced, but Alex bowed deeply. "Thank you for your hospitality," he said, sounding genuine.

Adrius scoffed and returned to his throne seat, waving his hand in a clear dismissal. Gwendolyn opened a portal, nodding to the two of them. *"Good luck. I'll be in touch once you get settled."*

She disappeared through that hole in reality, leaving them

alone in the dark. "Where are we supposed to go?" Violet asked Alex, sure that they weren't going to get anything else out of the king.

Instead, she heard another sigh from the shadows. "Go back to the foyer," Adrius answered. "Jaromir will find you a safe place to stay. You will address him as Prince Mender, as befitting his status."

"Yes, Your Majesty," Alex said crisply, shouldering their supplies and nudging Violet. They went back the way they came, breathing a shared sigh of relief to be away from the man and his wreathe of shadows.

"This feels like a terrible decision," she admitted. "I don't think abandoning us in an empty palace is the best form of protection."

"I'm inclined to agree, but we'll see." Alex's green eyes were a bright spot amongst the gloom, crinkled at the corners from a thoughtful frown. "You know how Gwendolyn walked into our safe zone without trouble? Any powerful vampire is like that, either through stealth or force. Being here, in the proximity of similarly powerful vampires, is worth more than being comfortable in New York if there's even a small chance it'll deter Lucia."

"Honestly, that's terrifying," she said. "After that showing, I wouldn't stake my life on King Adrius." Strong or not, they were wandering quite far from his throne of shadows and stone. The foyer was still empty when they found it again, so they set down their supplies and waited.

"There are more Ancients here than him. I look forward to meeting my first Blood Prince," he said, taking the moment to draw her close. She sank into his embrace and the safety of his warmth, his lips the only promise of protection she wished she needed.

That was how their first Blood Prince found them. A throat was politely cleared from someone who'd entered the palace on cat-silent feet. Violet jumped in surprise at his seemingly sudden appearance. "Are you Prince Mender?" she asked, blushing as she parted from Alex save for an arm around him.

The man before them was slender and stately, dressed in a

fine suit tailored to his narrow frame. A tentative smile rested on his lips. The only hint to his age were his maroon eyes, piercing and intense in a way she'd observed in the older vampires. His fair hair stood out in the darkness. "Call me Jaromir," he said. There was a sigh in his voice, a weariness he didn't wear outwardly. "Adrius has already shared his offer of sanctuary. If you would come with me."

She shared a glance with Alex, who shrugged. They gathered up their equipment and followed him down a different wing of the palace. "I must apologize if Adrius gave you a poor first impression. It's nice to see new faces. Perhaps you can tell us more of the outside world," Jaromir said, his voice echoing strangely down the white stone hallway.

"Could you answer a question for me first?" Violet blurted.

"Of course, madam." His courtesy reminded her of a butler of old, drawing out a smile. It was heartening to meet an Ancient vampire who was more open. They could learn more from this man.

"How do you know English?" she asked. It'd been bothering her ever since Adrius had opened his mouth.

"The first thing you should know of Nyixa is that it's steeped in magic. Myself and my fellows all speak the language we are most comfortable with, but the magic translates it instantly to something you recognize."

"Really?" she gasped. "That's so *cool*."

Jaromir stopped in front of a hallway that also smelled of cleaning products. He smiled politely, but his brows drew together in puzzlement. "Pardon?"

"It's cool that magic can do that?" she tried again. Maybe the magic wasn't working fully after all.

"Cool is slang. It means she admires the magic you just described," Alex said, biting his lip to hold in a laugh.

She elbowed him. "Yeah, that's what I meant."

"Well, yes, it is quite admirable." Jaromir gestured behind him. "This is the wing where I live with my fellow Blood Princes. It's the safest place on the island. We are currently using paving stones for privacy."

"When we get back to New York, remind me to buy these people the services of a carpenter," Alex murmured to Violet. As described, each doorway they could see was either partially or completely obstructed by a block of white stone. *Only vampires can live like this*, she thought.

"Let's just take them back right now and introduce them to technology," she whispered back.

Alex shrugged in reply while Jaromir led them to an unoccupied room with a freshly uprooted stone taller than Violet at the ready to serve as their door. "It's not much," the Blood Prince said, shaking his head. "We'll certainly know if you're serious about needing protection if you stay."

"Well, it's from Lucia, so..." she drifted off, lips quirking. From what she could see of the room, it was blank stone, without a window-hole to the outside world. Like a tomb in the dark of this unnatural place. Trepidation itched her spine to even go in such a place.

"You have news of Lucia? We haven't seen her since we woke up."

"Must've bolted straight to New York then," Alex remarked.

Jaromir blinked slowly, not comprehending. "A city you haven't seen yet," Alex supplied.

"I surmised from the context. However, she's left the island?" He stepped forward, leaning in like it was vital information. Violet exchanged a puzzled glance with Alex, as it was apparent that Lucia had left the island long ago.

He said as much, drawing a curse from Jaromir. "It makes far more sense than her hiding on the island somewhere...but it shouldn't be possible," he said, shaking his head. "Nyixa is a magical island from another land. It needs a tether to stay here, and for many years, that was Lucia. If she leaves, or—as we've experienced—falls into a state of deep unconsciousness, the island will sink."

"Maybe sinking the first time changed those rules," Violet suggested.

"Hmm." He eyed her more closely. "If anything, it proves how fickle magic truly is. The sun does not shine upon Nyixa, my new friends. More magic. But I can tell the end of our day comes to a close, so the other Blood Princes will be returning shortly. Before we retire, they should meet you."

"Of course. I'm sure there will be questions on both sides," she said.

"May we all come away enriched," Jaromir said mildly.

Chapter 24
Alex

Alex felt like a chihuahua in a dog park full of great danes as they sat in a semi-circle on unforgiving stone with some of the world's most powerful vampires. Sure, he'd thought up until the moment of meeting them that he was a big dog, but now he saw how far he still had to go.

These men and one woman were the origins of the vampiric race, the pinnacles of power and fortitude. And being in the same room as them was nearly as unbearable as Adrius's concentrated bitterness. There were no smiles or camaraderie, only sullen stares. Not that he could blame them, waking to an entirely new world after a betrayal and with more problems already afoot.

Five sets of haunted maroon eyes were fixed on him and Violet as they described why they were there. There were other Blood Princes, they'd shared. Prince Elandros, the Legion, had disappeared on the same eve as Lucia, and Prince Taryn, the Blade, was jailed somewhere for everyone's safety. They hadn't asked any questions of that.

"So, she's figured out a way to leave," said Prince Sirius, the Dawn, whom Alex had taken the keenest interest in. The eight main bloodlines of vampire kind were named after the Blood Princes, and he was primarily of the Dawn line. His inner beast cowed in his elder's presence, recognizing a powerful and Ancient beast within Sirius.

Of all of them, Sirius was the most alert, his hands balled into fists at his side and eyes blazing with furious conviction. He wore a workman's overalls and heavy boots, modern clothing found or borrowed from the mortals somewhere on the island. They were at odds with the shaggy, dark hair he wore long and a well-groomed beard patterned with several intricate braids and knots from battles long-ago won.

Alex wondered uneasily what these Ancients had told those mortals and if their secrets would soon be outed since they hadn't known better than to share. They'd discovered quickly that Nyixa was a dead zone for electronics. Any messages in and out of the island would have to be relayed when the sender was back with civilization. But if those messages were already en route...there was no way to stop them now.

Sirius shook his head with a frustrated growl. "She's always ahead of us. We should've killed her while we could."

"Gwendolyn squashed that plan, remember?" rumbled the big man to his side. Clearing nearly seven feet tall was the largest man in the room, Prince Korin, the Bane. He spoke with slow authority and gentle, languid motions, but Alex wasn't fooled by the gentle giant act. Korin had all the muscle and easy menace as the ideal warrior of old. Considering he'd survived the war on the Fell species, he must've been deadly indeed.

"How could I forget?" Sirius bit off, his lips drawing back in a snarl that'd make Alex's inner beast quake in fear. "We need a plan. A new plan. I'm sick and tired of cleaning and babysitting fat mortals."

Violet covered her mouth to conceal a gasp while Alex understood the insult for what it was. In their time, a well-fed person like the modern mortal was a rarity. These people had so much to learn; he wondered how exactly to get them started. To drop a Blood Prince in the middle of New York would be to overwhelm them with noise, lights, and technology all at once. But that's exactly what they might need to do so they could confront Lucia directly.

"Keep your head on your shoulders," Jaromir said, raising a

brow over at him. "Making decisions in anger will not improve our situation."

"At least I want to make decisions." Sirius crossed his arms. "Our glorious *leader* just wants us to rot away here."

"So we appoint another leader." Prince Qin, the Ascended, spoke. He was an East Asian man, his upturned eyes always roving. There was a calculating mind there. Unlike the others, Alex wasn't convinced he was a warrior, but it may have been his easy smile and a body gone softer with what he'd assumed was a courtier's life. He was constantly moving in some way, even if it were just with a white coin flipping through his fingers.

"He has a point," Jaromir said, speaking quickly before Sirius could snap another biting response. His tone gentled. "We've done what we can for your brother. Almost no one remembers the king he used to be. We can honor his edicts, as we have by taking in the two people he's offered sanctuary to, but we can also move on."

The last Blood Prince, the woman, shook her head with a scowl biting into her face. She hadn't said a word, not even in introduction, but Jaromir had told them she was Prince Neala, the Wraith, referred to as a "Prince" only out of old tradition. She was a redhead with a jagged, chin-length hairstyle, doing more homely features no favors. Her face was marred by scars, the most prominent cutting the corner of her mouth and preventing her from making full expressions.

He wondered if she was about to speak or just let the men lead the conversation. There were obviously thoughts there and rage barely leashed behind eyes of flaming red. Apparently, he wasn't the only one who noticed her gesture. "Yeah?" Sirius said, elbowing her. "Speak. I still cannot read minds."

She flipped him a more universal gesture with a glare. "Fine. Just sit there then. Useless as Adrius," Sirius muttered.

Jaromir sighed, sparing Alex and Violet a glance. "My friends have always been characters. I'm afraid our long rest has only brought out the worst in us."

"That's quite all right. I wouldn't expect anything less," he said.

"After the carpenter, maybe we could also hire a psychologist," Violet suggested privately. She'd nestled herself in the crook of his arm for comfort.

Alex chuckled to himself. *"Six. One for each Ancient here."*

They shared a tense smile, both as taut as bowstrings while they watched these Ancients interact. Neala in particular seemed like she was one bad comment away from snapping and punching someone in the face. He imagined she was only here out of formality for her status. He cleared his throat, nervous just to speak up to this group. "On the topic of plans, have you considered that Gwendolyn already has one?"

He immediately regretted mentioning her. Only Jaromir really listened while four pairs of hostile eyes turned to him immediately. "No!" Sirius shouted, a fist thumping on the stone. "We're not working with *her*. You're lucky we even let her leave you here!"

Alex held up his palms. "Okay. Just asking."

"I'll lead us if I have to. But we're not just going to sit around on our thumbs *again*. I'm done. I'm *done* with Adrius," Sirius continued, his pupils mere slits, as if his inner beast was close to the surface.

"And maybe I'd listen to you if you stop yelling," Korin complained in his slow roll of a voice. "You're scaring them. Especially the Sorceress."

To his credit, he seemed to listen, glancing toward Violet as he took a few deep breaths. "Maybe you two can give us more information about the outside world."

Though Violet nodded, Alex was the one who spoke for them, explaining modern vampirism to an increasingly horrified audience. They questioned everything. The territorialism, the secrecy, the numbers. As he'd predicted, the numbers were the most shocking part, with an exponential rise in vampires for the boom of the mortal population they'd been absent for.

"Gwendolyn made us weak," Sirius said at the end of it all. "Our blood runs thin. The young are barely vampires."

"At least she has a handle on the Fell Madness," Qin offered, smiling to himself when Sirius growled.

"Thank you, Elder Rehnquist. Perhaps we should retire," Jaromir said loudly as Sirius raised a fist, looking like he was about to start shouting again.

"*You* retire. I'm going to plan," Sirius muttered.

Jaromir rose to his feet with grace, offering a hand up to Qin. Everyone but Sirius and Korin stood, starting to leave the room. "Wow," Violet sighed, clinging to Alex's side as they headed for their room. The other Blood Princes retired to their own rooms, except for Jaromir.

Alex glanced over at him, raising a brow. "I have a favor to ask," the Blood Prince said. When he gestured to go on, Jaromir spoke in his mind. *"When you next see Gwendolyn, I wish to be present at the meeting as well."*

He looked to Violet, whom Gwendolyn had promised to train. *"You seem like a reasonable gent, but after that showing, I worry you're going to drag her to the wolves."*

"No. I wish to speak to her without anyone else's interference. She has to be coming back, yes? Only two women possess the knowledge to teach the new Sorceress her magic, and since you're here, that narrows it down to Gwendolyn."

He considered Jaromir, who'd proven to be the most stable of the awakened Ancients so far. *"I'll make a deal with you. If you take me to the mortals exploring the island tomorrow, I'll get you to Gwendolyn."*

"Deal." Jaromir offered his hand and they shook on it.

"What was that all about?" Violet asked as they parted ways and Alex inspected the block of stone that was supposed to be their door. The Blood Princes were dragging them on the stone below, the grinding sound nails to his ears. He ushered her into their room before setting to the task. While they made it look easy, he was sweating by the time the block was in front of the doorway. They *needed* real doors soon, he thought.

However, it was nice to have some privacy with her at last. She set up an LED lantern, lighting the bare stone of their new accommodations. As they rolled out their sleeping bags, combining them to make a fleecy bed, he said, "Jaromir wants to hear Gwendolyn's actual plan. I figure she may actually tell him... so I plan for us to be there too."

"You think she'll be back?" She was looking around at the stone walls, her shoulders drawing in.

"I know she will be." They were where he assumed a bed would be, a room away from the door, with a smaller room to the side where a bath might've once been. He drew her close to lay a kiss at her crown and distract her from her thoughts. "Hey. Just like camping," he said.

With her eyes on him, she relaxed. A cute little crease furrowed between her brows as she considered the description. "What? Bare bones stuff?"

He took a moment to steal a kiss while she looked so confused. "Well, think of it this way. It's just you and me, in the middle of nowhere. Nothing to worry about at home, everything taken care of there. We have time to explore. But more important-ly..." he hands drifted lower, molding to her curves.

"Time alone," she said, catching his drift with a coy blush.

"And we have the paving stone level privacy."

She muffled a laugh against his chest. "How'd my life get so weird?"

"You met me, love." He considered her silver eyes shining with mirth. What a wild ride it'd already been for them, going from a zoo pen to a stone room in an ancient palace. "I hope you don't regret it."

His inner beast began to purr when she smiled. "How could I regret meeting you? I...I really like you," she admitted, blushing faintly.

Simple pleasure flushed him as that little kernel of instinct cheered. *She likes us!*

Of course she likes us, he thought, but to hear her say it was a treat all its own.

"I really like you too," he said. Now was his time. He could tell her how, miraculously, she was his second lifemate. How they were *meant* to be together. If they continued down this path, they could court a real mating bond, a vampire marriage of sorts where their enhanced mental capabilities ensured they could easily share thoughts and emotions.

The mating bond was bliss. He'd felt it before, and a part of him yearned for it again. But he thought, *she isn't ready for that yet* and decided against saying a word about it.

They had nothing but time.

Chapter 25
Violet

Alex gladly showed her how he went "camping" with a lady well into the murky hours of what she assumed was morning. It was hard to tell with perpetual darkness pushing in around the lights they'd brought to chase those shadows away. She fell asleep in his arms when they finally turned out the lantern.

A part of her asked subconsciously, *what if that nightmare comes back?* She dreamt sweet nonsense with the foreboding that it was coming. Any second, her mind's eye would switch to the moment she couldn't fully remember, when an Ancient person in white forced her to drink the blood that'd changed her.

She woke up with a musty taste in her mouth and pressure in her head. Gwendolyn's voice had somehow pulled her away right before the first scream could start, and for that, she was grateful, even as she blinked a groggy fog away. Next to her, Alex was still sprawled out like a content cat, snoring into a pillow he'd stolen from his bed. They may have sleeping bags, but he'd made sure their heads graced something nicer.

She glanced around, wondering if she'd imagined the Ancient's voice. As she stretched, popping her back, the woman answered that question for her. *"Violet?"*

"Good morning," she answered.

"Good evening," the Ancient corrected primly. *"Sleeping in, hmm?"*

"Long day," she said, a shrug to her tone. She had nothing to be ashamed of. Still, she nudged Alex awake and kept him abreast of the conversation as Gwendolyn arranged for them to meet her outside where the palace garden used to be.

Alex stretched languidly, resting his eyes. "I suppose we should get Jaromir and go. Wonder if we'll run into any of the other Blood Princes today." He made mental contact with Jaromir and led her from the room.

She frowned, honestly hoping not. They may be decent people and ancient war heroes, but something about them rubbed her wrong. With Alex and the other vampires she'd met, she'd fully believed they'd been human at one point. Not so with the Blood Princes, save for Jaromir.

She kept the LED lantern on. Even though she didn't *need* it to see, it was better on her eyes. The palace seemed like less of a cave, and she spotted Korin and Sirius working together to haul driftwood and rotten things from further in the palace. They paused to watch her and the bright tool she held, blinking rapidly against the glare.

Out on the steps, Jaromir and Neala sat overlooking the island. It was another perfectly dark night, the heavens blanketed by a sheet of black velvet. Jaromir was mid-word when they turned at the sudden light gracing them from behind. "Ah, hello," he said, lifting a hand. "Don't mind us. Just a therapy session."

Neala's flame-red eyes seemed to hold less rage, but a part of Violet still quailed to be in close proximity to someone so palpably angry. "Bad timing, hmm?" Alex tilted his head, a cue that he was sending some mental message.

"No such thing. A walk would do us good," Jaromir replied after a few moments, his thoughtful gaze drifting to the burly woman next to him. She shook her head and stood, passing Violet with a stiff-legged gait on her way back into the palace.

He breathed a tense sigh once she was gone, starting the lengthy descent to the palace gardens and leaving Violet and Alex to follow. "I worry for her. There's little my Gift has been able to do to ease her pain," he said.

"What happened with her, if you don't mind me asking?" Alex asked.

She didn't think Jaromir would respond, as lost in his own mind that he seemed. She'd noticed the dark bags under his eyes were more pronounced, as if he were pouring all of himself into a task. But he slowed his gait halfway down the palace's staircase just as she was starting to puff from exertion. "When Gwendolyn decided to sink Nyixa, she snuck some magical elixir into our drink. I remember it as if it were yesterday. We toasted to Adrius and Lucia's good health with a dry, red wine. It was a delicious vintage. It was saved for a special occasion."

"Wait, Adrius and Lucia were getting married?" she interrupted, her eyebrows raising to her hairline.

"At political knifepoint, yes. It was either that or we would tear the island in half with a costly civil war. Not that any of that matters anymore." Jaromir sighed again, sounding as weary as the years on his shoulders. "My point is, Neala hates red wine. She sipped it to be polite while the rest of us enjoyed it highly. We fell into a deep, dreamless sleep."

"Except for Lucia, as part of the revenge," Alex commented.

"And Neala, who came aware before the rest of us, but only in her mind. I fear the experience has broken a fundamental part of her."

Violet imagined it was a lot like locked-in syndrome from her limited understanding of both things. She'd been able to understand what was happening around her, fully aware and thinking, but unable to move. "How long do you think she was awake for?" she asked, hushed with newfound respect for the mute woman and horrified that anyone would have that experience.

"Too long," Jaromir replied, shaking his head.

"Does Gwendolyn know?" Alex asked tightly. He looked of a mind to tell her exactly what her actions had caused.

Jaromir laughed without humor. "Oh, she knows. For all our posturing and rough words, only Neala has attempted to murder Gwendolyn. I imagine nothing would break her heart more. Gwendolyn raised and adopted Neala as her own...long ago."

"And this is why you don't try to drown an entire nation," Alex muttered.

"I respect that she stopped Fell Madness in its tracks. She acted in the best interest for mortal kind," the Ancient said in his most healer-gentle tone. "But most will think her too extreme. Especially when confronted with the consequences for the survivors."

She nodded to herself, appreciating how realistic he was. "You all deserve better than to live in an empty palace."

"Small steps, young Sorceress," he replied, guiding them through the marshy ground where there was plenty of space for an impressive garden. She was glad for her lantern, side-stepping anything that looked like it'd once been at the bottom of the ocean. It seemed he knew exactly where Gwendolyn would be, leading them to the stone foundation and benches of what may have once been a covered veranda.

The Ancient woman struggled to her feet when she spotted Jaromir. Violet wiped her shoes against the stone block, keeping a respectful distance with Alex as the Blood Prince hopped forward to help stabilize her. They shared a few private words before she covered her mouth with a shaking hand. Her shoulders shook as Jaromir drew her into a hug.

"Probably the easiest forgiveness she'll find here," Alex murmured as they turned away from the reunion to give them a moment of privacy.

"I think they all need something like this," she said, her lips quirking at how monumental a task that seemed. "We're all on the same side, but it sure doesn't seem like they know it."

"Trust. Hard to win and easy to lose." He played with a lock of her hair, his knuckles grazing her cheek tenderly. She leaned into his touch, wishing they were still alone. Maybe once things relaxed, they could go camping for real. Just get lost in the wilderness together without any worry for Haven, Lucia, or these morose Ancients.

He pressed his lips to her crown before turning to the other two. Jaromir had offered his arm to Gwendolyn, supporting her in the stead of her cane. "I promised you a visit to the mortals here," he said to Alex.

"We can practice as we go," Gwendolyn said to her. For the first time since meeting her, the Ancient seemed cheerful. If it were possible, she imagined there would be a bounce to her step. "Beginning magic is hand gestures until you have the proper tools to channel it. Come along."

"Coming," Violet said, a smile spreading across her face. In that moment, she decided she wanted to help make things right here. As much as one person could.

With Jaromir's support, Gwendolyn was able to walk at a reasonable pace. They headed into the city proper within the ball of light from Violet's lantern, revealing what was left of Nyixa's solid spine after its long nap under the waves. "We keep any visitors on the far side of the island," Jaromir said. "Gentle mesmerization only. They have no idea that we share this place with them, nor why no one has any urges to explore the palace. Their strange inventions do not work here, yet more and more arrive daily."

"They won't leave until they have answers," Gwendolyn remarked.

"Well, they're missing a huge part of the puzzle without knowing about vampires and magic," Violet said, wondering what they would do when there were too many people to mesmerize and trick. The men and women sent to investigate Nyixa were on the cusp of the findings of a lifetime. She wiped clammy palms on her jeans at how close vampire kind was to being revealed to the whole world.

"It's only a matter of time." She echoed Violet's thoughts. "We will choose how and when to reveal ourselves. There is only one chance for a good impression after all."

Jaromir glanced over at her, a thoughtful look on his face. "What are you planning?"

As they passed through a ghost town of plots and crumpled stone buildings, her voice echoed and bounced. "I was thinking of meeting with world leaders, explain—"

"No," he interrupted gently. "That, we can handle later. What is your plan to stop Lucia?"

Her gaze drifted to Alex and Violet. "You will not like my answer." It was unclear who she was referring to—all of them maybe. Violet certainly didn't like the foreboding of her tone.

"I would rather know the unsavory elements of your plotting this time," Jaromir said, seeming unsurprised by the grim turn of Gwendolyn's manner.

She breathed a sigh. "Of course. I have no desire to sacrifice you or anyone else, despite what I'm about to tell you. The summer solstice approaches in mere days. Do you know the significance of that?"

They all shook their heads. "Our young friends have lived in an age untainted by the evils of worlds beyond ours, Jaromir. Allow me to explain the old times to them," she said, and he inclined his head with a thoughtful frown.

Alex exchanged a dubious glance with Violet. It was clear he was about at his limit with tales of the past, though everything Gwendolyn had told them so far seemed to be true. "The Fell had a tool they used to open a portal to our lands," she began. As they turned a corner, Violet's eyes landed on a multi-story object, pristine amongst the destruction around it. "This tool, in fact. In Jaromir's time, we called it a Grand Occultarus. I've come to understand it more in the years that've passed."

They stopped so Violet could crane her neck up to behold it in its dark majesty. The stone blocks around its base were carved with a number of strange symbols. Its tarnished metal rose and thinned out like the stem of a wine glass before curving around in a giant sickle carved with more unfamiliar markings. Between the point of the sickle and the base was an orb as large as a house, glimmering by lantern light like an oversized black marble.

Gwendolyn crossed herself with shaking fingers. "Do not look too closely into its darkness. It has a mind of its own and takes delight in tormenting. This, my young friends, is an Eye of Worlds, one of two in existence. When the orb spins, it becomes a portal to another world. I sacrificed my life and light to close it when we took the island."

"Your light?" Violet repeated, feeling her shoulders draw in the more she gazed upon the structure. It was most unnatural in its pristine sheen, surrounded by the rubble of a lost age.

Gwendolyn shook her head as if it weren't important. Jaromir spoke up in her stead. "She was once a nephilim, half angel."

"That's *impossible*," Alex muttered.

"It's the truth if you believe it or not." She turned to Violet, who was still following along, willing to give any idea a try if it made sense. "Fell were an aberration from a different world, cursed husks of their former selves as the fair folk of Faerie. Their release on Earth was part of a plot to conquer it."

Violet bit her lip, her gaze drifting to Jaromir, who nodded along as if she spoke a truth he'd heard many times before. "Fairies?" she said, finding that hard to believe. But if vampires could exist in complete secret from humans for so long...

"Yes, though they prefer to be called fae. Before our time,"— she indicated Jaromir with a tilt of her head—"angels, demons, and fae all had the ability to come to Earth on the basis of a list of incredibly strict rules. A subsect of Unseelie fae broke all those rules when I was born by connecting Earth permanently to their land of punishment, which we call the Fell Lands. They set the Fell loose on the world to consume it so they could rule the ashes."

Alex frowned, raising a hand to pause her. "And why are there no records of this anywhere?"

"There are, but so much time has passed that they are little more than myths. We didn't realize it at the time, but silencing this Eye of Worlds made the boundary between Earth and other lands almost impossible to pass through. The Unseelie are permanently trapped in Faerie to punish their hubris." She saw the dubious looks both of them were giving her now. "How do I know this? I am friends with a set of Seelie who ensure the balance remains that way. They are only able to come to Earth once a year, when the sun burns longest in our sky...the summer solstice."

Alex chewed on this knowledge, looking like he was still

having a hard time with his disbelief. "So, you are waiting until the summer solstice to enlist your Seelie friends to help us?"

"That's right. There is a special place in Faerie I've taken those too dangerous to kill," she said, her tone resuming its grave tenor. "When any vampire dies, a portion of the Fell in them can pass on to an heir of sorts. It's how the Blood Princes earned their power so quickly—they took it directly from Fell."

"So those old vamp's you've curated..." Both Alex and Jaromir frowned at some implication Violet wasn't understanding as Alex's voice drifted off.

"They sleep, like Lucia and the Blood Princes did until recently. That way, they do no harm and have no chance of sharing their madness with others," she confirmed. "The Seelie help preserve and seal the Vault of the Ancients. Without a cure...it's necessary."

Violet's skin crawled with unease, realizing now why the others were staring at Gwendolyn. Alex with fear, Jaromir with something akin to resignation as he said, "You will place Lucia there to sleep until the end of time."

Gwendolyn nodded gravely. "It's the only way to protect everyone from her curse."

"And...you will try to take the rest of us," he continued, watching her shoulders stiffen. Disappointment lit his gaze. "You judged us too corrupted before. Likely to go Fell Mad at any moment or to share that condition with anyone we gave blood to. That's why you chose to let us drown."

Violet felt she could cut the air's tension with a knife. "Times have changed, Jaromir. I do not intend to take you to the Vault."

"But Adrius? Neala?" he prompted. "Even Sirius?"

"There is hope," she said in a small voice. She turned to Violet, taking her hands. "You are the new light in my darkness. You see the Eye of Worlds before you? Lucia has disabled it some-how. It won't budge from my magic, but I am no Sorceress. If you can get it to work again..."

"We will drown," Jaromir said sharply. His features were twisted in a scowl as he looked up at the monolithic object. "*That's* how she's left the island. She has outplayed us."

"Maybe if we can tether its magic to Violet..."

"Stop. Both of you," Alex snarled. "Don't drag my... Don't drag Violet into your plotting. She's cast what, one spell?"

"You don't understand. I worry that if we don't get it working again, there will be no crossing at the summer solstice. We have no other way of stopping Lucia," Gwendolyn said grimly.

He drew Violet away from her, baring his teeth as he recited names: Adrius and the Blood Princes they'd already met. "You don't understand," she repeated.

"What? You're not willing to kill her?" he aimed the question at Jaromir.

"I'm a healer, sworn to do no harm," he replied.

"Just listen—"

Alex shouted over her. "No, you bloody listen! Violet is not touching that damn thing! We're not playing experiment to things we don't understand."

"But—"

"Alex." Violet gave his shoulder a shake. She had a feeling they were missing some other important piece to this puzzle.

Gwendolyn ended up shouting back, "Anyone who kills Lucia will also inherit her curse! They'll go mad! Completely insane!" With him leaning away, she cleared her throat and continued in a calmer manner. "Lucia's curse destroyed her personality. It made her a megalomaniac and caused her to stab everyone she ever cared for in the back. Do you wish for your fate to be the same?" Grudgingly, he shook his head. "Good. Then—"

No one spoke over her this time. She stopped herself, watching shadows drift past them and coalesce into a man's form. He loomed over her just like he had yesterday, but now by lantern light, they could all see him clearly. Adrius had left his throne. Up close, she saw the resemblance between him and his brother, Sirius, down to the rage that twisted his expression under a black beard tied and braided with deeds of the past. He wore armor stained with shadows, the sword at his hip a relic from another time.

"I came to see what all the shouting was about. Imagine my surprise to see you *again*." He spoke through gritted teeth.

"You're moving about. That's good." If she wasn't mistaken, there was a tremble to Gwendolyn's voice and manner.

His dark eyes roved over their group. "I still need to feed. Don't worry. I didn't harm anyone."

A tense silence fell as they had a staring match. Gwendolyn wasn't willing to let him intimidate her into leaving this time, but that left Violet waiting uneasily for some sort of violence to erupt. She backed away with Alex, and a pun came to mind. "The past, the present, and the future walked into a bar," she whispered to him.

"Not right now," he whispered back, raising a brow at her.

"It was tense." She started laughing and found she could not stop. It was like a dam breaking, sweeping away thoughts of fairies and ancient feuds and the Eye of Worlds and how somehow, some way, she was involved in all of this. Both Ancients turned to her, Gwendolyn incredulous and Adrius's lips twitching.

"What did she say?" the king asked Jaromir, who repeated the pun. With what felt like everyone staring, she wiped at her eyes and regained her breath.

Then Adrius cracked a smile. His beard spread, and a little twinkle hit the dark depths of his eyes. "That's a good one."

"You...like puns?" she asked. It was the most surreal moment of her life, watching the tension leave Ancient King Adrius for even those spare moments. All too quickly, reality stole that smile away, and his stern countenance returned.

"Why are you back?" He turned back to Gwendolyn, his tone neutral once more. "Why won't you leave?"

"This young lady requires a tutor. Despite everything, you must realize it would behoove us to have a friendly Sorceress," she replied evenly.

His eyes narrowed. "Is this true, Jaromir?"

Though Adrius didn't turn to him, Violet did. The other Ancient slipped on a poker face immediately. "Yes. It's perfectly logical we would want the young lady as versed as possible in magic."

"We could ask Neala to teach her..."

"No. We can't." Jaromir spoke with the same firmness that Melanie did upon telling Violet that there was nothing wrong with her. *A doctorly tone,* she thought. Only summoned up by someone with a deep understanding of someone else's experiences.

Adrius nodded in acknowledgement. "Then there is no one else." Something passed between them privately, causing his expression to sour. A breeze caught his cloak as he turned pointedly away from them, moving on silent feet despite the armor he wore.

"King Adrius!" Violet called, ignoring Alex's desperate motion for her not to draw more attention to them.

Outside the halo of her lantern, the shadows were closing in around his form. Still, she saw his profile turn their way. "How do you say goodbye to boiling water?"

He tilted his head. She didn't hear a sigh or any annoyance in his tone, which was how she marked those who didn't like her punster ways. "I'm not sure. How?"

"It will be mist." She only smiled wider as Alex and Gwendolyn groaned behind her, but her heart was in her throat for Adrius's reaction.

A flash of white showed a smile before the shadows whisked Adrius away.

Chapter 26
Alex

Alex felt like a mess by the time the group returned to their initial meeting spot in the former palace gardens. As Violet finally received her first lesson in magic, he dusted off a stone bench still intact and sat with Jaromir to watch.

They did not talk for a while, leaving Alex to consider and brood. He was of a mind to leave after hearing how Gwendolyn wanted Violet to tap into the giant magical tool on the island. It seemed too dangerous.

But Violet herself had not protested. She'd heard the plan and had encouraged the Ancient to continue her strange rant about planets and faeries. How could she believe a word of that? His high esteem of the Curator and all she'd done for vampire kind was quickly plummeting upon getting to know who the woman truly was and how her agenda affected him.

Violet was a tool to one so Ancient, and it chafed to see it so plainly, standing next to her. By some strange happenstance, Violet was a Sorceress. Lucia had chosen her out of billions of women, to restore her while in the grasp of a hellscape. In doing so, Lucia had also chosen him as Violet's lifemate. There was a plan here. And the fact he couldn't clearly see what it was made it all the more dangerous.

The half-filled vial of silver blood felt like it tripled in weight as he thought. He carried it on his person at all times, assuming it was of value to be stolen if any of these vampires had even a hint of its smell. He didn't dare take it out with Jaromir seated beside him.

Lucia's direct gift was incredibly valuable.

He should destroy it.

Power was something most vampires would murder for. Why had Lucia given it to him in a bottle? *Why not use it herself?* he thought. He growled under his breath, knowing the trap of considering a future-seer's plotting too closely without enough context. It would make him mad long before she pulled the strings together for her ultimate goal.

And it could be months, years, before she called in the favor she'd done for them in saving Violet and giving him the rest of the silver blood.

"What troubles you most?" Jaromir asked, his gaze fixed on Gwendolyn and Violet as the younger woman attempted to mimic a series of increasingly complicated gestures.

"Where do I start?" He noticed Jaromir lean in. Even the soft-spoken Gifted man could be a politician. It hadn't escaped his notice how closely he had stuck to Gwendolyn's side once knowing that she was on the island. Even though he had offered an olive branch of forgiveness, the man was shrewd enough not to forget. Which meant any information shared could make it back to the other Blood Princes, or King Adrius if it pertained to Gwendolyn.

So, he searched his mind for the most benign of his troubles. "I don't know how anyone can live here anymore. When are you all leaving the island?"

"Possibly never. Unless the mortals leave. We have kept them on the least interesting side of the island."

"You know there's so much more out there? People and technology. It could be a fresh start for you." He saw the mulish line drawing on the Blood Prince's face. "We can remain a secret to mortals if they never find a hint of vampires here."

"Would that be so bad? We were never a secret in my time."

"Times change."

Jaromir grunted in agreement. "Sorry. That must be quite the understatement," Alex added. He felt a twinge of sympathy for the daunting task of learning the culture of the time. At least with magic, language wasn't an issue. "But if you're going to be awake, it seems right that you all would try to fit in with how things are."

While Jaromir considered that, Violet made one of her gestures correctly. A patch of fresh grass grew in a circle around her, flushing vibrant green. She pumped her fist, looking to Alex to share in her victory. "Excuse me while I go pick my jaw off the ground," he called once he'd recovered from his awe. He'd never met a vampire capable of making anything grow. Most of their powers centered on people, either affecting themselves or others.

"Think I should do more?" She smiled at the thought, her silver gaze already taking in just how much space she'd have to fill. Her circle of greenery extended about a yard around her.

"Great way to exhaust yourself. Let's try another," Gwendolyn butted in before he could encourage her, and he growled at the reminder that he wasn't listened to here with the respect of an Elder coven master.

Jaromir distracted him by finally voicing his thoughts. "I'm not sure there's a place for us in your world."

Alex considered him along with the smoke Violet curled over her arm like a languid snake. It flowed through her fingers, only visible in silhouette in the eternal dark of the city around her lantern's beacon.

It wasn't that the Blood Princes weren't of this world. Their magic was the foundation of the vampire race. Each and every vampire was their legacy in blood. But the magic their awakening had brought with them...Lucia and Nyixa and whatever truth there was to the tale of fae, nephilim, and other worlds. That was what made his skin crawl.

"I think everyone has that problem. You only have a place in the world if you make one for yourself," he answered.

The Blood Prince nodded, turning back to the training. Violet looked to be growing tired, her fingers fumbling the next few symbols. "Let's stop for now," Gwendolyn said. "The first spell in each element of magic is the hardest. I'm impressed you muscled through even two for your first lesson."

Standing straighter from the Ancient's praise, Violet seemed to hold a new spark of vitality, like the glow after a particularly good workout. "I have so many questions," she said. "You said there's thirteen elements of magic? What are they?"

Gwendolyn didn't answer directly, instead cutting a portal midair with a gesture from her walking stick. "If you would follow me, I believe I can give you this knowledge in a more concrete form." She gestured to the two men as well as she headed through.

He was last to follow, eyeing the hole with trepidation. His inner beast paced restlessly at the back of his mind, uncomfortable with the unnatural nature of stepping into a rip of time and space. However, he wasn't about to leave Violet alone. Once he mustered up his nerves, he saw they were still somewhere in Nyixa. The lantern was resting atop what appeared to be a lab table, illuminating the remnants of a room with vaulted ceilings and one incongruous sight that Gwendolyn headed for.

A wooden cabinet, lacquered and gently battered. "Only the magical items have remained here." Gwendolyn opened the cabinet to reveal it mostly barren save for a handful of glass vials full of unknown substances and a row of books. She drew the densest one and offered it to Violet.

Alex drew up behind her, peering at the gilt title on a weathered leather cover. He opened his mouth to ask how she was expected to study something written in a language of swirls and dots that was hopelessly foreign when those figures shifted into English before his eyes. "A beginner's guide, hmm," he remarked.

"This is very valuable and one-of-a-kind," Gwendolyn said.

Violet flipped the cover gingerly, drawing thick pages over until she found a table of contents. "Thank you," she said, sounding humbled. "I'll study this while we have time here."

"See that you do. I'll come around once a day to help you unlock the other elements when I can," Gwendolyn promised, laying a hand on her shoulder. "See you tomorrow."

"Until then." Violet waved, while Alex turned his attention back to the table of contents.

Broken down into fourteen chapters, it clearly labeled everything Sorceress magic could do, but his eyes skipped down to the last entry, titled "The Five Virtues," which drew a confused grunt from him. "Do you think this is going to answer all your questions?"

"Not even close," Violet admitted. "I'm going to need to study this. What even is this? The first chapter is titled 'Spring.'"

"Shapeshifting." Jaromir's voice nearly startled him. So curious of the book, he'd forgotten the Blood Prince was still there, leaning against a lab table and watching them both with inscrutable maroon eyes. "I believe animal familiars are tied to it as well, but none of us have gotten that particular power."

"That's a shame." She gasped at the thought, leaning her head back to Alex. "I could tame you."

He kissed the tip of her nose. "What's to say you haven't already?"

A joyful giggle escaped her lips. "We should study this together soon."

"Indeed. Study it very closely," he said, his gaze meaningful on her.

She cuddled back into him, the first to turn back to the book and reading out chapter titles to Jaromir for his help. "How about 'Summer?'"

"The element of fire. Autumn is earth, which includes botanicals and the ground itself. And Winter is weather and the element of water," he said.

"How do you know all this?" she asked, her brow furrowing.

"Lucia was and is able to do all of this. Plus...the symbols adorn every magical item the fae have left behind. Take another look at the cover."

She closed the book, holding it to the light of her lantern. The gold filigree started to fill the bottom third of its leather with symbols. A crescent of thirteen symbols with a circle of five arranged like points of a star set in the middle. It looked like a tiny version of the Eye of Worlds or Grand Occultarus. "Fae, huh," Alex said, casting a doubtful look toward him.

"The magic unfolds before your eyes." Jaromir gestured to the book.

"Other worlds?" he said more incredulously.

The Blood Prince chuckled. There was a sharp edge to it, something buried deep within him that hadn't seen the light of conscious thought. "Some folks need to be slapped with the truth to see it."

"Are you calling me ignorant?" he frowned. Pot and kettle there, he thought, offended someone asleep for centuries would imply such a thing of him.

"Never. Simply functioning within a set world view. Us old men get that way." He offered a tense smile.

Glancing between the two of them, Violet huffed a sigh. "Can we talk about magic without getting all snippy? Please?"

Alex tried to muffle a frustrated growl. Not with her, just with...everything else. The book and its glimmering magical inscription were just one thing too many. "Perhaps I should escort you to your quarters," Jaromir suggested. "Gwendolyn left us on the other side of the palace from them."

"Please do," he said, glad to be gone from this place and its magically intact cabinet.

Violet waited only a few paces from the room before she was asking questions again. She traced each symbol as Jaromir explained them. Alex listened with a frown. "The thirteen elements are connected into five sets, and usually, the seasons are depicted first. After them comes Day and Night, control over light and dark. Vampires borrow heavily from Night in particular."

"That makes sense," she said.

"Following that should be the magic that augments physical performance, which we all have a touch of. We call magic that improves strength or reflex Sword, while endurance, regeneration, and immortality come from Shield magic." He glanced to Alex, whose eyebrows were raised.

"I suppose you're going to say that our psychic powers, glamors, and auras are also a school of fae magic," he remarked.

He smiled as if having been waiting for exactly that comment. "The next set starts with Mind, which covers all of that. It's combined with Life, which is the Gift or anything to do with disease, and Metaphysical, covering dreams and portals."

"Self-explanatory," he grunted. He picked out that his bloodline wasn't as purely in one school of magic as he would expect. Spring covered his shapeshifting, Metaphysical, the dream walking, and someday, if he were lucky to make it there, as an Ancient, he could become a daywalker with Day magic, just as his father had been. He didn't know how it was possible to be torn in three directions that way.

"And finally, Language for the social aspects, and Wind to cover flight and the last element, wind itself." Jaromir turned to Violet. "With enough practice, you can wield all of the elements as a Sorceress, just as Lucia does."

She clutched the book close to her chest, chin lifting to face the challenge ahead. "Something tells me I'll need it before the solstice comes."

Chapter 27
Violet

Violet only realized there was something wrong when she and Alex retired to their stone room. He caught her hands before she could sit upon their bed of sleeping bags and pillows, leaning in earnestly. "We need to leave this place."

She recoiled, fumbling to place the spell book aside before she dropped it. "What? Why?" she asked. Sure, he'd seemed uneasy as they learned more about the island and where vampire kind had come from, but she hadn't expected this.

"Why?" he echoed, shaking his head. "If these people aren't off their rockers, Gwendolyn clearly plans to use you."

"Oh, to get the good fae here?" Her smile faded as his expression remained stern. "Look, she's the only one who can train me—"

"She gave you a book of spells. Now we can leave," he pressed.

"And how do you expect us to do that? She got us here!" She drew back from his grasp but forced herself to take a breath before she said anything she might regret. "I know it has been hard to learn all this stuff after so long. I only believe it all because, well..." She picked up the spell book. Its cover was completely blank, and she pointed to it as if to prove what she meant.

"All right. Say the magic and the fae are real," he said. "*If* so, that doesn't stop that we walked into a political situation I don't trust."

She bit her lip, thinking of the personalities they'd met on the island. "Adrius let Gwendolyn stay today. That's a good thing, right?"

"Do you think he would if he knew she planned to put him to sleep again?" he murmured back, shaking his head.

"She didn't..." Yet, she had. She'd only said she wasn't planning to put *Jaromir* to sleep. But he was the only Ancient she'd met who seemed like he could rejoin the world and learn to adapt.

Pressing while she considered, Alex said, "Gwendolyn is a plotter. The other vampires here have a good reason not to trust her."

"She did what she had to," she argued. "Why are we even talking about this?"

"Because one old woman, no matter how Ancient, can take on Adrius and the five Blood Princes. But if she had a Sorceress?" He tipped his hand. "With everything you can do? Or that she can teach you to do?"

"I think you've lost sight of why we're here. It has nothing to do with the politics. We're all on the same side. They're going to protect me from Lucia." She shook her head slowly. "Not to fight each other. Do you have another plan? Or someone Ancient enough to stand up to Lucia—"

"We can—"

"Stop interrupting me!" she shouted, pulling at her locks in frustration. "Stop being paranoid! This is where I need to be!"

His nostrils flared, the animal in him coming to the fore in his slit-pupiled eyes. "Very well. But we don't talk to the others. Especially Adrius."

Pinching the bridge of her nose, she thought of the man who'd smiled at her joke earlier. "Let me guess. Because he might try to use my power too." She definitely didn't appreciate the conjecture as to what these people may or may not do. They'd only met them yesterday.

"No. At least, I don't think he cares." He took her by the

waist, pulling her stiff form into his for a tight, one-sided hug. "He's dangerous. How can you look at him and not think that too?"

"Sure, but..." She turned her head from his lips to refuse the distraction of his gentle touch. She had the feeling his roaming hands were to divert her thoughts, and that only made her twitch with an angry flush. "Look, I don't need you pushing me around. If you don't want to be here, you don't have to be."

His hands stilled immediately. "What?"

"You don't have to be here," she repeated, lips pressing into a mulish line. "You want to leave so badly? Go. I trust these people. Just like I trusted you not too long ago."

His eyes searched her face as she drew from him again and took her spell book to sit on a pillow and read. The room didn't seem big enough for the two of them with him looming over her. She scanned the very first page of writing without really reading it, just scowling at the words as they reformed into English right before her eyes.

"Violet..."

"I'm *not* leaving Nyixa," she told the book.

"Then I'm not either," he said firmly. His clothes rustled, shirt falling to the stone by their makeshift bed. Pulling the book up over her face, she read like the most nearsighted person to avoid looking up at his muscled chest.

Be mad, damn it, she told herself. He knelt next to her, lips brushing her cheek. *Be mad. Be mad!*

Fur brushed her arm as he shapeshifted. She finally turned away, jumping at the crackle of bones as he shook off the rest of his clothes, taking the form of a fluffy black cat with his piercing green eyes. Her resistance melted away only after a few moments, and she set the book aside to cradle and pet him. "I'm still mad at you," she told that smug cat face with its whiskers splayed forward from the simple pleasure of her touch.

"No one can be mad at a cat." His voice was gruff and high like a cat's meow. He closed his eyes and purred as she placed him in her lap for his companionship while she read. A pang of homesickness hit her, reminding her of many similar nights with her cat cuddled against her. She rested her fingers in Alex's silky fur, feeling his breath even out as he fell asleep within minutes.

Careful not to disturb him, she flipped to the back of the book, starting chapter fourteen, which was on the five virtues. Jaromir hadn't explained what those were, yet she'd seen the symbols both on the book's cover and engraved around the base of the Eye of Worlds like the five points of a star.

She muffled a yawn and dove into it. After a few paragraphs, she was of a mind to wake Alex and read to him the detailed information on fae society she'd found. It turned out that there were five additional powers, and a person could only ever have one. They predominantly manifested in Sorcerers or Sorceresses, though occasionally, a "less gifted fae" would also be born with one of the virtues.

She bit her lip upon figuring out which of the virtues were hers. Something called true sight, or the ability to see beyond anyone's glamor or mind tricks. It explained why she saw beyond the beautiful façades of the vampires she'd met past being changed.

"I told you, my dear. I made you strong."

The voice! She nearly dropped the book in surprise. Her heart pattered against her chest like a caged bird seeking escape. *"Lucia?"* Upon asking, she desperately hoped the woman who kept creeping into her mind wasn't the Ancient Sorceress.

No reply came for long enough that she assumed she hadn't reached the other person, as always. But a reply crawled into her awareness as her eyes turned back to the spell book. *"It is not time for us to meet yet. But soon."*

"Wait! Lucia?" she called, the mental equivalent of grabbing at the other person. She felt the barest edge of awareness, as if someone else were watching...and listening. *"Why did you change me?"*

"I saved you, girl. No longer will you be a victim to the world."

"But...why?" she repeated desperately. Why her? Why use the Emperor's blood upon her, a random victim? So many questions bubbled to the surface, but she only wanted to understand

how someone so Ancient and storied had seen a kernel of potential in her.

Lucia's chuckle was melodious, like one a lady of old would make while hiding her mirth behind a fan of silk and lace. *"Possibilities. Pathways, dreams, hopes. A thousand thousand possibilities, but few are viable. Why you? You will see in time."*

That didn't answer her question, but she could already feel Lucia fading from her mind. Her hands tightened with frustration. *"Viable for what?"*

"Soon, my dear, I will call you to my side. You will see lies for what they are and the truth Gwendolyn nor the others will tell you. I am the future, and you are key to my destiny."

Violet's heart remained a jumping rabbit, even though Lucia obviously left her on that mic drop. She cursed under her breath. So that was the plan, whatever sliver of it Lucia was willing to share. Hands shaking, she clutched the spell book in two hands and forced herself to read of the other virtues, and when she'd memorized the five of them, she delved into the front of the book and read as far as her adrenaline would carry her.

She eventually joined Alex in sleep, deciding to disturb him and the others with Lucia's intrusion when they were fresh. Until then, she chanted the virtues like counting sheep.

True sight, future sight, empathy, druidism, mediumship.

Chapter 28
Alex

HE WAS DREAMING SOMEONE ELSE'S DREAM, HIS INNER beast tugging him further into the fog of rest. They weren't with Violet anymore, and he wasn't in control of where they were going.

Upon shifting, the inner beast had taken back its control of this new ability. Somehow, he thought it was showing him how it worked. He'd only experienced Violet's dreams, which showed only a drop of his potential to infiltrate others' minds. Together, he and the beast crossed to another's dream. Expecting a pop of stimulus to all senses, he instead felt them mute further.

He couldn't feel his body. Darkness as oppressive as the blanket over Nyixa surrounded him, punctuated by the slap of water against stone. His first thought was wondering if they were at the bottom of the ocean, drowning just as Gwendolyn had intended.

"Help! Someone help me!"

A woman's voice, muffled and desperate. "Where are you?" he called. There was no sense of direction here, but he still bent low and quested with his fingers, brushing against cold stone and the edge of a rug worn soft by the tramp of many feet.

"Help!" It sounded like she hadn't heard him. Her words had a hoarse edge. "Can anyone hear me?"

"I can. I can hear you," he answered, bumping into the solid bulk of a table.

"Is anyone there?" Despair threaded through her question. He realized all at once who this must be. Purring within his awareness was his inner beast, assuring him that they'd come to the person who needed their presence most.

Open your eyes, it whispered.

"Hello? Hello?" she was screaming now. The dream rocked uncertainly, a sign that the woman herself was fighting to free herself of this nightmare.

His fingers found someone's arm, and he shook it. "Open your eyes! You're not alone," he urged.

Light flared to life as sconces lit with fire around the room, bringing him nearly face-to-face with Neala, her freckles clear in a face bleached pale and coated in cold sweat. She shook him off and sat up, taking a look around. The room was one where he imagined many war councils took place, several half-finished maps pinned to the wall. A long table in the center of it all was still set with a bottle of wine and a few waiting glasses.

"You're dreaming. None of this is real," he assured the redheaded woman as she pressed fingertips to her face, brailing out the contours of a crooked nose and the long scar that marked the side of her mouth.

"Dream walker," her voice grew hoarser still, as if she'd shouted it to its limits.

"So it would seem." He tilted his head back as she stood, towering over him. Awareness lit her red eyes like living, furious flame.

With a gesture from her, they were accompanied by the bodies of sleeping men plus a raven-haired woman sprawled out in a wedding dress like a discarded doll at the end of dress-up. "This is what this really looked like," Neala murmured. He recognized all the sleeping faces, save for three. "I opened my eyes first, but I couldn't move."

"How long did you lay here?" His voice hushed respectfully down to her own as memories flickered at the edge of the dream.

"Years. I don't know." Her fingers balled into fists at her side.

It was hard to imagine a worse hell than to be awake and aware, but trapped in a cold tomb for so long... "I would ask a boon of you, dream walker." Gesturing for him to follow, she walked out of the scene and into the quiet of her unconscious mind. Where Violet's mind, when not dreaming, was a calm, starry night, Neala's was like walking into a windstorm. He was pushed and pulled by invisible forces, hair knotting above him as if it were caught in the top of a twister.

He understood what she wanted. His inner beast didn't have to tell him, even though that bundle of instinct screamed it anyway. *Calm!*

"Long ago, I had a friend who walked in dreams," Neala said, standing unaffected by the chaos filling this space. "She helped me erase the memories that held me back. We could remove exactly what was needed."

"Like surgery." He nodded. "Instead of erasing full days...you could take away specific scenes of memory." He'd already done something similar with the hellscape he'd pulled from Violet's mind.

But Neala was about to ask for more, he thought. She confirmed his musings a moment later. "I wish to forget I ever woke up before my friends." Erasing bits and pieces of foreign memory was one thing, but she was talking the experience of years. "Restore me, and I will give you a boon in return."

He closed his mouth on voicing any hesitations. He could at least give it a try for a boon from a Blood Prince, especially if it would soothe the fury that'd gripped her the couple of times he'd seen her in person. Win-win if it were possible.

It's possible, his inner beast assured, stretching out its claws. This time, he let it take control, and together, they led Neala deeper into her memories, searching for the moment she woke a prisoner in her own body. They walked for hours, though it could've been minutes, fighting the raging wind that impeded progress while screaming of revenge and betrayal.

Neala herself grew less aware as they went deeper, blank eyed like a sleepwalker. He finally came to the moment he was looking for. Together, man and beast stretched out their mental influence, telling Neala to forget. She would still know of Gwendolyn's betrayal, but the bottled volcano in her mind would be put to ease.

Neala's mind calmed as the memories faded to nothing. Her sleeping self turned to him, a smile tugging the unscarred side of her lips. "Thank you."

"My pleasure. Really." He hoped he could hone this side of his magic without needing his shapeshifting instincts leading the way. If it worked for her and Violet, many more could use a gentle hand to erase the most painful of memories.

"Is there anything I can do for you now in return?"

"Yes! Don't wake up," he said hastily. "I would like proof."

She raised a brow silently, beckoning for him to continue. "I've heard two stories and some outlandish claims. Fae. Portals to other worlds. Show me proof in your own memories of such things."

"Who told their tales to you?" she asked in her hoarse voice. In the silence of her mind, he could hear her, though he imagined it would be harder if she didn't speak in the waking world.

He reluctantly shared Lucia and Gwendolyn's names, watching her face crease with hatred. "Of course. I honor your request."

The air warped until they stood together before the Eye of Worlds on a dark day not unlike any of the others he'd already spent on Nyixa. They flanked a woman wearing a moonstone crown, regal and proud as an army of men and women waited tensely around them. Her eyes and hair were golden, skin flushed with vitality under a simple gown of rose petal pink. A butterfly perched on her shoulder, its wings the only jewel that otherwise adorned her. "This is Nyah. My sister by choice and adoption," Neala said. The memory of the woman didn't twitch as they spoke of her. "She's also Gwendolyn's daughter and Adrius's lifemate. We lost her long ago."

He put a hand over her shoulder as her voice cracked. "I'm sorry. We don't have to—" he cut himself off as Gwendolyn and the dark-haired woman from before worked together to make the Eye of Worlds spin its giant glass orb. He assumed the other woman was Lucia. Faster and faster the orb went until its spinning surface flattened out to a sphere-sized portal.

"Nyah thought we could reason with the Fell after their defeat," Neala said. Words spoken long ago passed like murmured background noise. *Forgotten to time,* he thought, watching the body language instead. Neala and Sirius joined another woman with rich brown skin, a delicate sari wrapped around her form and eyes of Blood Prince red, to surround Nyah.

He and Neala followed the memory beyond the portal, their feet landing in a dune of ash. Ashy mounds stretched as far as the eye could see, a ruin where no one would be able to survive. The vampires spoke with a single Fell as it led them into what looked like a refugee camp not far from the portal. "I assume it didn't go well?" Alex asked, watching hungry Fell peer out of their tents. The creatures were worse in person, hunched over and frog-like, with lips permanently stretched around prominent rows of fangs. Hunger lit many a face.

"Not because of the Fell," she answered. Nyah and the Fell spoke while the other Blood Princes looked on with disapproval. She passed it a vial not unlike the one still sitting in his pocket, except this one was filled with a glimmering, golden liquid.

He meant to ask of the similarity but stopped when the Fell started to change upon gulping down the vial's contents. Pale, paper-thin skin flushed with color. Bones popped and shifted to turn the creature into something with a humanoid frame, only a loincloth to cover his modesty. The only thing that left Alex's mouth was a confused grunt.

It couldn't be possible. But here was the proof he asked for. A living, breathing fae from her memory, transformed from a Fell by miracle. "This is Caladorn Nightweaver, son of the Fell Emperor. Back then, at least, he was the leader of this group of Fell," Neala told him. "He's an astral fae."

Pointed ears poked from a tangled nest of hair. The fae was everything the Fell wasn't. Tall and built to be slimmer than a human's form, his obvious starvation showed the outline of rib bones. High cheekbones made his gauntness more apparent. But all of this didn't stop the fae from being mesmerizing in his own way. His skin was black as night, crushed diamond flecks just below the surface. Eyes transformed from cold pits into overlarge depths that glimmered with stars.

"So, it's true," Alex breathed. "Fell...fae. It's all true."

Neala nodded. "It is true. Lucia also trapped my friends here this day. Nyah and Chandra." She gestured to the blonde queen and the Blood Prince next to her, freezing in this memory. "To see them again..."

"Just a dream. A memory of the past," Alex said, feeling bad as Neala took in the sight of both of them. He knew that feeling of rending old wounds wide open and seeing the faces of those long dead.

She pulled herself away. He had a sense of time passing as the dream sped up around them. "One good thing came from this day," she said wistfully. "Caladorn entrusted me with two fae children. I miss when they were this small."

When he looked up, he saw her cradling a newborn baby, cleansed of Fell corruption. The child's eyes glimmered silver, full to the brim with stars. "My Sorsha." Neala smiled fondly down at the baby girl before her gaze turned to a fae toddler standing close to her leg. "And Keegan. Do you know if they are still alive?"

He closed his jaw, holding in his astonishment. "I...I don't know. Sorry. Gwendolyn wants to reunite us with friendly Seelie fae. Maybe they're amongst them."

Neala's attention turned to him, her expression schooling to an unreadable mask. "You have your proof. Give an old woman some time with her family as she remembers them."

The next moment, he was a cat again, waking with a sudden shove of his dreaming self back into his own head. He blinked blearily to find Violet sprawled out across their sleeping bags, the spell book open and laying across her face.

That tome was full of magic he now acknowledged along with a secret heritage from creatures beyond their world and understanding. They had a lot of work ahead of them.

Chapter 29
Julian

He had to be dreaming. Reminded of this moment in person, his mind supplied the time and place. Nearly two hundred years ago, Julian prepared for an honorable duel first by praying in the church. He knew he faced judgement later in the night. No one had cut down Marcus Hartson, no matter how many battles he fought or duels he was challenged to. What would make this any different?

A withered hand rested over his shoulder, startling him. An elderly nun held out a cup of water. "God bless," she said, offering a shaky smile. With what he knew now, he saw Gwendolyn's features, easily taking on the disguise of a nun feeling the winter's chill as she returned to her chores. He hadn't thought twice about the gift at the time, but when he gulped down her offer, it tasted off. Metallic.

He drew himself up, heading outside to face his fate. He knew how the night went and swallowed nerves anew. This could easily be a nightmare where he and his friends were instead murdered for their attempt to overthrow his father's coven before anyone else could die in his pointless wars.

But something else was off. A woman was waiting for him right outside the sanctuary of the church, raising a hand for his attention. He cast her a glance as she fell into step with him.

"Hello, Julian. I've waited so long to meet you." Her voice was a silky smooth purr, putting his hackles up immediately.

"And who might you be?"

Moonlight filtered down through trees stripped of their leaves. Slim branches creaked as the woman smiled, bearing too many teeth to be friendly. She was vampiress-lovely, though, her black hair tied back from her face in an elegant twist. A silvery robe hugged her generous curves, cut just low enough to show the vee of her cleavage. But his biggest hint to the answer was her eyes, glimmering like silver coins as she looked up at him. "I am your queen."

"What are you doing here?" His eyes roved over the forested path they passed through on their way to a nearby village, where his father warmed up his body and prepared for a duel to the death. He had no weapons at the moment, not that it would matter in a dream.

"Alexander isn't the only one who can dream walk," she purred.

"But this memory?" he asked, unimpressed by the woman who'd caused such a panic. She was no monster here, just a beauty used to using her charms. Even in his dreams, he knew, *no, she wasn't the one.*

He'd searched high and low for his lifemate, not allowing himself to even consider another woman. It was his father's fault, the memory of him putting his childhood love to the sword as fresh as his memory of this day. Or perhaps Lucia was at fault for that, as many painful memories started to resurface in the back of his mind. She smiled his way like a cat with its paw over its prey's tail.

She was playing, but she still had his full attention. "I just wanted to see the day for myself. My scrying isn't nearly as detailed as seeing the event from someone who was there."

"Got some skin in this game, hmm?" he said, starting to feel a twinge of discomfort from how easily her tone turned to venomous silk, the hint of a threat lurking under her pretty façade.

"You killed your father," she stated outright, "a man I knew."

He grunted, realizing he'd been right. His father attributed a silver-eyed woman—Lucia—as to why women and love made a man weak. Perhaps she was to blame for his womanizing, murderous ways, but at some point, someone needed to take accountability for their actions. "A man you loved," he said, seeing the truth across her face and those silver eyes filling to the brim with contempt. For him.

"He was my lifemate, you *wretch*." In an instant, she was a screaming banshee, clawing at his arm with nails suddenly sharpened to lethal points. He leapt away too late, feeling stinging wounds all the way down his forearm.

Lucia brought her bloodied claws up to her lips, all coy pretense abandoned as she painted her lips red. "Consider this your warning. I will have revenge in his name. Come. Show me your sins."

She crooked her fingers, and his feet moved on their own to return him to her side. Sweat started to freeze down his spine on this chilly day when he realized just how much control she had as the older of them. A Sorceress used to getting what she wanted. Her magic wouldn't allow him to tug free of this chance meeting and wake safely in his body, and this was when he knew he was trapped in a nightmare.

In an instant, he was before his father, a sword in hand. He and Marcus were identical on the surface, big men with a manner as arctic as their icy blue eyes. The same squared jaw, though Marcus wore a shaggy beard while Julian remained clean shaven. The memory halted as Lucia stepped from his side to Marcus, running her hand covetously down his cheek. "My love, how I miss you," she said.

Julian tested the balance of his sword behind her. He didn't look around, knowing he'd be caught in the nostalgia of old faces. His mother amongst a crowd of worried concubines, each woman a trophy wife for Marcus's many conquests. The women who raised him and counseled that he needed to be a good, honorable man. Most of them were long deceased now.

Their children, his half-brothers and sisters, were also gone. The great Marcus's line was down to two men, himself and his nephew Armando, who stood to one side with the small coven of British vampires who'd taken Julian in. Despite himself, he chanced a glance over at Samuel and Melanie, arm-in-arm, frozen with nervous smiles painted on their faces. Alex was somewhere else, waiting in an animal form to make a nuisance of himself should Julian need the assistance.

The moment felt so real. Julian wished he could walk the annals of his memories and spend more time remembering. But this long-lost moment was a distraction from the true danger at hand, and she was nearly done whispering to the still image of his father.

Julian glanced to his sword. He could wake himself with pain, yet Lucia's claws hadn't done that for him. If he killed his father as Lucia fawned over him, he could be assured she would find a way to keep his sleeping mind here for her to torture.

But the Sorceress herself...she was the only thing in this scene that didn't belong.

He lunged, blade catching a glint of moonlight. Her blood gushed from the stab wound, not silver, but an inky black. "You," she snarled, turning with his sword still embedded in her body. Lucia's face split in a sneer, her beauty ruined by a maze of black veins riddling her face.

Her teeth sharpened as she raised talon-tipped hands glowing with magic. Julian felt her fading as he opened his eyes, wrenching from his dream with a gasp to find his face resting on the floorboards next to his bed. He'd thrashed his way out from under the sheets, waking to a puddle of cold sweat.

Despite his freedom from the nightmare, Lucia's deceptively smooth voice was still with him. *"You will pay for what you've done, Julian, son of Marcus."*

Julian cursed, dressed, and strapped on extra weapons to face the coming day. He doubted his dream, as many do when waking to a head full of fog, but couldn't shake the feeling of impending doom lingering over his shoulder.

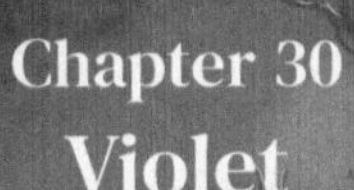

Chapter 30
Violet

Violet wished for the wonders of modern plumbing after waking to another early-evening summons from Gwendolyn. They had four days before the coming solstice, and she imagined there wouldn't be much time for the softer things in life during that time.

Alex was already awake and dressed by the time she'd opened her eyes, finding him studying her new spell book intently.

Her first thought was a mental sigh. *Not this again.* She didn't want to fight about something neither of them could prove nor disprove. If she had faith that Gwendolyn was telling the whole truth, that's what it was. Faith.

But Alex's skeptical frown was missing. He was intent on reading something toward the beginning of the book, eyes flickering to her as she sat up. "Evening," he said.

"Hi. Have you been awake long?" she asked.

"Long enough to peel this from your face. Was your night as long as mine?" His lips quirked with humor.

"You could say my night was totally booked." She grinned as he muffled a groan within the pages of the book.

"If you're punning, does that mean you're not mad at me anymore?" he asked, sounding hopeful.

She bit her tongue, realizing how quickly she'd fallen into joking around with him again. It was too easy for him to distract her with a hint of his charm, but this time, he hadn't been trying. "I don't know. Are you over trying to boss me off this island?"

"I am, for real. It's in our best interests to stay."

She worked her jaw, wondering what had changed. This was a completely different attitude than he'd had last night when it seemed like he was about to throw her over his shoulder caveman style and steal one of the research team's boats to get away from this island and its ancient secrets.

"Yeah?" she asked.

"Yeah. Plus, if you're staying, I'm staying." He put the spell book aside, gazing at her with such tenderness that it stole her breath away. "I meant it last night, and I mean it now. I'm on Team Violet. Whatever is best for you, that's what I'll do. I don't care about prophecies, Ancient Sorceresses—"

He was smiling when she interrupted with a kiss. "I wasn't done," he teased.

"It's fine. I get the idea. And I like it...the Team Violet thing." As she thought back, she wondered if she'd always been alone in Team Violet, even with her family. Between her parents, there'd been little love. Without role models, she hadn't seen what such a beautiful emotion should look like.

But now, it felt like her heart had swelled up. She could face her challenges as long as she had Alex by her side. In time, when she managed her powers, they could be equals rather than always having a gulf of age and strength between them. Hope spread its wings for what lay ahead. For what they could make.

Was that feeling love?

If so, it paralyzed her with possibilities. Should she tell him now, out of the blue, or save it for a special moment and hope that he felt the same? It felt too early. In the same moment, it also seemed just right.

Alex brought her back to herself as he drew his fingers through her hair, drawing her closer. She let her lips do a different kind of talking to show him what she meant.

Gwendolyn's impatient voice came some time later while she was still tangled up in him. *"Do you intend to keep an old woman waiting in the dark?"*

Violet gasped aloud, earning a languid glance from the content man beside her. "My training! I'm late."

He smirked, quite content with himself. "Just tell her you got a little distracted."

She felt the heat of her blush reach the top of her ears as she donned new clothes. "Then she'll know exactly what happened."

"She seems smart. She probably already knows." He followed suit, tousling his hair. It was longer than she recalled, and his beard had passed the shadow stage to cover his jaw. Spending a night in shapeshift form had made it grow at double the speed. Not that she was complaining.

"*We're coming now,*" she said back to Gwendolyn, not saying a word about being distracted.

"*Bring the book,*" the Ancient grumbled. She sounded like she had a good guess as to what'd held them up.

Violet scooped up the spell book as he moved their makeshift door aside. She grabbed a second lantern, fully charged, and used it to illuminate the hallway. The other Blood Princes were gone about their own tasks, their doors also ajar.

She sighed to herself in relief. Maybe there would be no weird tension today, as all these people and their old dynamics brought out the worst of them. Especially if Gwendolyn was involved.

"I walked into a different person's dream last night," Alex said, breaking up the monotony of wet stone and parting darkness while they walked toward the exit of the palace. Gwendolyn waited in their first meeting place, the old garden.

"I thought that'd gone dormant." Ever since she'd confessed to hearing Lucia's voice, he hadn't spent time in her dreams, despite his attempts to control and wrangle the new magic.

"It seems my inner shapeshifting beast controls the magic to do it. Since I was an animal last night..." he drifted off with a shrug.

"Who did you go see?" she asked.

As they emerged into yet another pitch-black night, Alex pointed out a figure in that dark. "Speak of the devil. Neala."

The muscular woman was with Sirius in front of the palace

entrance, which provided a stage-sized area for them circling each other silently. They held slim pieces of driftwood like swords. Neala's fury shone on her face as Violet picked up what he was saying to her. "...talk. Just say *something*. I'll let you hit me if you just talk."

Violet and Alex exchanged a glance. He seemed keen to watch, though gestured that she should stand behind him. *"I helped her out. This is probably safe."*

"Probably?" she yelped. Being around Neala's concentrated anger wasn't her idea of a good time. She watched from her safe spot behind him as the woman lunged. In an eye blink, Sirius had dodged with the fluid roll of a viper. He tapped the back of Neala's neck with his driftwood.

"Maybe if you weren't so useless, you could hit me," he taunted, leaping away as she lunged. She stopped her forward momentum within a step, whipping around with her face set in a snarl.

Violet glared Sirius's way. He had no sympathy, only more hard words as he moved out of every strike with the grace of a dancer. He was *too* good, able to adjust his body with ease that belied his abilities and age. It seemed time didn't dull his sharp tongue, however.

"Goodness, what a bore. If you fought like this against the Fell, I'd be cleaning your guts from my sleeve," he said, covering an exaggerated yawn disguised as a duck away from her makeshift weapon.

Violet tried to tug Alex away, but he held her hand firm. He didn't look away from the fight, whispering, "C'mon. C'mon."

"Or maybe going to your funeral after Lucia put you out of your misery," Sirius quipped.

Violet felt her stomach turn as vibrations hit her ears. She could feel it straight through to her gut before it became audible. It burst into a high-pitched shrill on the heels of a mental shout. *"Shut up! Shut your filthy mouth!"*

Neala grabbed a grinning Sirius by the throat, bringing them eye to eye. *"You loudmouth cur. More mongrel than man."* She had plenty more insults for him. He was laughing even as his face reddened.

"I know, I'm terrible," he gasped, trying to pry her fingers from his neck. "You got me. Hit me good, free shot."

She paused in her litany, head butting him and dropping him to the ground. The next moment, he rolled to his feet and they hugged fiercely. Violet looked on, baffled. "What just happened?" she whispered.

"I erased most of Neala's memories of being locked in her own head last night," he murmured back.

"Okay, but...they're not trying to kill one another," she said, waiting nervously for them to start brawling now that they'd set their driftwood weapons aside.

"Tough love," he replied as the two Blood Princes finally seemed to notice them.

"You there!" Neala's mental voice was still a force, and now she was pointing directly at Violet. The anger had softened from her face sometime during her outburst. Determination had taken its place.

"Yes?" Violet asked in a soft voice. She'd never wanted to get the Ancient woman's attention.

"Where is Gwendolyn?" she asked, eyes as flinty as granite.

She swallowed thickly, remembering that Neala had tried to kill her on their first reunion. "Why...I...I don't know!" she replied in a nervous chatter.

"Don't bluff me, girl." Neala stepped close enough to draw a warning growl from Alex. She glanced toward him, a rasping chuckle leaving her lips. *"I want to use my words, not my fists, this time. You told me Gwendolyn wants to make sure a few Seelie fae can make it to Earth during the solstice."*

"That's my understanding of it, yes," he said, his face schooling to a neutral mask.

"Then I have to know if they're my children." After seeing Violet's confusion, she added, *"My adopted children."*

"Oh, wow, okay." She hesitated when Neala's attention sharpened. The woman looked fit to shake the truth from her. "So...you want to help her?"

"We don't help traitors," Sirius put in, glancing between them. A tic formed over his brow as the thought worked him up toward the same rage that had fueled his first anti-Gwendolyn rant.

So much for a tension-free day, Violet thought to herself, resigned to it after the last couple days.

"Shut your mouth for a minute," Neala snapped.

"She's just going to use us again," he hissed.

"I will see my kids," she insisted.

Sirius stepped away from her. "And if she uses them against you? Against us? What are the chances Keegan and Sorsha are even still alive?"

Instead of following after him, raising the fist she balled at her side, Neala fixed Violet with a piercing stare. *"Where is she? I tire of pointless what-ifs. I would hear her out directly."*

"The gardens. There's a block of stone—" Neala was already gone, racing down the stairs.

"Neala!" Sirius chased after her, leaving Violet and Alex alone.

They turned to each other. He lifted a shoulder. "I vote we go back to bed."

"I'm supposed to be getting trained," she sighed. "You know, something I only have four more days to do?"

"I don't think you're getting anything from her today. That's all. But we can walk all the way down these stairs and see." He let out an exaggerated sigh.

She didn't admit how tempting it was to leave the humid murk of Nyixa outdoors to go share some intimate time, but she started taking the stairs downward anyway. "These are the bane of my life. No, thigh life." Her thighs and calves would definitely not be thanking her for the return trip.

"I hope this is worth it," Alex remarked. "Also, that pun was a stretch."

"I'd like to see you come up with better."

"I've been saving one for King Adrius if we see him again," he admitted.

"Really? Me too." She laughed. "It was nice to actually see

him, you know, laugh. That's a gloomy guy." Another Ancient that was hard to be anywhere near.

"Not that a pun or two will fix that," he pointed out.

"Sure. But smiles are free. And in short supply around here."

That certainly felt like an understatement as they found Gwendolyn, Neala, and Sirius arguing in the gardens. Sirius was the most heated of them, pointing accusing fingers and swapping insults with Neala once again. "Yup, that's what I expected," Alex remarked. "Can you believe they're on the same side?"

Chapter 31
Violet

She and Alex started making out in a shadowy corner, just within earshot of the Ancient trio. He'd promised they'd go back when they resolved their differences but that made for a long, inevitably frustrating tease by the time Alex parted from her.

"Sirius left," he said. They took a moment to cool off and then went to rejoin the two women. They sat opposite one another on the stone benches that remained of the garden's gazebo.

Complete silence stretched between them, so there had to be some sort of mental communication. Violet was hesitant to interrupt, though their footsteps alerted Neala, whose fiery gaze turned to them. Her voice came into focus as she beckoned them closer. *"Gwendolyn was telling me of modern affairs,"* she said, standing and nodding to the elderly woman. *"Have a good training session."*

She left at a brisk pace. Gwendolyn sighed out her tension. "Come, sit. Did you have an opportunity to read any of that book I gave you last night?"

Violet nodded, eager to talk about what she'd seen from the book. "I understand what the elements of fae magic are and read a few chapters."

"She fell asleep with the book on her face," Alex pitched in, pulling her to his side as they sat together.

"I really wanted to read more," she said, a blush creeping up her face.

Gwendolyn's stern expression broke with a rare smile. "I'm glad to hear it. Let's try to activate the rest of your elements. Then we can figure out which of the five virtues you've inherited."

"Oh! I already figured that out," she exclaimed. "I have true sight. I haven't seen any vampire's glamor this whole time."

"Maybe you've gotten more than one." Gwendolyn, despite the smile, seemed disappointed. "True sight is considered the fifth virtue. But it does make you unique. In retrospect, I know my daughter Nyah had empathy. And Lucia inherited future sight."

"It's possible to have more than one?" she asked, her enthusiasm dampening when she read between what Gwendolyn was saying. True sight must be considered the weakest of the five powers. Being unable to be tricked probably didn't stack up compared to seeing into the future or into the spirit realm to talk to lost loved ones.

"I have heard rumors of a fae who was born with all five. But that does not matter to us. We have to train the gifts you were blessed with," she said. "All Sorcerers and Sorceresses have at least one virtue and one element of magic they're exceptional at. Once we've figured out which element that is for you, we will focus on that one to get ready for midsummer."

With more time to train today, Gwendolyn led Violet through the thirteen hand motions. Some came easily after a night's rest, but she got stuck when trying to make a portal or shapeshift into an animal form. Her cheeks burned from the irony, with Gwendolyn and Alex a master of those respective talents. However, she told herself eleven out of thirteen wasn't bad, especially as she turned and realized they'd gotten a silent audience.

King Adrius and all five Blood Princes were gathering to watch at the edge of her lantern's halo, murmuring to each other. The hair raised on the back of her neck as she glanced to Alex, whose attention had snapped over that way the moment the Ancients had appeared. "Talk to your boyfriend for a minute. Maybe he can help your shifting," Gwendolyn said to her, standing a little straighter to see this group. After the blowup with

Sirius earlier, Violet imagined they were all there to talk to her, one way or another.

She went to Alex's side, murmuring, "Sure would be nice to train without interruption." She was sweating from the sheer effort of pushing her newly discovered magic to its limits and felt gross as it remained in the humidity of Nyixa. A shower was desperately needed.

"I think you've done bloody well for yourself today," he said, kissing her forehead. His gaze had gone slit-pupiled, his animal close to the surface as he focused its more sensitive hearing toward the meeting going on between Gwendolyn and the other Ancients. "Well, I'll be damned."

"What? What is it?" she asked quietly.

"Neala's demanding a portal to where Lucia was spotted last. They're arguing."

What else is new? she thought with a sigh.

"But Gwendolyn is willing to send her if she promises to bring Lucia in alive," he added, eyebrows raising. As he said that, Neala's attention turned their way. "She wants us to help her blend in."

"Yes," Violet gasped. "At least for a bit. I need a shower!"

Her outburst startled a laugh from him, and he hugged her close. "I don't begrudge you one. But we should come right back."

"When I figure out portals, we're going back so we can shower every day," she said emphatically.

He nodded in agreement, going stiff with alert as the group of Ancients headed their way. "Good evening," Adrius said, positioning himself so his bulk was between Sirius and Gwendolyn. The Ancient shapeshifter looked like he'd swallowed something rotten, clearly the most displeased. The rest of the Blood Princes seemed more curious than anything, especially Qin, who'd stopped his constant coin flipping to turn his full attention on the proceedings.

"Good evening," Alex replied for them both.

"I'm glad to see your magic is progressing," he said to Violet, offering a brief grimace that might've been a smile. "We have something to ask of you. Consider it a request to match your plea for protection here."

Alex considered him, unblinking. Violet wondered why he didn't accept that right away when they already knew what the request was. Then she realized this was completely political, tying one deed to another. If they didn't perform to Adrius's liking, he could take away his permission for them to stay here in Nyixa or chase away Gwendolyn for good.

"I would hear the request first," Alex said finally.

"We have come to a truce of sorts." Adrius's gesture included all the Ancients, Gwendolyn included. "Despite our...differences, we are still on the same side." He spoke with a heavy sigh, as if reluctant to even have this conversation.

When Neala stepped forward and nudged him, Violet figured that was her taking charge. She wasn't very surprised when he nodded to her. *"What he means is that some of us are tired of sitting around in self-pity. I, for one, am very tired of pity. My request is thus: I need an escort to modern lands and have been warned that things are quite different now. You are a coven master. Assign me someone who will help me find Lucia and bring her to justice."*

Alex nodded slowly. "I know of someone. You're the only one going?"

"For now."

"Then we need a portal back to my home for an hour or two," he said to Gwendolyn.

"I'll be going with you." She gestured as she spoke, opening a doorway-sized portal. Without hesitation, Neala plunged straight into it with shoulders squared like a soldier marching to battle.

"Okay, looks like we're going now," Violet remarked, going through with Alex and Gwendolyn. Her shoulders sagged with relief to see the mansion's foyer and one of Alex's maids dusting the mantle. The woman turned and froze upon the sight of their sudden appearance.

"It's all right," Alex said quickly, raising his palms. "Would you fetch Samuel if he's in?" She bobbed her head and rushed off.

Neala had covered her eyes with a hiss at the sudden influx of light from the chandelier and lamps set out to create a cozy atmosphere. Gwendolyn went to have a seat in one of the lounge chairs set up for visitors. "Get used to it now," she said to the other Ancient. "Humans hate dark nights."

"Something tells me this is the least of my new concerns," Neala replied.

Violet, at loose ends as soon as Sam arrived to chat with Alex, slipped off to have a blissful shower and change clothes. She wondered who he would pair with Neala to really get her ready for modern vampire life. When she emerged, she realized she shouldn't have even questioned the choice.

He'd called in the same woman who'd first helped her, Petra. Her thick Russian accent preceded her as Violet turned the corner and saw her plucking at Neala's old-fashioned suit and clucking over the shaggy, careless cut of the Ancient's hair. She had to kneel for petite Petra to reach that far. "This will not do at all. You'll stand out immediately," she was saying. "Also, no mortal speaks with their mind!"

Violet joined Alex and Sam, who both watched this interaction with amused smiles. Her own mirth faded as Neala opened her mouth and spoke aloud for the first time. What came out was a labored rasp instead of words. Petra's perusal paused with a surprised gasp. "Oh, my apologies. I did not know..."

"I have tricks to make mortals think I'm speaking aloud," Neala responded.

"Of course, of course." Petra clasped her hands before her, looking mortified.

"Think nothing of it. Handicapped vampires must still be a rarity," she said, sounding more bored than offended. *"Let us get started. I suppose I must try on these...jeans you speak of."*

"You'll love them," Petra said, bustling off for the taller woman to follow and catch up in a few fluid strides.

Sam turned a casual smile toward Violet. "I see you two have been having fun without us. Care to show me a magic trick?" His eyes twinkled with mischief. It was a relief to see someone who wasn't a ball of stress and anxiety or wanting her magic for their own ends. She thought about what would be the showiest spell of the few she knew off the top of her head.

She clapped her hands thrice, lifting her hand straight up from her palm on the third clap. In the air between her hands appeared a tender new flower. She'd meant to make a violet, but the buds at top unfurled into a meek cluster of buttercups instead.

"Aww, look at that. You shouldn't have," Sam said, plucking it from her palm and pulling up a network of roots that rested on her skin, ready to be buried in the earth. He took a sniff of one flower and nodding approvingly. "You want to make about a dozen more of these so I can give them to my wife?"

"I could try." She giggled at the thought. "She'd probably be more impressed with roses, though."

"Want to make an entire bouquet with your hands so I can give it to my wife?" he teased.

Alex snorted and elbowed him. "Stop trying to take advantage of my girlfriend."

"Not my fault she's cooler than you, mate!"

He pulled a long-suffering expression. "Two centuries of friendship and she's cooler because of a flower? I see how it is."

"You could say I won him over once and flor-al." She grinned as they face-palmed at the same time.

"Is it just me, or are those puns coming out more?" Alex complained.

"You're seeing my true self," she said with a wink.

His expression grew more tender as he drew her to his chest. "Good thing I like it." If they were alone, she knew where this moment would be going. For all his complaining, she thought he might like her little plays on words, so she looked for more opportunities to make them.

Gwendolyn cleared her throat before they could go on any further. "It's about time to return," she said.

"I think I will shower first," he said, parting from her after a quick kiss. "Violet had the right idea."

"Good, you smell," Sam said cheerfully, waving when Alex shot him a dirty look and went off to his room. He turned his attention to Violet. "Melanie says hi, by the way, and wanted me to remind you that she's thought all along that there wasn't a thing wrong with you."

"Thank you," she said, smiling to herself. She missed the kindly surgeon who always seemed to be working. "Did Alex tell you what we've been up to?"

He nodded, his smile fading. "I don't like it at all. We've always tried to dodge the big guys making moves on each other. Politics is the easiest way to find a knife in your back."

"I bet," she said, frowning as well. "How are things going here? Are you playing politics too?"

"Sure am, but don't you worry. I haven't signed on to anything. Don't be alarmed or anything by this, but..." He held up his palms preemptively. "Haven and Coven Rockefeller have both declared for Lucia, giving her a mega coven larger than even the former biggest, Coven Deveaux."

"What?" Her voice was a disbelieving squeak. In a couple of days, as far as Violet understood, Lucia had assembled enough people to become the ruling power in New York City. "What about the Deveaux Accords?"

He worried his bottom lip. "Too soon to tell. But they're probably overruled. Coven Deveaux hasn't declared a side, but we're really screwed if they lean Lucia's way too."

"It won't be a problem in a few days. Gwendolyn has a plan," Violet said with a nervous laugh. "Lucia will be gone by then."

"I sure hope you're right, love." He sighed, brushing a hand through haphazard curls. "We needed a bit of good news. The more superstitious of us are freaking out, for lack of a better explanation. Julian hasn't slept since this whole thing started. I'm of half a mind to send him with you and Alex."

She hesitated at that thought, imagining the brooding man following her and Alex around. She really enjoyed having more private time with Alex, but that was a selfish thought. "He could come if he wanted."

He shook his head. "It's fine. He'll get over it. We're going to seem weak if our most powerful people keep disappearing. Outsiders will think we're hiding."

She nodded to herself, fitting that information with her understanding of vampire logic, which was definitely focused on appearing as strong as possible. Alex going with her and disappearing at a time like this must have seemed like weakness when they couldn't afford to be weak.

Alex's talk of Team Violet came back to mind. He walked a dangerous tightrope, arranging events to keep both her and his coven safe. When he emerged a few minutes later, showered, shaved, and with new purpose in his step, she eyed him with new appreciation. She'd need to show him what his dedication meant to her when they were next alone.

Chapter 32
Alex

THEY RETURNED TO NYIXA AND ENDED THEIR EVENING WITH Gwendolyn having Violet study her portals and the magic that created them. Alex pretended to be interested as their talk grew more technical until Violet had a breakthrough of her own in creating a portal. Twelve of thirteen unlocked, except for what he was best at—shapeshifting. His lip quirked that she would have trouble with that of all things.

He decided to teach her himself as they settled back into their quarters. Eyeing their bed, he wished they could spend the night back at the mansion. Now that they'd seen how easy it was to go there and back with proper portal magic, he yearned for the comfort of home with the privacy of this room.

When he started stripping, Violet turned an eager look his way. "I want to try something first," he said, waggling a finger. "You need to be naked too."

"I like where this is going," she said. His mouth went dry as she endeavored to be as naked as he. Silver veins stood out through her skin as she shivered with the chill of the room, but he pushed her out to about arm's length. "Okay, never mind. What are you doing?"

"Gwendolyn's trying to teach you shapeshifting through fancy gestures. We're going to embrace your wild side."

Her gaze drifted downwards. "Uh huh."

He tilted her chin up with a wink. "Focus."

"I'm not sure what you're trying to do," she admitted. And honestly, he didn't know either. He thought she might be more comfortable letting out a possible inner beast of her own if she was away from prying eyes. Just the two of them, without the barrier of clothes.

He thought it might work to bait out his own beast and follow its instincts. He gave it an ounce of control, waking it from its fearful torpor from spending so much time with Ancients much stronger than he was. His eyesight narrowed to a laser focus as it roused, lending its keen senses to his own.

Violet saw the change come over him, a flush coming to her cheeks. His inner beast was a part of him that liked to come out in moments of passion, and as it woke it, it purred to see her naked. *Mate. Mine,* it said with certainty.

How to explain to that beast that he wanted to awaken something similar in her? His thoughts grew hazy with its much simpler needs. *Is she like us?* he thought, trying to steer it to focus. His brow furrowed in confusion.

"Are you all right?" she asked, more confused than his beast.

Maybe he was mistaken. Often, his instincts had answers he couldn't see on the surface, but this time, it seemed unlikely. She made magic with gestures and phrases while his magic was a part of him, melded into his instincts like a living thing.

Her fingertips brushed his hand as she took a step forward, lips parted on another question. In that moment, man, instinct, and magic alike understood.

He crushed his lips to hers, fingers laced through her hair. They swallowed each other's moans, coming skin to skin. "Be mine," he whispered, their foreheads brushing as he pulled from their kiss only by an inch. Her hot breath washed over his chin.

"Yes," she said, her touch drifting lower on his back.

He knew what she thought he meant. The beast in him spoke without inhibition. "I mean, be *mine*, lifemate."

Her touch stilled, eyes widening. "Lifemate?" she echoed, the first thread of uncertainty entering her voice. "But..."

"You can't tell me you don't feel it too." He stroked a lock of hair from her otherworldly silver eyes, breathless with tenderness even as he waited for her reaction to that rush he'd felt between them since the moment they'd first kissed.

Surely, she knew. Even without his level of instinct, she should've felt it by now, the flame of their attraction.

"I thought...but you've already had..."

He interrupted that thought with a kiss. "Had. But now I have you. Team Violet, remember?"

Her expression softened. "How is it possible? I thought you said there was only one..."

"One of the only times I've been happy to be wrong." His heart soared to see her smile in agreement. "I know we haven't known each other long, but it feels right."

"What are you asking of me?" She still hesitated. She was a new vampire, he had to remind himself. Mortals didn't have such things as lifemates and a shapeshifter's inner beast, lacking the certainty he embraced so readily. If he didn't phrase it just right, she would push away such an ambitious move in their relationship.

He took a mental step back from plunging headfirst into explaining a mating bond. "I love you. That's what I'm trying to say." His heart beat harder to be presented to her so soon. He hadn't felt this way for another in a longer time than he could remember. Had anyone really come before Violet? He barely thought of the distant memory of his first mate, who paled to a cherished glimmer compared to the blaze of potential before him.

She touched her fingertips to her lips, eyes sparkling like polished coins. "I love you too. I thought...maybe it was too early to say it."

"You don't have to hide how you feel with me." He bent to kiss her fingertips until she moved her hand aside, their lips meeting in an unhurried embrace. The first time they'd kissed, she hadn't recognized the electric certainty that passed between them like a static shock, but this time, she sighed through her nose with the bliss that lingered behind.

"You don't have to hide anything," he whispered against her lips. "Do you feel it too?"

"Yes," she said in breathless entreaty. "I think...I think I'm ready. What do we need to do for me to be yours?"

Alex showed her the way, melding body and mind in a dance and binding as old as the vampire race. They became mates, following the promise of the lifemate call that they were secretly two halves of one beautiful whole. The bond between them sang of shared emotion and pleasure, their mate's attention only a thought away.

Laying tangled together to rest, Alex's inner beast called. Something within her called back, new and wild.

Chapter 33
Violet

Violet greeted Gwendolyn the next day in the shapeshift of a cat, a great bushy one with sandy fur and a proud purr in her throat as the elderly woman startled and looked down at her in confusion. "You mastered your last element. Good," she said, scratching Violet under the chin.

"How did you know that it's me?" Speaking from an animal's vocal cords was still a challenge, but she'd barely practiced. She and Alex had been far too occupied last night, only catching a few short hours of sleep before Gwendolyn called for her.

"Your eyes are silver still." Gwendolyn set her aside on cool stone. A part of Violet wanted to flop down and rest there. She was still getting used to the idea that shapeshifting magic made her a little like the animal she'd become, inheriting the instincts and bad habits along with the fur coat.

"Show me what else you can do," she continued. She glanced up to where Alex watched, holding a bundle of clothes for Violet once this demonstration was done.

Violet could feel his pride in her even from that short distance, mingling with the simple joy within herself to be able to do this. How jealous her childhood self would've been to know she'd learned to become an animal herself! She smiled within, her cat face remaining rigid and incapable of the same expression.

Drawing from Alex's knowledge, she became various animals

with ease. A twittering robin, a mastiff, and then plunging into the darkness as a squeaking bat. She shifted quickly into more animals, growing larger as she went. It felt like showing off after the thirtieth form, but Gwendolyn simply stood back to give her more room and gestured for her to go on. She stroked her jaw as Violet continued until her bones ached from shifting and resizing.

"This is your strongest element," the elderly woman said in a tone of complete certainty to the horse Violet had settled on as her final shapeshift.

"You think so?" Violet neighed enthusiastically.

Gwendolyn turned her face away, her shoulders shaking. If she didn't miss her guess, her mentor was laughing but holding it in with a stiff upper lip. "If you would shift back into a human form, I have a gift for you," she said once she'd mastered herself.

Alex followed as she trotted to a shadowy corner of the garden and took a deep breath. In the couple of times they'd practiced this, shifting back into herself was the hardest part. The part of her that was a horse wanted to remain a horse. She twitched, her bones crackling unpleasantly as the magic twisted and reformed them into a human's skeleton. Buck naked and on all fours, she shook herself and stood, flexing her hands to return some of their flexibility.

"Think I impressed her?" she asked, dressing quickly in the clothes he'd brought.

He offered a languid shrug. "You surprised her. When you get as old as her, I imagine that's the closest thing." His emotions flowed to her, expressing what his words did not. While Gwendolyn might not have been moved by her performance, Alex was certainly impressed and proud of her progress. She got onto her toes to kiss him. They shared a moment until her curiosity compelled them to return and see what Gwendolyn intended to give her.

The Ancient was making slow progress out of the garden when they rejoined her. "Let's go for a walk. It's good for my old bones."

They fell into step with her, walking at her pace as she took the cobblestone path toward the city ruins. "Did you know that two moons rise over this island?" Gwendolyn continued, tilting her head up to the pitch-black heavens. "It is incredibly rare that any light shines through the magic shrouding Nyixa. But when it does, all vampire powers are at their strongest."

"Like during the full moon," Alex remarked.

Violet gaped up at the sky as if two moons would suddenly make an appearance. "But why *two*? That doesn't even make sense."

"There are two that hang over Faerie, wherever in the cosmos it lies," Gwendolyn said. "And Nyixa is the closest place in this world to Faerie. Anyway, a fun fact for you."

"Cool," she said with a smile. Even though he didn't verbalize it, Alex was quietly impressed as well, though she felt he was also wondering why Gwendolyn would mention it now.

"I've looked into every nook and cranny of these buildings, searching for anything that survived Nyixa's stay under the sea," Gwendolyn continued, gesturing them toward a mostly intact building close to the palace. "Anything magical. And I was lucky indeed to find these."

Within the building was a slab of white stone toward the back, located where a bed might be in a one-room cabin. Upon it, glittering like gems in the dark, were five orbs reminiscent of the Eye of Worlds in the center of the island. Gwendolyn picked up the largest of them and offered it to Violet. "This is my gift to you. A Sorceress's best friend."

The glass was heavier than she expected, dropping into her palms with all the heft of a bowling ball. Under the surface lay cloudy darkness, hiding beneath the veneer of shine on the orb's exterior. Like a globe, it was attached to a crescent-shaped piece of copper etched with the thirteen symbols of fae magic. She glanced to Gwendolyn, puzzled as to how this could be her "best friend" when it seemed like a tourist's replica of the Eye of Worlds.

"Lucia first translated the same word for what you're holding and its larger counterpart, the Eye of Worlds. This is an occultarus," Gwendolyn explained. "The fae manufacture them as tools to help with magic. In short, I'm giving you a focus to push your magic through. You don't need to make the gestures if you're holding it, which will make your spellcasting much faster."

"How does it work?" Violet eyed it with eagerness. She was merely a beginner but already could see how much better it would make her at magic if she didn't have to telegraph exactly what she was doing. Very good in a fight.

"Give it a shake. The magic within it will imprint to you."

"Imprint, huh?" she murmured to herself, giving it a solid shake. The shadows within it circled like a mini cyclone, individual motes branching off like grains of sand. Darkness turned to light, becoming a new beacon to replace the lantern by her side. The orb floated of its own volition, circling around her torso. "Is it supposed to...?"

"Yes. For your convenience, when it's active, it'll circle around you to your natural movements. I'll teach you how to do this, but you can send it magical signals to jump into your hand if you need it." Gwendolyn watched Violet interact with her new magical tool with a troubled frown—as if her thoughts were miles away.

She barely noticed, enamored with the copper occultarus as it established an orbit around her shoulders, spinning as if she were a planet. "That being said, I need you to take a look at the Eye of Worlds," the Ancient continued, sweeping from the room abruptly and cutting short her admiration of this gift.

"Isn't it cool?" Violet whispered to Alex, catching it on its way past her right arm. It floated right above her palm as if awaiting its use.

"I'm jealous I don't have fancy enough magic to get my own moon." He winked, reaching for it. It rolled out of the way, toward Violet's chest, staying just out of touching range. "Makes me wonder if the big version is as cheeky as this thing."

Gwendolyn, not far ahead of them, shot a stern look over her shoulder. "The Eye of Worlds is *evil*," she snapped. "You might toy with Violet's occultarus, but you do not touch the Eye. Ever."

He worked his jaw, and Violet felt him weighing and fighting against firing a barbed response back. Taking a deep breath, he responded, "Of course. But perhaps you should share how an inanimate object can be evil?"

"I'll show you," was all she said on their walk to the monolithic structure. Violet and Alex held hands and took simple pleasure in watching her new occultarus make a loop around him in apparent approval or understanding of their mating bond.

When they reached the Eye of Worlds, Gwendolyn leveraged her cane on its base, climbing until her face was mere inches from its surface. "Come. Look into its depths. Tell me what you see."

Exchanging a glance with him, she did so, getting up close with the shining dome. Beneath the surface lay darkness, just like with her occultarus when it was dormant. However, the longer she looked, the more she noticed cloudy shapes and movement. Sprites gathered at the corner of her vision, pointing at her.

Laughing.

Her anxiety spiked as she realized how many of those sprites there were, jeering and jostling to stare down at her. Her gaze turned to her reflection.

"What a mistake. You never stare into the Grand Occultarus, dear," came Lucia's voice, purring into her mind as her reflection started to blur like a heat mirage.

"I don't want to talk to you," she said, her mental voice breaking with a shrill of fear.

Alex gave her shoulder a shake, but she couldn't look away. Her reflection changed, donning a silver gown with a waterfall of ruffles and taffeta curls beneath a fitted bodice glittering with sequins like miniature stars. *"What is your heart's deepest desire? Where do you wear this dress?"*

The backdrop changed from ruined buildings to a church's pews, lined with familiar faces. Next to her, Alex's concerned expression smoothed to one of love and devotion, replacing his old t-shirt with a fine suit. *"Is it to your wedding?"* Lucia asked.

"Stop. Stop this," Violet said, her hands trembling within the folds of a dress she could almost feel.

"I'm not doing anything. Isn't it incredible? This tool responds to my will and mine alone. You may have an occultarus of your own, but it's a mere toy. Feel the power pinning you in place."

Lucia's voice was mere narration as Violet tried to blink and shut out what she was seeing. A dark-haired woman appeared over her shoulder, her features beautiful and cold as if sculpted from marble. Her eyes were a silver as pure as an ingot, marking her for who she was.

Her hand ghosted over Violet's shoulder, there, but not. *"In mere days, we will meet."* Her mouth moved, but the words pushed into Violet's head, inescapable.

"Let me go. You can't hold me like this," she protested, tears starting to slip from her eyes.

Lucia tilted her head. *"Why do you cry? Why do you fear me? I found you dying. I gave you new life. We are one of a kind, you and I."* She raised her hand, a flame burning white-hot in her palm. When Violet moved to speak, she held up a hand sharply, silencing even her weak protests to leave her helpless. *"Hush, my dear. Weep not. I have a special plan, just for you..."* She leaned in, her cold lips brushing Violet's cheek.

A sting of pain followed. Violet tumbled backward into the dirt, her cheek smarting and Gwendolyn looming above her, trembling. "I'm sorry," she said, her shoulders sagging. "I needed to know—"

Alex grabbed her collar, snarling. "How dare you strike my mate."

"This is much worse. I had to see what would happen," she said, shoving him away easily with Ancient strength. She landed hard in the dirt, offering Violet a hand up with eyes full of remorse. "I know what she's done to the Eye of Worlds now."

"Did you see...?" Violet asked, feeling light-headed from the rush of blood to her head. She sat down on the base of the Eye, holding her head and shutting her eyes hard, trying to squeeze the vision of Lucia and her words from her head.

Alex's warm arm covered her shoulders, pulling her into his side. "I didn't see anything," he murmured.

"And I didn't see anything, but I felt Lucia's magic," Gwendolyn said, sitting heavily to her other side. She rolled her cane between her hands, head bowed. "What did she say?"

In Alex's embrace, she found it easier to repeat the conversation. It hadn't been a long one, but it'd *felt* nauseating, and Lucia's phrasing seemed more ominous on repeat. Gwendolyn nodded slowly to it all, breathing out a sigh. "Lucia hasn't disabled the Eye of Worlds. She's made a pact with it."

"And how do you know that?" Alex frowned, a growl edging into his voice as he held Violet protectively. She could tell he didn't appreciate Gwendolyn using her for bait with the magical tool.

"I, too, have a special relationship with it." She chuckled without humor. "The Eye is one thing all fae are mum about. There is an intelligence inside of it that can see your deepest desires, and it taunts you with them. If you try to use it for magic and are weaker than it, it will find a way to destroy you."

She turned watery eyes their way, her face etched with pain. "Long ago, when I used it, it showed me what I could've been. An angel with burning wings, fully invested in the light I used to wield. I don't dare attempt to command it now."

Violet opened her mouth to ask but realized Alex understood. He glanced her way and shrugged. *"She's been alive for a long time. If this thing really is that powerful, her desire to move on from this world might break her like a twig."*

"So that's why you think it's evil," she said. "It would compel you to kill yourself?"

Gwendolyn nodded slowly. "I don't know how religious you are. I can't believe that hasn't come up," she said. "Suicides are in the realm of Hell. And Hell is how I measure evil. Anything that tells you that you should kill yourself is *evil*. Maybe that's why it has a pact with the other great evil in this world...Lucia." She said her name on a sigh. "The island itself, in its long submersion, allowed the Eye of Worlds to attune itself to her. It waits, dormant, for her to return and command it. And while it slumbers, no other may cross the veil between worlds, so very engrained is this thing with the rest of fae magic."

She slapped the base with her cane, trembling with fists clenched.

"So what do we do?" Violet asked in a small voice. She imagined the island sinking at any moment from Lucia's command, waves closing in on them as the world shook at the elder Sorceress's whims.

"We train, you and I," Gwendolyn said, a dime-sized portal glimmering as she opened her fist. It sized bigger and then smaller at her whims. "Midsummer day, between the two of us pulling and our fae allies pushing, we will get the Eye of Worlds to budge for our collective wills."

"And if Lucia comes back to foil us?" Alex asked, dubious that it would work.

Through the portal fell a pouch, which sagged in her palm. She waved away a puff of cobalt dust from its drawstring top. "I have more tricks up my sleeve, Alexander. Behold from a safe distance—languor dust. A breath of this will render complete body paralysis. The same that grips you in your sleep." She tweezed its drawstring between her fingertips, offering it to him.

"Thanks...I think," he said, eyeing the pouch as he held it away from himself gingerly. "Do you have the cure?"

"No, but my fae friends do. Lucia should pray they make it over here if she takes a face-full of it," she said, taking it back from him and hooking it into her belt. Standing, she offered her palm to Violet. "Come. We have work to do."

Chapter 34
Julian

He rubbed at his eyes in the passenger's seat, glad that Armando was driving. His partner and nephew's seemingly endless chatter filled the night air between them, his words blurring together. At least, that's what Julian heard. But he hadn't slept well in several nights, haunted by nightmares that left an oily feeling at the back of his throat come the kiss of the night sky and the dawn of another duty day.

All of Coven Rehnquist was on high alert, expecting danger big and small. The enforcers under Julian's command were patrolling their territory for any vampires who didn't belong. They'd essentially closed the borders, especially to anyone swearing allegiance to Lucia and surrendering their territory to the Ancient Sorceress to form a new mega-coven.

Coven Deveaux hadn't declared for Lucia yet, but they expected it any day. Cossette had hosted her since her arrival in New York City and thus had the most pressure at her throat to conform. But that wasn't what was on Armando's mind, and while they waited for the dam to break on the brewing inter-coven tension, he sought to fill the space with one of the only things he cared about.

He prattled on about women.

More specifically about their newcomer, Blood Prince Neala, the Wraith. "Man, you should've seen her," he was saying. "Ugly as tree roots. You know that chewed-up look the ladies dig on their men? Just put that on a woman instead with a bodybuilder's muscles."

Julian roused himself long enough to scan their perimeter. They were between businesses now, the late-evening traffic breaking as mortals retired for the night. "Talking trash about an Ancient gets you hurt, Armando," he said, muffling a yawn.

"I'm, like, prefacing. That's not what she even looks like anymore," he said, laying on the horn as another vehicle cut them off.

"Uh-huh." Julian sighed.

"Petra got a hold of her, and she put on the strongest glamor I've ever seen. Now she's got legs for days. Big red hair that you just want to put your face into—"

"Armando," he put in.

"What? You don't put your face into ladies' hair? You gotta try it. Anyway, she's a total bombshell now. I wish you could've met her too. Maybe she's that woman you've been looking for." He took his hands off the wheel to clasp them under his chin in a playful swoon, flashing his bright teeth. After all the bored practice during their nightly patrols, he easily steered with his knees as he batted his eyes at Julian, who rolled his.

"C'mon, you gotta smile sometime," he said, transitioning to easy charm with the smile that won over the ladies he loved so much.

Julian forced himself to look more cheerful for Armando's sake. It wasn't his fault that his head was full of worry for some unnamable *something* that sank its claws into his heart with cold disquiet. "I might smile more if you had more to talk about than women."

"Like how our boss is off canoodling without us?" he asked.

"On an abandoned island, save for the strongest vampires in the world, who, apparently, don't even get along." He'd heard it all from Sam, who'd caught Alex on a quick trip to shower and shave for some form of decency in the middle of nowhere. "I don't begrudge him any of that political sinkhole."

"Whatever. He's still probably having a bunch of—"

"Could you focus?" he put in before he could suggest anything compromising about one of Julian's oldest friends.

"Whatever, man," he laughed, turning onto an abandoned stretch of road with his knees as he spoke with his hands in full Italian verve. "I'm just saying, I wish I could do that. I'd take a sweetie and hide out where the Ancients couldn't find us."

Julian scanned the area while he spoke, spotting the silhouette of a man before Armando did. He lunged over to grab the wheel, turning at the last moment. Their rover clipped the stranger, who fell to the street. Both men cursed. Julian thought the poor soul might be dead from his nephew's moment of distraction, and his dread spiked with a sick lurch.

He *knew* something bad was going to happen.

Bringing their car to an abrupt stop, they ran back to the prone body that lay where it'd fallen. Armando cursed, his olive skin paling. "He looks dead." He leaned down and felt for a pulse at the man's neck.

Julian watched his chest rise and fall shallowly—not dead then—and Armando breathed a soft sigh of relief. There was evidence of a broken arm from the awkward angle it'd been bent at, but if they rushed him to the hospital, there was a chance this would be no more than an expensive mistake.

The man's undamaged arm shot out at vampire speed, grabbing Armando by the throat. Eyes shooting open, the man blew out a cloud of green-tinged gas into Armando's face. In only moments, Armando's eyes rolled back, and he went limp, thrown to the side like a ragdoll.

Jumping to his feet, Julian palmed two daggers, his favored weapons when dealing with other vampires. No gunshot noise to draw mortal attention.

"Ah, my queen gives me all the unpleasant jobs," bemoaned the other vampire as he drew himself up, rolling his shoulder. His arm popped back into place with preternatural healing. Julian frowned to himself because no one should be able to heal *that* fast.

He didn't bother mincing words, lunging forward to stab him

straight in the heart. The other vampire had said the right word. *Queen.*

And he caught Julian's wrist without trouble, twisting viciously. "Put down the toys. Make it easier for both of us," he said. The dagger fell from Julian's fingers as he felt tendons snap.

With a grunt, he went for a stab with his other dagger, just to have it caught too. He butted foreheads with his adversary, seeing black spots as they disengaged. His wrist throbbed, hand hanging limply by his side. While his opponent had easily healed something far worse, this wound would take hours and a fresh transfusion of blood to fix for Julian.

"Give up, boy. You can't win here," the other vampire said, flexing his hand. In a burst of psychic influence, Julian's discarded dagger flew to his palm.

Julian released his aura, a blast of frigid cold that dissuaded most vampires. Chuckling, his opponent did the same as he threw the dagger point-first with sheer brute force.

Two things hit him at once. One, this man was the eldest vampire he'd ever felt the aura of. It blew aside his cold shell to scorch his skin with violent heat. Second, the dagger embedded in his thigh up to the hilt before he could even twitch.

His teeth clenched down. He barely uttered even a grunt. Long ago, his father taught him that only weak men reacted to pain.

Still, he knew he was up against someone far older and more experienced than himself. Someone who grabbed his jaw, forced their eyes to meet, and began a different battle. Set within sunken sockets were maroon eyes, the same he'd heard marked a Blood Prince. He mustered all his concentration on avoiding the older mind trying to turn him into a puppet to command.

Vampires put mortals under thrall all the time. To remain a secret in the night, it was a necessity to make mortals forget they'd been bitten by another person. But between vampires, putting another under thrall required either a willing participant or a massive power gap of age between aggressor and victim.

Julian felt himself losing this battle as the power of a thousand-year-old mind bore down upon him. His thoughts and struggles faded as the other man commanded obedience. His expression simmered from a pained grimace to a blank. Fury evaporated to...nothing. His worries for Armando became ash.

"There, that wasn't so bad, was it?" the other man said, clapping his hands twice in a signal Julian's enthralled mind knew meant *pay attention*. He stood straighter despite the blade still embedded in his leg. "You are permitted to agree with me."

Julian dipped his head mechanically.

"We're leaving. You will be in command of the... vehicle." His maroon eyes flashed toward the car. "Take the weapon from your leg and go."

He pulled the dagger out, feeling the blade scrape tender bone. His master had not permitted him to make a noise, so he didn't. But his body started healing the wound immediately, closing the worst of it before he could hemorrhage to death.

Julian took limping steps toward the driver's side, stepping over Armando. Glancing down at the momentary distraction, his nephew's face brought on a moment of realization. *Armando!* He couldn't leave him behind, yet they were doing just that. The Blood Prince didn't even spare a glance back at the man he'd dropped with a dirty trick.

"Do you know where Rockefeller manor is?" the Blood Prince asked as they got into the car. Julian's fingers turned the ignition as his mind screamed in denial.

He didn't answer until the other man clapped his hands twice. He went on the alert like a trained dog. "Answer my question."

"Yes. I know where it is," he said through gritted teeth.

"Take us there. And play music. I require modern music."

"Yes, master." It was the only task he'd been given so far that he was completely willing to fulfill. He turned the dial to Armando's favorite heavy metal station and upped the volume until his ears rang.

"What is this trash?" the Blood Prince asked.

"I can't hear you, master," he said blandly.

"I said... *what is this trash?*"

"Modern music, master. Just like you requested."

His cold blue eyes showed nothing of the emotions brewing within. Thralls weren't supposed to have emotions or thoughts. But all he could think about was Armando, left behind in the street like a sack of garbage. He clung to that image and burned it into the back of his mind. He could be ordered and pushed around, but he'd been around long enough to know one thing that could save him.

No master could control an unwilling thrall perfectly. He would only need to wait for his new "master" to grow complacent and take advantage of a poorly worded command, just like he interpreted the definition of modern music.

Chapter 35
Julian

No one at Coven Rockefeller's mansion headquarters batted an eye to see a Blood Prince leading a Master vampire from a rival coven into their midst. They passed dozens of vampires, both ranking members and servants. The coven master, Ada Rockefeller, was stuck many years in the past, requiring her people to dress their station.

Julian, in his combat uniform, pant leg ripped and soaked with drying blood, stood out amongst them like a modern man at a cosplay exposition. When he got his first good look at the Blood Prince, staring at his back as he followed obediently, he realized the Ancient fit in as a relic himself.

He wasn't dressed for combat and had gotten through the process of apprehending Julian without getting a drop of blood on his cravat. His shirt was ruffled at the sleeves and hem, crisp and white against dark pants and a slim leather belt. His dark hair went to the shoulders and was slicked back by a generous applica-tion of gel. A cynical side of him thought he looked like he was dressing for the part of a vampire prince.

Too bad his fall had scuffed gray dirt into his back and sides, and a hint of red on one sleeve showed where his stunt had initially broken his arm. From behind, he wasn't nearly so immaculate.

They walked into a private bedroom, where the Blood Prince

gestured that he should sit. "The queen will be here shortly. Put on your most pleasant face."

Julian's face twisted into a forced smile which aged to a grimace as the minutes ticked by. A bead of sweat dribbled down his forehead, the only outward sign of the dread threatening to rend himself in two. He knew something bad was coming, and here it was.

Gliding into the room on silent feet was the queen herself. His master had not bidden him to turn and look when the door creaked open, but he felt the air shift. Her voice followed, smooth as silk. "Ah, at last, we meet in person."

He knew that voice from deep in his nightmares. *He was my lifemate, you* wretch!

Night after night, he knew the clothes of silver and white she preferred, but when she stopped before him, one thing was different. Her head was completely shrouded by a veil. But it was still Lucia, and to see her in person woke memories of long nights of dodging her and her accusing stare. She'd threatened retribution. But he'd forgotten, his waking mind shaking off her nightmares like the bad dreams they'd felt like.

He should've remembered. He should've taken her threats as promises because there was no waking up from the reality of this situation as she loomed over him. "You have done well, Elandros. Barely a scratch on him."

"Thank you, my queen," the Blood Prince said behind him.

"And the other one?"

"I gave him a special brew, just like you requested. The disease met your every qualification." He spoke with pride while Julian recoiled inwardly. *Disease!* So that was what he'd blown in Armando's face.

But qualifications? Lucia had wanted this to happen in a tactical manner. If Armando was found and taken to the hospital on their coven grounds with an unknown disease in him...he could unwittingly spread it to their friends and allies.

He had to get a message out to someone before it could happen. Yet here he was, glued to the chair by an order from

Elandros, waiting for them to turn their attention back to him once they were done patting themselves on the back.

"Truly outstanding," Lucia breathed. "I knew I made the right decision in taking you first. Our victory is soon at hand." Elandros's clothes rustled as if he bowed.

"Now, for you." He felt Lucia's attention turn to him. An odd magical orb circled over her shoulders at the same time before gliding right into her palm. "Even your face oozes of deceit. You are the spitting image of my lost love. What a lie."

She gestured, creating a rip in midair. *A portal,* he thought, his gaze fixed on her uneasily as she fished within it. What torture implement would she pull from nothingness?

Lucia withdrew her hand, holding the handle of a briefcase. She tossed it before him with a contemptuous sniff. And then her hand flexed on the orb, creating crushing pressure within his skull. *"You will go to Nyixa and give this to Prince Qin, the Ascended. He is expecting you. Tell him his information is past due, and collect what he has to say. You will remember every word."*

He had a new master, her orders adding to the ones already in his head. It wasn't that Elandros lost control of Julian but that Lucia somehow added herself. He'd never heard of a thrall with two masters—but most vampires didn't exploit one another in such a way without dire consequences. Gritting his teeth, he struggled against the words. But he had an order to follow. "Yes... mistress."

Lucia's voice returned to a silky purr, sounding pleased. "You will learn your place, Julian Marcuson. You serve me now. Go, do as you're told, and return as quickly as possible. Do not be seen. You are weak enough a vampire that no one should notice you."

She beckoned to him as she opened another portal, this one big as a doorway. He picked up the briefcase, hearing something rattle within. It was heavier than he'd expected. And then he passed through the portal, into the gloom of a place shrouded in full night. Where was this person he was supposed to meet anyway? She'd dropped him in the rubble of an ancient house, under a surviving archway that'd once been two walls and a section of roof.

The sky was pitch-black, the stone beginning to glow as the only thing white for miles around him.

"You there," came a quiet voice. Out of the shadows slunk a man dressed in fine, dark clothes from an older time. His silhouette flipped a white coin, and his slanted eyes burned maroon.

"Prince Qin?" He must've been expecting company to have been so close.

The Blood Prince nodded, grimacing below a pencil-thin mustache. The words spilled from Julian, compelled from his tongue. "Queen Lucia says your information is past due."

"So is her payment. I presume this is it here?" He gestured to the briefcase, which Julian handed over. His eyebrows rose as the Ancient man opened it up flat, revealing bars and jingling coins of silver and gold. A king's ransom lay within, and he had no idea how Lucia had gotten it except for exploiting her new covens or theft.

"So she has not forgotten about me after all," Qin remarked, shutting and clasping it with a nod. "I have not forgotten her either. Tell her that her victory is assured. Adrius sits uselessly on her throne, waiting while the world passes him by. Without a leader, the rest of us spend more time fighting than anything else."

Julian leaned in, memorizing every word, though he felt his sweat sticking his clothes to him as his nerves reacted to what he was hearing. How had these people not realized there was a spy amongst them? And what did it mean for Alex and Violet, who stayed here under their protection without knowing one in their midst would knife them in the back for money?

"However, she should not discount that there's been a breakthrough for them recently. Adrius allowed two people to stay here —one of Sirius's bloodline and the woman she chose to turn into a Sorceress. They've spoken some sense into the group, and now Neala and Adrius are tentatively accepting Gwendolyn's presence."

He reported at length on individuals, revealing that Neala

had gone to New York to hunt for Lucia and was taking shelter with Coven Rehnquist. Julian winced because he knew he'd have to repeat that to her. He dreaded telling her any of it, recognizing that it made him complicit. Lucia would have to keep her thumb on him permanently to prevent him from warning his friends of the coming danger.

"The young Sorceress is progressing well. She's unlocked all of her magic and mated to her companion, meaning she is ready for the queen's purposes," Qin said, leaving the briefcase in a shadowy corner before he beckoned to Julian to follow. He put a finger to his lips and headed through the ruins, dodging piles of seaweed and rubble with practiced ease.

He scaled a building that was mostly intact, using loose bricks for handholds. Resting on a pillar sturdy enough to take his weight, he beckoned to Julian again and made room for him. From this vantage, they were able to see a halo of light around two people. With a lurch in his heart, he realized it was Alex and Violet practicing. She was holding a glowing object and gesturing with her free hand, sending out a wave of fire in a bright lash.

Alex dodged to the side with his inherent grace, hands behind his back as if taking a stroll in the night. "They are...they mated?" Julian asked quietly. Lucia and Elandros hadn't mentioned questions in their orders, but he technically wasn't barred from asking them.

It was just...his eternal bachelor of a coven master was *mated*. Maybe Armando wasn't so off with his comments about what the two of them had been doing here. "Yes. Just as Lucia was waiting for." Qin nodded, casting him a glance askance. "I'm sure the queen will be interested to know how she fights. Luckily for us, clumsily."

Gwendolyn's stooped form came within the halo of light, shaking her cane. He couldn't hear what she was saying from this distance, but she corrected Violet's stance. "Her strongest magic is in shapeshifting," Qin added with an edge of scorn. "She won't be able to hold Lucia off."

They watched quietly as Violet trained and tried a variety of magic under Gwendolyn's tutelage. Julian was impressed inside, cheering her every success. She'd already come so far from the scared woman who'd arrived at their coven barely alive from her brush with a hellscape. Now she was Alex's mate and capable of slinging lightning, fire, and even spikes of ice. Incredible.

He didn't know Lucia's plan, but he didn't need the specifics to understand she was posed to destroy it all. And all he could do was watch. She meant to torture him with this knowledge that he was so close and couldn't tell them of the danger lurking just beyond the halo of their light.

Qin glanced over his shoulder and nudged him. "Seems the queen is calling you back. One more thing before you go—Taryn is not constantly watched. We will be able to release him when she is ready."

Julian looked back as well, seeing a portal waiting for him. If it were that easy to place one, she could've easily called Qin through to report by himself. She wanted Julian to know his friends were in danger.

Chapter 36
Alex

Time passed too quickly. Alex helped Violet as much as he could, even if all he could offer was the rock of his emotional support. She was as ready as one could be in a few short days of training. Gwendolyn gave her rare approval, even though Violet struggled to hit a target with magical force. Any magical force. She hadn't grown up a fighter, and to think she would become one in less than a week was foolish talk.

Perhaps their best breakthrough was an advanced shapeshifting move that not even Alex could attain for long. She sprouted fangs and claws at command, shifting only part of her body to gain the best attributes of an animal while maintaining the control of a human form. Gwendolyn called it a demi-shift. "I've only seen it in Sirius," she remarked. "This may not help you fight a Sorceress, but having enhanced reflexes and strength by being only *part* animal will help you against anyone else."

"I don't want to fight anyone," Violet said with a sigh.

Gwendolyn patted her shoulder. "You have a good heart. Soon you'll face someone who will exploit that goodness and use it against you. But it's time to retire early. I'll rouse you both when the sun rises on midsummer day." She glanced up at the dark sky. "Elsewhere in the world."

"Sounds good," Alex said.

"Meet me at the Eye of Worlds." She made a portal to return

to her own home, wherever that might be. And Violet, proud to show off something she could do, cut the air beside them to make a doorway back to their room.

He kissed her before heading through. "Showoff."

"You like it." She laughed as he caught her on the other side, her curves pressing to his chest as he drew her close. "I don't think I'll be able to sleep."

His beast was more than willing to push her behind it, ready to protect with the snap of fangs. But he recognized that, should anything involving magic come up, their only hope was something she and Gwendolyn could do to counter it. "I wish we had more time," he said, not liking the feeling of the unknown before them.

He wished they could consult Cossette. Their last talk had been cryptic at best and felt like it'd happened years, rather than weeks, ago.

"I can make us a portal back to New York," she said, feeling his turn of thoughts. "I wouldn't mind a night in a real bed either."

He echoed that sentiment with a sigh but shook his head. "It's not safe."

Chewing her lip, she gave a half-hearted shrug. "I can portal us out of danger if any presents itself. I'm not a damsel in distress anymore."

He smiled with pride, hoping she could feel it over their bond. "You've come a long way. I just think a future-seer will know when we spend time in New York and plan around it. We should just stay here and get some rest while we can. When it comes to Cossette...well, she originally hosted Lucia and gave her a platform."

"You think we can't trust her now?" she asked.

He hesitated to answer, considering how long he'd known Cossette. The little girl and her coven were allies in the past. He'd always trusted her before, even when her prophesies were cryptic nonsense. When had she ever lied?

"You know what, what's the harm in asking?" she said. "I can make us a portal to the mansion, we'll be together for however long it takes, and then we can come back."

There was less risk in that, he thought. As long as they stayed together, he was more amenable to the idea. At his nod, she made a portal to his—their—bedroom back at the mansion. They both flopped into the bed's plush warmth. His mind wandered and strained, trying to make mental contact with Cossette as Violet curled up against his chest with a content sigh.

"Good evening, Mister Rehnquist," Cossette's young, chipper voice echoed in his head.

"Got her," he said aloud, petting Violet's hair idly as he responded. *"Good evening, Cossette. I need some guidance."*

"Don't we all?" She sounded grave and mature, a good sign for getting something serious from her.

"Can you help me?" he asked.

Cossette didn't reply right away, but he heard her hum. He gave her that time, watching Violet doze with a warm feeling in his chest. If only they could stay in this moment, just the two of them. In this calm between storms. He could lay here and hold her forever in a safe and warm embrace.

Cossette's voice intruded on the moment too soon. He sighed to himself but paid close attention for any double meanings. Any advice was valuable. *"Future sight isn't as straightforward as you might think. It's not like I can close my eyes and see what's going to happen ahead of time like a movie about my life. Things come in bits and snatches, out of order and context."*

"Yes, but that's not what I wanted to ask you about..." His brow furrowed. What did this have to do with Lucia and what might happen tomorrow?

"But I can search the future for things I'm involved in or conversations others have about me. You see, the focal point is always me in one way or another."

Oh. Good thing he hadn't said any names. Cossette was sharing valuable information after all, assuming Lucia's future sight acted anything like hers. If they didn't mention her name, this conversation would seem like one of little interest to Lucia—it wasn't directly about her.

"I see what you mean now," he said.

"Okay, cool. So, as I was saying, if I had a lot of time to see the future, I still would need something to focus on, namely myself and things I was going to do. If I wanted something to happen, I would try seeing different possibilities and actions, which creates a new layer of visions. Things that would never actually happen unless I made them happen."

"You're giving me a headache, but I think I follow." Lucia had seen the future in her sleep, and with plenty of time to play with the odds, she was manipulating her way to some end goal. That's what he heard in Cossette's wording.

"If you want to beat a future-seer like me, you have two options. You can pick out the strange behavior and what results from it. That way, the end result isn't a surprise. Or—you're really good at this, Mister Rehnquist—you can act erratically instead. Change the variables that no future-seer could predict. Does that help?"

"Immensely." He wished they could've had this conversation sooner. *"Are you all right?"*

"I haven't agreed to anything yet." Her response drew a sigh of relief from him. With their covens combined, they could feasibly match the mega-coven Lucia was already assembling if it came to that.

"What does tomorrow bring?" Despite her advice, she hadn't said a word about what would happen while the midsummer sun hung in the sky.

"What does any tomorrow bring?" Cossette giggled girlishly. He sighed to himself, wishing her serious phases lasted just a while longer. Just one more answer, that's all he wanted. *"Excitement. You'd best rest up, Mister Rehnquist."*

He wondered how he could rest, his mind pulling apart the few clues they had as to Lucia's end goals. He kept circling around to things that he'd been told *about* her from Gwendolyn and the other Ancients.

The strangest thing she'd done was save Violet with the rare and valuable silver potion he still carried on his person. If his mate was involved, he was sure to have a hard time resting until he'd solved the puzzle of her behavior at last. *"I will try,"* he said, gently rousing Violet with a shake to her shoulders.

"Mmm? Did she tell you anything?" she asked. She stretched as languid as a shapeshifter.

"I'll tell you once we're back in Nyixa," he said, hoping it wouldn't distress her as much as he was troubled.

"Oh, one more thing," Cossette said as Violet flashed him a concerned look upon sensing his shift in emotion. She opened a portal back to the dark island with a frown.

"Yes?"

"Go to her dreams tonight." With that, the Ancient was gone from his head.

Shaking his head, he followed Violet through the portal. They traded a solid mattress for a nest of sleeping bags and pillows. Once settled, he repeated everything to her despite the growing unease he felt building over their mating bond. "I just don't see why she made me a Sorceress and then didn't kidnap me or something. I mean, why me? I'm nothing special."

"You're my lifemate. I think you're rather special." He said it to tease but wondered if that was really the point.

"But her worst enemy is training me to use the magic that she gave me."

He shrugged because that's where he lost the logic as well. "We could go in circles about this for hours. I think it's time to be erratic instead. Follow our instincts." His inner beast purred in agreement.

Now that it was active, he baited it with thoughts of dream walking. *With mate?* It purred harder, always keen when Violet was concerned.

"Are you trying to tell me to go to sleep?" She nestled into his arms with a sigh, sounding tired enough to do just that. Once she drifted off, he then allowed himself to do the same. His worries faded as his inner beast tugged him quickly to unconsciousness, obliterating thoughts of plans and convoluted schemes.

They drifted into darkness. At first, they were cocooned in a general warmth of togetherness, a dreamless sleep spent entwined. But that gloom mounted and deepened, creeping in on restless tendrils of night. Alex felt them shift into a dream all too familiar as screams and cursing echoed in a small room. A room where Violet was trapped and bound.

Elsewhere, wood smashed, and glass tinkled to the ground as it shattered. Those sounds drifted closer.

Open your eyes, the beast whispered.

"You there, check out that noise!" Kim Cox ordered.

When this really happened, Alex knew that Violet had been near death, unable to see what was going on. He still agreed with his instincts. "Open your eyes," he urged. Somewhere in the dark, Violet groaned. "This is a dream. You're a Sorceress now, far, far past this."

Wavering at the edges, when she opened her eyes, the rest of the dream came into focus. They watched Will Jaxom's body fly past and turned to the doorway as it slammed open. The dream blurred, as if she struggled to remember. "Focus," he urged. This could be their missing piece to Lucia's plan.

When Violet focused, a part of Alex really wished she hadn't. There was a sense that they both recoiled from what floated there while Kim Cox screamed, "What the—? What *are* you?"

"Is that Lucia?" Violet asked. They had manifested bodies to lucid walk through the scene, and she paused what lay before them with a lazy gesture.

Alex's inner beast was impressed. *We haven't figured that out yet.*

Take notes then, he thought back to it, his face set in a grimace.

He inspected the feminine figure, not wanting to get closer even with it frozen in time. It had Lucia's dark hair, but that's where the resemblance ended. Her lips were pulled too far back, revealing sharp teeth dripping with blood and bits of flesh. That blood ruined the collar of a fine wedding dress still shrouding her in white silk and pearls.

Her eyes were Fell-like, twin pits of pure black, and inky veins ran over her face and the exposed flesh of her neck. "I daresay that is Lucia," he agreed.

"That's not how she looked in the Eye of Worlds." She rubbed a rise of goosebumps from her arms.

"If you had incredible magic at your fingertips, would you want to look like that, love?" he asked dryly.

Instead of replying, she let the nightmare play on. Lucia turned and lunged, ripping a vicious bite into Kim Cox's neck. As she fell, she stayed down, knocked unconscious. When Julian had reported on what he'd seen in the warehouse, apparently, all of the Haveners were taking a nap at the time. Now they knew why.

The veins around Kim's wound stood out red and black, like an infected spider bite, before healing over quickly. By then, Lucia was turning to the chair, where a version of Violet was still tied up and dying. She stroked her cheek tenderly with the backs of sharp claws that'd punctured through a satiny pair of gloves.

"I...I think I'm going to be sick," Violet said beside him, the real, dreaming one. He didn't turn away, morbidly transfixed as Lucia drew a full vial of silver blood from a pocket.

"Just a little longer," he urged.

He'd heard most of Lucia's whispers before.

Poor thing.

Fated to die so senselessly.

You are victim no longer.

But she turned to leave as she finished feeding the old blood to Violet. "Now rest. I will call for you when it's time."

The nightmare shattered as Violet woke violently, throwing herself to her feet in a wake of cold sweat. She covered her mouth with her hands, gesturing to open a portal, but put her palm up to him afterward. "I understand," he said, knowing she needed a moment.

After what they'd seen, he didn't blame her.

Chapter 37
Julian

Julian spent what felt like days sitting in one place, left only with the image of Armando's unconscious face and the slow creep of cold. It came from himself, his own aura turning against him as it trickled up his limbs like liquid ice, starting at the fingers and toes. He figured it was another slow torture from Lucia, of whom he saw none of. Instead, it seemed he was sitting in Elandros's quarters. The Blood Prince came to occasionally check that he was still under thrall.

He was otherwise left to wonder how Lucia had turned his aura into an icy punishment. Under the influence of another vampire, his thoughts were too blank, even with Armando's memory to remind him of who he was. That left his attention to drift to the slow creep of ice crystals over his exposed skin, as if he were turning into a statue.

In those quiet moments, he vowed that he *hated* magic. He would put a blade through the real Lucia's heart for doing this to him.

As if his vitriol had summoned her, she glided into the room not five minutes later. Her shroud hid her expression as she took his hand, turning it over for her inspection. He thought uncharitable thoughts as he sweated in her presence, and those salty droplets froze upon his back. "Yes, I think it worked," she said.

She flexed his hand, ridding it of its icy coating. His skin did not warm even upon exposure to the air.

"I have another mission for you." She seized her magical orb, looming over him as his heart beat at his ribcage for escape. Her voice crushed into his head, speaking an order he couldn't fight. *"Within the heart of the palace rests my old laboratory. Beneath it is a jail, and inside waits my most loyal servant, Blood Prince Taryn. You will release him and bring him back to me."*

"Yes, mistress," he said from between gritted teeth.

"But first, there's one more thing you need." She drew the shroud from her head. On the inside, Julian gasped, but his expression remained one of obedient blankness.

Under her skin pulsed blood as black as night, staining every vein like the stroke of ink. He'd seen her true face in his dreams. The reality was so much worse. Her breath stank of old meat as she tossed her perfumed veil aside. Two rows of sharped teeth spread too far on her face in a Cheshire cat's grin. Her brows drew together over eyes like two black pits.

"Take a good look. Know that your beloved *Curator* saw fit to do this to me. I'm ruined. My body needs to be replaced to match my majesty." She placed a gloved hand over his cheek. Now he knew why she kept her whole body covered, including veiling the horror of her face. She was something ripped directly from the past, the definition of a Fell from what descriptions he'd heard.

She tilted his chin upward, those soulless eyes inspecting his face. "Are you afraid in there, wretch? Answer me."

"Yes," he said, if only to avoid her ordering him with his magic. His body trembled with more than the cold as he looked upon a monster who could eat him alive with fangs such as hers.

"Good. You should be," she purred. "I will destroy you for what you did to my lifemate. No, no, *you* will destroy yourself. You will tear your own life apart, brick by brick. But maybe I will have some mercy if I hear you beg for my forgiveness."

He pressed his lips into a thin line, staring at her with the blankness only a thrall could accomplish. She didn't *order* him to beg, and she wasn't his true master. Had Elandros told him to beg,

Julian would be forced to grovel and kiss the ground Lucia walked on.

But he wouldn't do it of his own free will. If she'd truly been Marcus's lifemate, she would understand that he and his kin would never beg.

Lucia snapped her teeth as the silence drew on. "Very well. Allow me to give you a taste of what's to come."

Quick as a viper, those sharp teeth closed around his shoulder. Pain flared in twin half-moons from multiple punctures. Black spots danced in the corner of his sight as numbness spread from those points like a dark tide. It dragged him under to a feverish blankness, his body flushing hot for the first time since his captivity began.

In that void, he started seeing things.

A tall girl wearing an extravagant yellow gown on a stage, dancing with another man as a song about true love was sung by a live choir. She had a generous scattering of freckles on a plain face, innocent and heart-shaped, with a button nose and rose petal lips. Her face was framed by a few brunette curls, hair up in an elegant bun. Lucia was generous enough to creep the vision closer until he saw only her face and the crease of concentration between her brows as her lips moved silently to the lyrics of the song. She looked lively, in her element under a spotlight.

He knew her on sight, like a punch to his wounded leg. The woman he'd been searching centuries for. His *lifemate*.

Tainted by the inclusion of Lucia's voice. *"What a cute girl."* Julian knew true horror for the first time, not from Lucia's presence or her bite, but for the fact that she was the one to find his lifemate.

"I passed her name on to a very interested party. Someone willing to put his men to my service for even a hint of information on someone so close to Alexander Rehnquist."

The scene changed, showing him his woman sitting on a shabby couch. She jumped to her feet in surprise as her apartment door was kicked down by a man shrouded all in black. He could've screamed with her when he realized who they were.

Haveners. Thugs of Bryant Collins, always determined to stick a dagger in the back of Alex and his closest friends.

What better way to get Julian than to steal his lifemate? Forced to watch it happen, he was proud that his lifemate punched one thug in the face. But it earned her a beating before being hogtied and dragged from her home. They taped her mouth to muffle her shouts.

Not so muffled, Julian made a sound of pain. Just one. He opened his eyes to find Lucia licking his blood from her teeth, her expression pure pleasure. "Now you are marked as mine. This will be easy." She gestured to make a portal and jerked her chin toward it. "Do not dally."

He drew himself up, every muscle protesting the motion with how the cold had seeped into him. Nothing pained him worse than the sucking wound she'd delivered to his emotions, even if he couldn't express it. He limped through her portal and covered his face under the cover of darkness, taking a deep breath as his body threatened to betray him.

Haven had his lifemate. And he didn't even know her name.

He'd searched the world for her. No one other than his true match would do, not with the final promise he'd made his childhood love.

Lucia meant to dangle temptation before him just to snatch it away. He had no means of getting a message to his coven and ask for help. And he had no one to tell what he'd just learned of his lifemate and Lucia alike. There was no way he could stop her plan with him positioned directly under her thumb.

"Quit feeling sorry for yourself and move." Lucia sounded impatient but, more importantly, quite present in his head. Had she read his thoughts?

Could she do that?

He stood straighter, his breath turning to cold mist before him. The portal had led to a room inside of the palace, pitch-black as was the rest of the island. His hair stood on end as he glanced out of the square where a window once was, seeing only an endless stretch of blackness.

"Wrong way." Lucia ordered him to turn around, and his feet

moved obediently to her task. He walked past the portal still wavering there in the dark and followed her instructions up a flight of stone stairs. As his eyes adjusted to vampire keenness, he started making out what was before him by shades of gray.

The worst part about the ghost town this palace had become was the smell. The stink of rotting fish and other sea life matched his wretched feelings. He moved with her orders just to get out of this place faster, locating her old laboratory and a set of stairs at the back. *"He is bound by nephilim chains. You now have enough power within you to remove them. Be honored. Their magic will recognize Marcus within your wretched self."*

Down in the laboratory's depths was a six-cell jail smelling vaguely of cleaning solution. He took a breath of that with a sigh of relief, pacing to the only cell with closed bars. A pair of eyes fixed on him in the dark, a flash of maroon in the light of the chains he wore. Julian was able to walk into the cell, its lock long turned to rust.

The only thing holding the man captive was two lengths of golden chains. They glowed of their own light, simple as iron locks but obviously infused with magic. A longer set hooked into a stone ring, anchoring the captive there. His wrists were bound with a second set. "Has my queen sent you?" His voice was a roll of thunder, belying someone of great size and strength despite the way he'd had to sit in the corner to stay comfortable while chained.

"Yes. I have come to free you and return you to her service." Julian parroted Lucia in his head at her command.

"I knew my love wouldn't forsake me."

"Taryn has always been smitten." Lucia sounded like she was laughing at some private joke. *"Look at the chains and find a knot of upraised metal. Press down upon it to free him. Bring me the chains."*

A portal opened not three paces from them, another sign that Lucia could've done this herself. She wanted him to further damn himself by setting up the dominos to fall as she wished.

Forced by her command, he turned over the chains Taryn thrust forward until he found a circle of metal raised over the rest.

He pressed his thumb into it, feeling his skin prick on the metal's sharp edge. A bead of blood pooled on the surface of his skin, and the manacles sprung free a moment later. He repeated this for the second set and carried both through the portal Lucia had left for them.

Upon reemerging into a room with light, Julian got his first good look at Taryn. The last Blood Prince had skin as dark as night, nearly blending in with a fine, old-fashioned suit he wore. Judging by its condition, he'd been wearing it a while. His head and jaw were graced by scruffy hair, unkempt in his captivity. His expression changed from a monotone thrall's stare, to a loving, coveting look upon seeing Lucia, still unveiled.

"My love. I return to your service," he rumbled, kneeling before her.

"Just in time to help me in my ultimate victory. I'm sorry our fellows saw fit to chain your strength." She left him on his knees, motioning to the chains Julian held. "It's a miracle these survived. Nothing magic touches can be fully destroyed, it would seem. Did these sap your strength permanently, Taryn? Or was it only while you wore them?"

"I am strong again, my queen," he said.

"Good. I am pleased." Even her words seemed to cause Taryn to lean in, eager to continue his service.

Instead of acknowledging him, she turned to Julian. Her fangs were fully bared in a vicious smile. "I have another task for you. Gather up the one person missing so I may begin anew. Bring me the little Sorceress, Violet. It's time she paid her debt for me saving her miserable life."

Screaming on the inside, Julian's body obediently stepped through her next portal.

Chapter 38
Violet

Violet took her time to scrub herself until the nightmare and the slimy feeling it'd left on her skin faded. She pressed her forehead to the tile, gazing at the reflection of her silver eyes.

A monster had saved her life. And she *still* didn't know why! She pounded her fist against the bathroom wall in futility before shutting off the stream of warm water. After emptying the contents of her stomach and washing herself crown to toes, she at least felt more ready for the day.

She donned a new outfit she'd picked out for herself after drying her hair. Without the whine of the dryer, she heard the clack of hangers sliding on the rack. Someone else was in Alex's walk-in closet, where she'd already moved in her things. "Who's there?" she called, hoping for Petra or even one of the maids who kept the mansion tidy. She missed the vampires who'd made this place feel like home so quickly.

"Julian," came the response. The hair on the back of her head rose despite a confused smile crossing her face. She'd missed him and his stern manner, too, but why was he in her closet?

He carried out a dress still wrapped in a sheet of plastic from where it was purchased. A shiny, silver number very reminiscent of...

Oh no, she thought. She'd seen that dress in the reflection the Eye of Worlds had shown her.

"What is your heart's deepest desire? Where do you wear this dress?" Lucia had mocked. She didn't realize she already owned the very same dress.

Julian turned toward her, his expression completely blank. Her questions guttered in her throat. She'd seen a face like that before, stripped of its natural life to resemble a mask's stiff, lifeless form. It felt like a lifetime ago when her coworkers at the zoo were butchered by Haven thugs, wearing that same expression.

She turned to take hold of her occultarus, but he was on her in a flash of vampire speed. He grabbed hold of her wrists and pinned them behind her back. Screaming, she realized she was immediately beaten without the ability to make magic symbols with her hands or touch her occultarus.

"I'm sorry," Julian said quietly. He held her with one hand, the other pulling something from a back pocket. Cold metal shackled her wrists, but that wasn't all. She felt her control of magic seep from her. Her occultarus fell to the ground with a dull thump, its light extinguishing.

"How could you?" she gasped. Of all people, she wouldn't expect Julian to attack her. But the only response she got was his blank look.

She thrashed in his hold, digging in her heels as he gathered the dress and her occultarus. He threw her over his shoulder without a problem, uttering only a grunt as she kicked his chest repeatedly to get him to let go. The air thrummed with the opening of a portal before they were suddenly in a different room.

He placed her on her feet before a creature of her nightmares, clutching her shackles so she couldn't escape. "Hello, Violet," purred Lucia, her black-veined face unveiled as she leaned in, blowing a gust of foul breath over her.

Violet released another scream, this one pitched higher as her terror mounted. A swift smack silenced her. "Do that again, and I drive this through the back of Julian's head. Are we clear?" Lucia held up a sheathed dagger that looked familiar. *A weapon he used to wear,* she realized. Who else carried weapons like that?

Still, Violet pressed her lips together. She knew Julian hadn't suddenly experienced a change of heart on his own. "Better." Lucia chuckled as she toyed with the blade, unsheathing it and checking its sharpness. A bead of black blood rose from her fingertip, seeping through her glove.

"What do you *want* from me?" Violet asked desperately when the other Sorceress started inspecting her instead.

Lucia glanced over her shoulder. "Think I should tell her?" she asked two men Violet hadn't realized were standing there. Though they shared Blood Prince eyes, as maroon as a glass of fine wine, they otherwise couldn't have been more different. One was thin and gangly, with slicked-back hair and fine clothes. The other was a Black man looming over everyone as the most muscular in the room. His expression was nearly as blank as Julian's except for when he glanced to Lucia and gave an enamored smile.

"What harm would it be to show your brilliance now, my queen?" simpered the one she had a hard time believing *was* a Blood Prince. "They'll both be dead soon anyway."

Violet's heart plummeted somewhere around her toes. "W-what?" she whispered.

"Oh, it's nothing personal, my dear. Almost anyone would've done," Lucia said, patting her cheek. Her fanged smile spread to encompass most of the lower half of her face. "This body of mine is ruined, and I am in desperate need of a replacement."

She gestured when Violet opened her mouth, closing it with an unseen force. Brows pinching together, she made muffled curses at the other woman. She wanted to steal her *body*? Only how outnumbered she was stopped her from lashing out with a kick or headbutt. Anyone here could hold her down if they needed to. "You do have a pretty face, but I already tire of your voice," Lucia said. Violet felt her face redden further as she tried to speak.

"As I was saying, almost anyone would've done. But I needed a special woman who could survive the transformation to a Sorceress *and* establish herself with a powerful mate. I tire of ruling alone, despite my lifemate's untimely end." She shot a glare at Julian.

Violet could gag. In her body, Lucia could trick Alex into thinking it was still her. "With the right events in place, Alexander will ascend to Ancient and bend to my will," Lucia continued, her expression growing smug as she read Violet's reaction. "He's no Marcus, but he will do. Meanwhile, you will bear my curse for however long it takes for your friends to find and execute you. Whomever swings the sword will inherit the curse, as that's how Fell magic works. But that won't be my problem anymore." She shrugged casually, ignoring how pale Violet had turned.

Snapping her fingers, she sauntered from the room. "Bring her. It's time."

The two Blood Princes followed her. Julian tried to prod her into motion before resorting to carrying her again. This time, she went completely limp. "Help. Please. Tell me you're still in there," she whispered, finding Lucia's influence left when she left the room. He was her last hope here before her body could be stolen.

"I'm sorry," Julian repeated. "I would never..." He marched her from the room even still.

"Can you call to someone?" she asked, seeing a hallway decked with lavish portraits and painted landscapes pass by. She sniffled, realizing belatedly that her tears were soaking into his shoulder. She cried for both of them as he shook his head because whatever these chains were, they had sucked away every ounce of her magic. There was no escaping this moment, so expertly plotted as Lucia had lain dreaming beneath the waves for so long.

Everything had been set up, leading her to the gallows. From saving her from the Haveners, gifting her magic long lost to the past, to setting her on the path to meet Alex. She sobbed as she thought of him laying with Lucia and thinking it was still her. Him kissing her, telling her that he loved her.

They entered another room, and all the furniture moved to one side to reveal wooden planks. The surface had been scored deeply in a circle as wide as Violet's arm span, complicated symbols engraved at intervals on both sides. "We are fortunate this ritual doesn't require an Alchemyst's blood. There are none left after all," Lucia said, having a private chuckle at that.

She drew out Julian's dagger. "Reposition her arms in front of her. You can unlock one side by holding the other closed as you press the release."

Julian's cold hand closed around her left wrist as the right shackle unlocked. She whirled to elbow him in the ribs, but he merely took the impact with another grunt and grabbed her free wrist, locking it before her. Lucia watched, amusement tugging at her lips. She grasped Violet's elbow, standing at arm's length as she cut a series of symbols into her forearm. She stopped only to make a pinching motion when Violet began to curse her out and tell her where to go, silencing her magically and finishing the task.

"Put her on the ground. Press those marks to their match where I cut them," she instructed Julian as she turned her knife on herself.

Julian wrestled Violet to the ground. His reluctance and her resistance made it a difficult task, but she realized she was only amusing the Ancients in the room watching the futile struggle. Eventually, her bleeding wounds were pressed to identical symbols on the floor. Her ears popped as her silver blood pooled in a channel before flowing to an ornate mark on the other side of the circle.

Lucia knelt and pressed her own carved arm to a matching setup of symbols that ran the other way, like an unholy yin and yang. Her occultarus floated to the middle of the circle, glowing brighter and brighter as it threw off jagged cracks of lightning.

Violet felt a tug and then nothingness, as if a great hand had reached within and pulled out her spirit. Her body went limp.

Chapter 39
Julian

Both women flattened to the ground when the spell concluded. It hadn't even taken five minutes, just a donation of blood and a flux of magic from the orb returning to Lucia and floating by her side.

Violet stirred first, groaning. Letting her go, Julian gave her space. "Violet?" he asked quietly, his heartbeat throbbing in his ears.

She sat up, checking her arm before looking up at him. "Julian? What happened?" she asked.

"Are you still you?" he asked, unable to mask the relief in his voice, followed by a wave of dread as she smiled viciously.

Different face, same smile. "Sure I am. I am as I have always been—beautiful and eternal. Elandros, command the wretch to free me."

The other man turned his attention Julian's way. "Free her," he ordered, and Julian obeyed with great reluctance. The chains sprung from her and hit the floor with a clatter.

"Come, I have a kingdom to claim," she remarked, standing and stretching. As she did, the marks on her arms vanished, healing over to pink, new skin. Before sweeping from the room, she made a gesture for magic with her thumbs and forefingers. A portal cut itself into existence.

"One last order for now," Elandros's voice echoed back long after he left the room and left Julian there, standing uncertainly. *"Stay there until Neala arrives. Cooperate with her and tell her the portal goes to Nyixa. But do not tell her the truth of who is really in Lucia's body."*

"Yes, master." Julian could do a lot with the command *stay*. He rushed to the side of Lucia's body, giving it a shake before turning it over. Violet was in there now, out cold.

Maybe he couldn't leave the room, but if Violet woke, she still had a magic orb and a Sorceress's magic. She could get a head start out of here. Because he had no doubts about what would happen when Neala, who'd come to New York to hunt the woman before him, found them. With him mum on what had actually happened, her only hope was escaping before Neala could kill her.

He was sure it would happen any minute. Lucia had to have tampered with this, too, predicting the timing exactly. But he didn't expect *just* how good she was when a booted foot kicked in the door right away. An angry redhead stood in the threshold, finding him looming over Lucia's body. As Armando had described, Neala had glamored herself heavily, looking like a curvy woman rather than a hardened warrior. Yet he had no doubt this was her.

"Did you knock her out? Good job." Her lips moved, but he was an old enough vampire to know she was actually speaking with her mind. She stopped short and eyed the drying blood on the floor. Her nose wrinkled with distaste, but she didn't linger on that long, scooping up the set of golden chains and motioning him aside.

She clapped Lucia's wrists in those chains, so conveniently placed for this purpose. The silver occultarus circling over the unconscious body dropped to the ground. He frowned uneasily behind her, seeing the puzzle pieces clearly now. *"I've waited so long to bring her to justice."*

Neala stood, gazing at him long enough that he shifted with discomfort. *"You look so much like someone I used to know. It's uncanny."*

"My father was Marcus," he said. No need to play coy with her. If Lucia knew him, he was sure the Blood Princes did too.

A smile lifted a corner of her mouth. *"Ah! Did you inherit his blood tracking?"* At his nod, she gestured to the body. *"Why don't you have a taste of her? If she manages to squirm her way out of this one, at least you will know where to find her."*

It wasn't a bad idea. His friend was in there now. If anything did happen, he'd be able to find her—no matter if she were Lucia or Violet. Bending down, he nipped her wrist enough to get a few drops of blood to swallow. He nearly threw them back up, the taste of rancid flesh festering in his mouth.

Pinching his nose, he kept it down, feeling his magic identify her now that he was focused on her. But a strange thing happened. With him tracking Lucia's body, he felt an awareness of dozens of others in the same building. And more still, farther out. It rendered his blood tracking worthless to sense so many people at one time.

"More damn Sorceress magic," he muttered to himself, shaking away that feeling.

"Does the portal go to Nyixa?" Neala asked him. He nodded, wanting to tell her that it was too convenient. That they shouldn't go through. But his will was bound by Elandros's orders.

As she picked up Lucia's body, he realized she was awake and looking directly at him. Lucia's face, Violet's horrified expression.

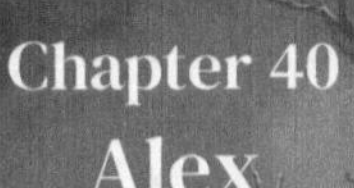

Chapter 40
Alex

ALEX MUST'VE DOZED OFF WAITING FOR VIOLET TO RETURN because the next thing he knew, Gwendolyn's voice was in his head. *"Sun's up. Is Violet still asleep? I haven't gotten through to her."*

He cracked open his eyes, turning to feel that the other side of his makeshift bed was empty and cold. Jumping to his feet, he checked every nook of their room. No sign of her. *"She must still be in New York,"* he said.

"New York?" She sounded outraged. *"Why would she be there?"*

He paced, wondering just how much time had passed. After vowing to always be by her side, he'd left her out of his sight to clean up and recover from that harrowing dream...just for her to go missing. So many terrible things could occur in minutes, and she'd been gone for hours at best.

A portal appeared as he pondered what to say to Gwendolyn. *Perfect timing,* he thought with a relieved sigh as Violet emerged, not a hair misplaced. She came in on a soft cloud of perfume and hair product smell, her platinum blonde locks curled in delicate ringlets. She clutched a garment bag to her chest.

"Where were you, eh? Take a trip down to the salon?" he asked in disbelief.

"I just wanted to look good. It's been so long that we've been

239

here...smelling so terrible," she said, glancing down at the bag and then back to him, biting her lip with a coy look. "Want to help me get dressed?"

His inner beast overruled him, purring at the thought. "We can't keep Gwendolyn waiting long," he said, closing the gap between them and putting aside the silver dress she'd picked out. He bent down to kiss her brow tenderly, pulling her to the line of his body. For those pulse-breaking few seconds, he'd thought he'd lost her. As close as they'd been in the last week, it'd felt so strange to be parted from her.

No, there was something else wrong. His instincts were no longer so content, and he opened his eyes to look her over more closely. "What's wrong?" Violet purred.

What was wrong? His nostrils flared, picking apart what lay under the sweet perfume. "You smell like blood."

"Oh, huh. Must've cut myself with the razor," she said, shrugging. Her hands drifted lower, fitting into his rear pockets. "So this is where you keep it."

In her grasp was his half-filled vial of silver blood. "Why haven't you drunk this?" Her tone was almost accusatory.

He reached toward their mating bond for some insight to her sudden flash of anger, coming up empty. That's what was really wrong, putting his inner beast increasingly on edge. The bond was either gone or so stretched by distance that he couldn't feel it. Which made no sense with Violet right in front of him, her expression smoothing out as she offered the tube back to him. "Do you want me to drink this?" he asked.

"Well, yes. How else are we to survive this day?" She crossed her arms, looking at the floor. "The stronger you are, the stronger *I* am. Why don't you drink it while I change?" Retrieving the silver dress, she started to undress right in front of him. The body that had enticed him so much before did nothing for him now.

Not my mate, the inner beast whispered. *Can't trust.*

Alex slowly tucked the potion back in its hiding place. He thought to Cossette's advice, to be unpredictable. This was certainly an unpredictable event, but when he felt his lifemate bond snap into place with someone else on the island, it really clicked for him.

The woman in front of him was only wearing Violet's face. She had her back to him, struggling with a zipper. "Let me get that for you," he muttered, embracing his beast's heated reaction to realizing someone else was impersonating his mate. He both zipped the dress and grabbed her wrists, pulling her flush with him for a very different reason.

"What are you doing?" She looked up at him with such innocent confusion, lips parted to ask more questions. For a moment, he faltered, thinking himself mistaken.

Open your eyes, his inner beast demanded. He had no bond with this woman. She was no better than a Violet-like stranger.

"What did you do to my mate?" he demanded, baring his teeth like the angry animal inside of him.

There was no hesitation there. A smile split her face as she laughed. "Oh, Alexander. You should've just played along." Her hands flexed behind her. The next thing he knew, he was holding a live wire of electricity, forced to let her go lest he electrocute himself. Crackles of lightning made their way up her arms.

She grabbed her occultarus from orbit, gesturing out to him. Every muscle in his body froze. He couldn't breathe. "Behold what a true Sorceress can do. Newly turned, little training." She gestured to herself. "Yet stronger than an Elder vampire in one spell."

"*Lucia,*" he projected out to Gwendolyn.

"*Yes, she's here. Neala brought her in nephilim chains. We've won,*" she replied in elation.

"*No—*" He felt the connection sever from an outside source. The Lucia before him wearing Violet's skin watched him like an entomologist studies a particularly interesting bug. Something novel but otherwise easy to crush.

"You *will* drink this potion. It may not feel like it, but you are still bonded to this body, and I need a strong partner for what's to come." At her gesture, he could breathe again as his jaw was wedged open.

He tried to project uncharitable thoughts toward her, but it seemed she had somehow cut off all his mental speech. As still as a statue, he could only watch as she sauntered toward him in a feminine strut, showing off her new and untainted body with a proud lift of her head. She took out his vial and uncorked it, smelling the fumes coming from it with a sigh. "Ah, the last of its kind. This blood has waited for you for a thousand years, Alexander. Aren't you honored?"

He hoped the murderous look in his eyes properly communicated just how little he appreciated this situation. He should've followed Gwendolyn's advice and destroyed the vial and its contents while he could.

Instead, she pressed the glass into his mouth, pushing the lip of it past his frozen gag reflex. Cold liquid poured slowly down the back of his throat. "Don't worry, though. Such a big influx of power will knock you right out. And once my old body is dead, I'll be sure to come back and erase your memory of this ever happening. We can be a happy family together. Just like you've always wanted, right?" She rubbed her belly and gave him another coy look.

His thoughts immediately flashed to Mary Ann and how she'd always cradled her pregnant belly so tenderly. *Yes,* he wanted a family. But the thought that Lucia would sink her talons into his dream turned him cold in no way anything else had. That she thought erasing this ordeal would trick him into otherwise believing she was Violet...maybe she was insane. Truly out of her mind.

She didn't let him respond, though. *The woman must like to hear herself talk,* he thought bitterly. As the dregs of the silver blood emptied out in his throat, he felt it take effect like a kick to the stomach. His whole body thrummed with new power, building and building with mounting pressure at the back of his head. It didn't stop when it reached the pain threshold, making his whole body throb as if it had nowhere to put the influx of power.

That was when he felt lightheaded. Lucia removed the vial from his mouth and let him collapse to the floor as she released her spell. He curled up with a groan, feeling his body go limp.

"Sweet dreams, my love." She chuckled to herself as she turned, making a portal out of the room.

She hadn't stayed long enough to watch Alex grit his teeth, taking every wave of agony as his powers aged years in moments. He didn't pass out as he lay there a few moments longer, as if expecting her to come back as he played possum.

Instead, he pushed himself to his feet. Sweat soaked through his clothing in an instant. It felt like his whole body had turned to lead. The room blurred as his eyes filled with pained tears. He tottered to get his balance. Managed a step. Fell. He stood again, limbs shaking. He had a mate to save, and determination pushed him forward another step.

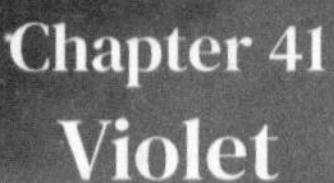

SHE DIDN'T KNOW HOW LUCIA HAD GOTTEN UP SO EASILY IN her new body. Now that she had awoken, Violet felt like her whole body weighed double. Her limbs lolled on the rocky soil as Neala half-dragged her toward the massive Eye of Worlds. "I'm... I'm not..." she tried to say, her lips dry and chapped. Licking them lacerated her tongue on dozens of needle-sharp teeth.

Neala turned a hateful look her way. She'd dropped the pretty glamor at some point, looming over her like a hulk of woman warrior. *"Save your breath. No one's listening."*

Violet wondered if Lucia had drugged her body right before the swap. It seemed like the kind of thing she'd do, to leave her only magical competition disabled. But she needed to get a grip somehow because she was being dragged to her execution, which would permanently leave Lucia with *her* body. Tears burned at the corner of her eyes, leaving ink trails on her face.

"I'm not... Lucia," she rasped.

"You are lucky I'm saving you for Adrius," Neala gritted out, her grip on the golden chains binding Violet's wrists tightening. *"I'm tired of your mind games."*

"But—"

"Shut up!" Her face curled up like a snarling bulldog's. It reminded Violet distinctly of the mute, red-faced Neala she'd first met, who'd looked seconds from exploding.

She kept her lips sealed, shooting Julian a desperate look. Following behind them a few paces, his face was still blank and ready for commanding. He was paling further than a creature of the night who hadn't seen a hint of sunlight, his skin taking on a cold sheen where she could see it. He met her gaze, only showing his inner turmoil with a twitch of his brow. There had to be some thoughts in there, some pushback from the terrible things he was forced to witness.

They came up to the Eye of Worlds, where Gwendolyn stood with arms crossed over her cane. She turned, adjusting her spectacles as she did a double take. "You found her," she gasped.

"*I did. I am taking her to Adrius,*" Neala said gruffly. She paused with Gwendolyn for a moment, drawing a sigh of relief from Violet. As smooth as the white stone Nyixa was built upon looked, she'd started to feel every bump and hard edge as her clothes wore down.

"Remember, she cannot be killed yet. Whomever swings the sword will inherit her power and curse," Gwendolyn cautioned. The line of Neala's body grew more rigid.

"*There's always an excuse for why we cannot end her. Have you no better solution?*" she grumbled.

"I'm not...not...Lucia," Violet said, her voice small and weak. Both women turned toward her before exchanging a glance.

"*She keeps saying that,*" Neala said, flipping her hand dismissively.

Gwendolyn frowned, tapping her cane against the ground as she inspected Violet at length. She held a hand up as Neala moved to continue dragging her toward the palace. "I'm..." Violet rasped before she noticed a disturbance in the air across the square. Out stepped...well, herself. Lucia piloted her body, except she'd taken some time to primp and put on the silver gown she coveted so much.

She lifted a clawed hand and pointed. Lucia was making the symbol for "portal" behind their backs, retrieving a familiar-looking satchel that she hid behind her back with both hands. "Lucia," Violet said. "It's...Lucia."

Gwendolyn and Neala turned, both smiling to see who they

thought was Violet. "Good morning, dear. Looks like we don't have to worry about a fight today," the older Ancient said. Only from another's ears did Violet realize that her tone turned warm and almost motherly. Her heart ached to hug her mentor for putting up with her for a whole grueling week of intensive training.

"What a relief," Lucia said, flipping her hair. "Sorry to keep you waiting. I wanted to put my best foot forward for whomever comes to visit today."

"I see that. This is the most formal you've ever been. It should've waited." Just like that, Gwendolyn was back to being her severe, professorial self. "I need you to try communicating with the Eye of Worlds with me. Together, we will have the power to command it."

"N-no," Violet said. No one saw what she did. Lucia had taken her occultarus in hand, the satchel still behind her back. A subtle breeze kicked up.

"*I will take Lucia to her cell then,*" Neala said, sounding displeased.

Lucia chuckled. The breeze blew in behind her back, picking up speed. She ducked as a cloud of blue dust rose behind her— the languor dust, aimed directly at Gwendolyn and Neala's faces. Julian sidestepped it, and Violet held her breath until she felt herself growing dizzy.

"In truth, I don't need any help with the Grand Occultarus. It actually listens to my commands," Lucia said, her face splitting with a vicious smile as the two Ancient women dropped like discarded clothing. Neala's face was turned toward Violet, her eyes bugged wide in silent horror as she returned to her old torment of being locked in her own body.

Lucia knelt, grabbing Gwendolyn's chin, and cooed over her. "You should've killed me when you had the chance. Look where your revenge has placed you."

"L...Lucia..." Gwendolyn choked out. Her body was already limp as the dust did its work.

"Languor dust hmm? That's what you used on me." Lucia clucked her tongue. "The only substance in the world that makes you fully aware as you sleep. For a thousand years, I was stuck only with my thoughts and visions. I needed revenge. I needed you to *suffer* for the hell you put me through."

Standing, she let Gwendolyn's head thump on the stone dais. She strode up to the Eye of Worlds, placing her hand on its glass surface. "While I slept, this magnificent tool slept with me. We developed a kinship." Motes of shadow danced around her palm. Those sprites, which had laughed so viciously at Violet, welcomed Lucia like a celebrated friend. "In exchange for its cooperation, I promised to reconnect it to the one place it misses most. The Fell Lands."

"You're...mad," Gwendolyn said on a mere gasp of sound.

Lucia tilted her head. "Am I? I've seen so many variations of this moment. The Fell haven't had a Sorcerer or Sorceress to lead them since we slayed their last Emperor. They'll follow someone who will put them back on the winning side."

She turned to Julian when it was apparent there would be no more reaction from Gwendolyn. "You will try to kill anyone who comes near my old body, except for Adrius. Understand?"

Julian's throat worked, a frown turning down his lips. "Yes, mistress," he answered.

Nodding to herself, she cast a complicated spell with her hands, her bare feet buoying off the ground as if carried by invisible wings. She floated up over the Eye of Worlds, her hands spreading. Spinning around her like a moon, her occultarus flared to brilliant life as she started muttering an incantation over the massive tool.

"*Violet?*" The voice whispering in her head was Julian's, his gaze vigilant as he scanned the eminent area for threats.

"*Yeah?*" she responded quietly, as if Lucia could hear her even in her thoughts.

"*Lucia isn't my mistress. A Blood Prince called Elandros is. I don't have to follow her order.*"

She breathed out a tense, shaky breath. "*What does it matter? We've lost anyway.*" Another hail of dark tears leaked from her eyes as she blinked, watching tiny bolts of lightning flow from Lucia's hands down to the giant Eye of Worlds. The shadows within swirled harder and faster the more energy was poured into it.

"You are our only hope. And you're giving up?" Finally, he sounded like himself, a stern frown pulling at his features. She held up and shook the golden chains, and he released a sound like a small "ah" and nodded curtly. *"I can remove those. From what I saw with a different person...your magic and energy should come right back. But she'll probably attack me the moment she realizes what happened."*

"So...we have one shot. But I don't have the occultarus that's attached to this body," she murmured. Julian wordlessly held up the silver-plated occultarus that'd made the body swap between her and Lucia possible. She still didn't like her odds, but it was better than laying here and watching Lucia—in her body—open a giant portal to release terrible monsters back into their world.

Determination hardened her from the inside out. No, Lucia wouldn't succeed today. She had miscalculated and picked the wrong person to mess with. If there was one promise she'd made to Violet that would come true, it was thus: she was *not* a victim any longer.

She held up the chains. Julian fumbled them over for a few excruciatingly long moments before his thumb pressed to a certain ridge. The shackles sprung free, and she felt a wave of power follow. Magic filled her every pore, so much stronger and concentrated than what she'd been able to wield as a newborn Sorceress. Even her connection to her occultarus felt stronger, and the tool flashed once in recognition that its mistress was back in control.

Above them, the Eye of Worlds started to rotate for the first time in a thousand years. It *screeeeeeeched* Lucia's deeds to the whole island.

Chapter 42
Alex

Alex stumbled his way out of the palace, gaining back his more fluid stride in stages as he fought the worst pain of his life. He'd emptied the contents of his stomach twice until all he had left was water and bile. Still, he persisted. He eyed the grand staircase that descended into the city and held fast to the side so he wouldn't tumble several stories to his death.

He felt his new power trickle in through his inner beast. The animal instincts were always a manifestation of his magic, growing stronger over time to the point where he had to assert dominance and control of his own body. Now, he felt those instincts more and more strongly until he and his magic were one and the same. He understood Sirius and his constant anger so much better when his own beast bayed for blood.

He and the beast were in complete agreement—they would tear Lucia limb from limb for what she'd done when she was in the proper body. A part of him hoped she could feel his fury over whatever shred of bond remained between him and the body she'd stolen.

His boots were a few short steps from steady ground when a piercing shriek boomed from the center of the island. Grunting, he covered his ultrasensitive ears and felt a shift in the night air. Every pore on his body prickled to instant awareness moments before it happened. Silvery moonlight burned above him, breaking through the palace in the shape of a full disc. In the land of constant gloom, the moon was like a spotlight. The white stone of Nyixa started to glow from its cold glare.

Only one moon, though—and it wasn't from Earth. He knew the sun was up on this midsummer day. This island was just a step away from magical Faerie.

He mustered his resolve, at first jogging and then sprinting toward the center of the island and the Eye of Worlds. The massive orb's swishing was audible to his sharpened hearing. From what little he knew of the thing, it was a bad omen.

A cloud of darkness swept by him as he ran, turning pitch-black eyes his way briefly. Adrius inclined his head with a severe frown. He bore himself swiftly on magic.

Alex returned the acknowledgement, glad the king got off his throne for something. *"Lucia's not Lucia right now,"* he warned.

"What do you mean?" Adrius demanded, taking his full form as he emerged into the ruined square where the Eye of Worlds sat.

Julian was bent over Lucia's body, helping her to her feet. He wondered fleetingly when his friend had gotten here, but now wasn't the time to ask questions. Several stories above them, Violet's body channeled magic into the magical tool as it picked up speed. *"Lucia and Violet have swapped bodies."*

"That's impossible," Adrius said flatly, drawing his sword in a scrape of metal. He marched swiftly across the square until two people emerged from the shadows. Alex only recognized them by their Blood Prince maroon eyes.

"The queen requires full concentration," said the thinner of the two, drawing two pistols with a fumble. Adrius scoffed, probably not realizing how much deadlier the smaller, modern weapons were compared to his sword.

The other Prince cracked his knuckles, face hardened with determination. He said nothing, charging directly at Adrius. "Step aside, Taryn. I don't want to hurt you," the king said. He caught Taryn's fist, thrusting him away.

Alex rushed the other man as he took aim at Adrius with both pistols. One went off, the bullet embedding harmlessly into the side of a collapsed building. "If it isn't the queen's new plaything," said the Blood Prince.

Snarling like an animal, Alex tried to force a demi-shift and felt his body responding to the technique for the first time. His hand transformed into a heavy bear paw, scoring deep furrows in the other man's face. *"Never,"* he snapped.

Disengaging and touching the wounds, he shook his head. "My queen said you'd be asleep."

"Surprise." Alex didn't give him a moment to rest, trying to wrest one of his pistols away as he hulked up with a gorilla's strength. The demi-shifts were the pinnacle of shapeshifting strength, giving him the control of his human side with the best aspects of his inner beast.

A bullet whizzed past the two of them. Julian was on his feet, Lucia's body gone. He was holding the smoking gun, cold gaze focused on them. His fingers jittered on the trigger, sending a second shot awry. But it was the distraction Alex's adversary needed, landing a punch to his sternum and sending him to the ground with a wheeze.

"It's really too bad the queen needs you," he said scornfully, bashing Alex over the head with the butt of his weapon. "I don't know what she was thinking, picking you for a mate. Taryn and I have both served her faithfully since before you were born."

Alex saw stars as he dodged the next bludgeon, rolling to his feet with a cat's grace. "Maybe she wanted someone with a brain in their skull," he grunted.

His outraged reply was drowned out by a flash and a loud crack of thunder. And then another. They both glanced up to see Violet and Lucia circling each other midair, tossing projectiles at once another. From Violet's body's hands came lightning bolts, which she shot one after the other, her head thrown back in a soundless cackle.

Lucia's body only dodged, wavering uncertainly as she made a clumsy symbol midair. She threw a fireball back, but it tumbled past to fizzle on the rocks. His heart lurched at the display, not needing to see how vicious the real Lucia fought to know that his mate was outmatched in experience.

He took the other man's momentary distraction and used it to grab one of his weapons. He fired a bullet into his kneecap, sending him howling to the ground and grasping his bleeding leg with a pitiful moan. "Shoot him! Kill him!" he screamed back at Julian, who turned his gun reluctantly toward Alex.

Realization hit him a moment before the bullet did, whizzing off his arm in a hot trail of pain. He couldn't see Julian's enthralled expression this far out, but it was the only explanation. Bending down, he slammed the butt of his weapon down on the Blood Prince's head, silencing his cries as he knocked him unconscious.

Julian's arm dropped. Alex glanced to where Adrius and Taryn were still fighting, equally matched as they traded blows with growing ferocity. He decided that they could handle each other and rushed over to his friend's side. "Are you yourself?" he demanded.

The other man breathed hard as he turned a hooded look Alex's way. "Elandros was controlling me, but you knocked him out...I'm so sorry—"

"Save it." They'd have plenty of time to talk it out later. "Do you see the occultarus orbiting around them both? The magic orb?" Julian nodded curtly. They watched the Sorceresses trade magic.

"It's made of glass," Alex said, lifting one of the two pistols he'd stolen from his opponent.

Chapter 43
Violet

Violet may have been in the stronger body, but she found herself dodging lightning strikes rather than making her own magic in return. She knew why Lucia went for the spell and started using it back, her eyes feeling like they were melting in their sockets as flash after flash blinded her. To make a lightning bolt, the hand gesture was to extend her fingers and thrust out her arm. It was one of the least complicated gestures to make for such a devastating effect.

Below them, the Eye of Worlds picked up speed. She was worried it would open a portal any moment, spilling out the creatures that'd made vampires a necessity all those years ago. There were maybe minutes left before their darkness was unleashed on the world again. And Lucia wasn't going down without a vicious fight, firing magic constantly.

"Give it up, girl. You've lost." Lucia spoke with Violet's voice. She'd even taken that, assuming everything about her.

"Never," she hissed.

"I won't have the Fell spare you. They'll eat you all—even your mate."

Violet gasped, her gaze flashing downward. She saw Alex's graceful figure sprinting across the courtyard, heading for Julian. As she did, Lucia hit her square in the chest with a blast of electricity. Her muscles danced erratically with the surge, and she dropped several feet with a panicked cry.

"Think I would spare him, did you? I only needed him to power the portal. He is not trustworthy enough to sit by my side," Lucia laughed.

"You mean...he won't lick your boots," Violet managed to say, floating out of the way of the next blast of lightning at the last moment. *"He saw through you, didn't he?"*

"Shut up, girl," she snarled, clawing both hands and charging a ball of electricity over her head.

She couldn't help it, she snickered. *"Even in my body, you couldn't seduce my lifemate!"*

Lucia roared wordlessly, the energy building and mounting between her palms.

Violet heard a more subtle popping noise from below, her eyes widening with shock as a bullet struck the occultarus orbiting her real body and sent it hurtling backward. She watched Lucia turn toward it too, just in time to watch a spider web of cracks form around the impact point. It wobbled violently, exploding the next moment in a hail of glass shrapnel.

Lucia screamed as her spell failed, falling straight on her head. Her body went shock-still midair, tipping backward and falling head-first toward the ground in a flash of blonde hair. "Violet! I got her! Stop the portal!" Alex bellowed.

Violet turned to the giant tool spinning furiously and generating its own version of electricity in pitch-dark sparks of lightning. She grasped Lucia's occultarus with a shaking hand, knowing she had seconds. Reaching with her magic, she stared directly into its dark surface. Her reflection showed the body she'd been shoved in, riddled with black veins and a Fell's soulless stare.

It shifted and changed while she watched, becoming her true self looking back at her, wearing that beautiful silver gown.

"Stop!" She shouted the command with everything in her. *"You have to stop!"*

Something within the massive tool pushed back at her. She had the sense it was asking something.

"Are you willing to pay the price?"

Her reflection changed to that of a different woman, a blonde with a crown of golden hair and eyes of the same shade. She stood against a backdrop of ashy dunes, surrounded by shadowy people. *"Nyah, long-lost queen,"* it whispered. It *was* talking to her in a chorus of quiet voices, like its laughing sprites all whispered in her ear.

"You have to stop," Violet said, not recognizing the woman who wore tight-fitting leather clothing, her gaze piercing and fierce.

"Are you willing to pay the price?" it repeated. It projected a monster creeping up behind the woman, its many-fanged maw sinking into her flesh. It ate the proud queen in great bites right before her eyes as she cried out in shock. *"This fate awaits her. You could save her."*

She wavered but realized that it was stalling once more. For whatever reason, the Eye of Worlds *wanted* this particular portal open. *"You're lying!"* she shouted. *"Stop! I command you to stop!"*

"As you wish."

It didn't slow down so much as try to abruptly change direction. It was like throwing a car in motion into sudden reverse. Metal grinded on metal, and the whole structure wobbled with a piercing shriek. Its metal support buckled as she watched with her mouth hanging open in shock.

Sheets of glass cracked with the sound of shattering ice. It shook as violently as Violet's occultarus had before it exploded. She scrambled to fly out of the way, thinking the same thing would happen here. Down below, she saw several shocked faces— all the Blood Princes had arrived to tackle either the threat or each other. Friend and foe alike watched cracks thread through the glass dome.

It didn't explode—yet. But the first chip fell from it, landing on the white stone with a splintering crash. *"A thank you for my freedom, Sorceress,"* the chorus of voices whispered in her ear. A massive pulse of magic followed, invisible but *felt*. It raced over Violet with the force of a tidal wave, and she felt herself freeze, pinwheeling through the air as she began to crash. She squeezed her eyes just before the moment of impact, hearing the muffled *thump* of flesh and clothing hit the ground. But she didn't feel any pain from the landing.

She gasped and opened her eyes just to find herself in Alex's arms. Her whole body hurt, still twitching uncontrollably from the massive surge of electricity it'd taken. Her body! She lifted a smooth, silver-veined hand, seeing a glass shard sticking out of her forearm. "Violet?" he said tentatively. "Is it really you?"

"I couldn't be happier to see you if...if I fried. Which I feel like," she said, working a stiff jaw.

Alex made a choked sound somewhere between a laugh and sob, bundling her close.

"Sorceress!" Adrius bellowed. "Get us to safety! Now!"

They startled apart. Violet spared a glance for the Eye of Worlds, which continued to rock violently. It would explode at any moment, and this time, the blast would be much worse than her occultarus shattering from a bullet. But that meant she didn't have her magic tool to help her spell work, and her arms felt like putty now that the aftershocks were subsiding.

"Put me down," she whispered to Alex. He steadied her as she wobbled, her fingers trembling. It felt like an eternity before she locked her thumbs and forefingers in the symbol for portal, connecting it to the only place she could think of—Alex's mansion. Jaromir went through first, transporting Gwendolyn's body in a fireman's carry. Korin followed with Neala. A massive wolf with a bloodied muzzle came next, whom she assumed was Sirius. His red gaze flashed to her briefly before he was gone.

"Where's everyone else?" she asked, quivering all over with effort.

"Lucia made a portal for herself and her lackeys," Adrius said curtly, bashing her fingers apart instead of going through to safety. "There are still mortals on this island. I will not leave them here to die."

Alex snarled as he loomed over her protectively. "Make me a portal there now," Adrius commanded.

Violet felt her sight swimming as she made the symbol again. Alex carried her through this portal as they emerged into an encampment with several men and women scrambling around. "Now another to safety. One more, Sorceress," Adrius commanded.

"You can do it," Alex murmured, now holding her upright. Their mating bond punched back into being at just the right moment. She felt his focus on her, feeding her an influx of his steady strength. She forced a third portal into existence, also leading back to the mansion.

Adrius did most of the work, shouting orders and shoving every mortal he could find through the portal. "I don't sense anyone else. Do you?" he asked Alex, who flared his nostrils.

He shook his head, his eyes on the horizon. The Eye of Worlds was a distant dome now, leaking a steady stream of darkness. It rocked one last time before bursting with the fallout of a nuclear explosion. The sky around the center of the island parted, its eternal darkness pierced as a second shockwave of magic erased it in a rapidly growing circle. Deadly sunlight flooded in in its absence. Violet's mouth hung open, frozen by the display. Luckily, someone had more presence of mind, dragging her through the portal she'd made before she could be burnt to a crisp.

Her hands fell to her sides, the portal disappearing before the fallout could follow them through. She leaned back into Alex's strength, feeling her body sag with relief. "Scariest hours of my life," she said in an undertone for his ears alone. The front foyer was a chaos of people and one very confused maid, who observed panicking humans mixing with wounded Ancients, two semi-conscious vampiresses, and a large wolf.

"Of *your* life?" he sighed, giving her a squeeze. They laughed together, subsiding to a tired lean as the morning's events hit them both. Over their mating bond, she felt that he was as exhausted and battered as her.

"Of both of our lives," she amended, leaning her head back on his shoulder.

He turned a tender gaze her way, brushing a ringlet from her eyes. "I thought I'd lost you," he said. "That, somehow, my protection just wasn't enough."

Shaking her head, she said, "It happened so fast. There was nothing you could've done. I just wonder...if Lucia had planned this out so perfectly, why did she fail at the very end?"

Alex smiled knowingly. "She forgot that I am, forever and for always, Team Violet. But I can tell you the full story later." He glanced up as Samuel approached them, his curly hair pulled every which-way.

"You two look knackered," he said by way of greeting. "What the hell is going on?"

"That's about how I feel. We're both in need of your wife's services," Alex replied, looking over the foyer and everyone milling about. He sighed. "We need to extend hospitality to all of these new vampires. It's only right when they took Violet and me in."

"And the mortals?" Sam asked.

He scratched the back of his head. "Them as well. I think they need to have a full memory wipe of what they just saw on Nyixa. If there's even a Nyixa anymore."

"That sounds like a story," his deputy remarked, his lips quirking. "Why don't you two go to the infirmary? I'll send for Melanie and take care of the rest."

"You're worth your weight in gold, Samuel Rainey." Alex clapped him on the shoulder.

"I'm getting a raise?" He laughed, waving them away.

Taking a good look at Violet, Alex swept her off her feet as her gait grew more sluggish. "Hey. You did great today," he whispered in her ear. "You saved all of us."

She sank into his hold, letting her eyes close. "I decided I wasn't going to be a victim anymore. And that no one, not even Lucia, could force me to be one again."

The last thing she remembered was his proud voice as she promptly drifted to sleep. "That's my mate."

Chapter 44
Alex

A good Gifted healer could get most vampires back on their feet after a life-threatening injury within a few days. Alex stayed awake long enough to confirm that it was Jaromir, not Melanie, who would see to their injuries. After a peacefully dark, dreamless sleep, he woke tucked under the white sheets of an infirmary bed, feeling groggy but mended. His phone read that it was a little over a day later. Midsummer had come and past.

In the bed next to him, Violet lay sprawled out with her blonde hair forming a halo around her. His heart swelled immediately to see her whole and healed of all the scratches that'd marred her arms and face.

She'd asked what had gone awry in Lucia's plan and he'd immediately known what it was. Lucia wasn't expecting just how much he loved the woman resting just out of reach. He would've walked through the sweltering desert barefoot if it meant another day together with Violet.

They'd done it; they'd thwarted Lucia's immediate plans. Something told him a future seer such as herself would have some sort of backup—but that wasn't important now. He sat up, feeling how fluidly his body rolled into motion. His inner beast was a content, if heavy, presence at the back of his head. Its strength reminded him of what he was now.

There was a very real possibility that Lucia's stunt with the silver potion had catapulted him to Ancient status. He would see very soon if he were truly like his father, a daywalker from Sirius's bloodline. A change in status would be both a blessing and a curse. On one hand, he would no longer have to play second fiddle to Cossette in the political frontier. But on the other, he had lost the ability to stay low and avoid strife. He would also need to watch himself for signs of the corruption Gwendolyn worried so deeply about stopping. Lucia had painted a big, silver cross on his back the moment she'd stepped into his life.

By his bedside rested an envelope with his name written in Julian's bold hand. He frowned, taking a look inside to find a typed letter and two shoulder badges with Coven Rehnquist's lion insignia. Their presence alone made Alex dread reading the letter. He symbolically asked for the insignia back of anyone leaving his coven who'd served as one of his enforcers.

It was worse than he'd thought. He was in the middle of reading it a second time when Violet stirred, groaning as she swiped at her eyes. "Is something wrong?"

"Nothing we can fix right now," he responded, offering her a hint of a smile. "Julian wrote out everything you both went through and more." His smile shaded to a toothy grimace. "I've never wanted to kill someone more than Lucia."

"Do we really have to talk about her right now?" She covered her head with a pillow.

"No, love." He set the letter aside with a sigh. "The only other thing you need to know is that Armando is in the hospital right now but making a recovery. And Julian has gone rogue."

"Rogue? Like, he's left the coven?" She peeked out at him with a soft gasp.

He flipped Julian's old insignia against his palm, lips quirking. "He knows I would never accept his resignation in person, so he told me in a letter. Apparently, he's about to do something he doesn't want reflected on the rest of us, which is utter rubbish because it will anyway and I'd help him do it, whatever it is."

Sliding out of her bed, she slipped in with him, her arm circling over his chest. "Hey, it's all right," she said.

He turned, catching her lips with his own. Her presence

was a balm on his jagged thoughts, smoothing out the uncertainty of the moment. Julian would come back to them when his business was done, for better or worse. But they had each other. Lucia had only succeeded in bringing them closer together.

JAROMIR CAME TO CHECK ON THEM A LITTLE LATER TO FIND Violet dozing in the circle of Alex's arms. He checked them over to give them both a clean bill of health. "You may want to change and head to your meeting room," he suggested. "Adrius is holding a war council as we speak."

"I'm sorry. Did you just say Adrius was doing something productive?" Alex asked dryly.

Violet smothered a yawn and elbowed his side. "Don't be rude."

Glancing between them, the soft-spoken Blood Prince cracked an amused smile. "He is indeed doing something productive."

"Well, I have to see this," he remarked. They parted ways for him and Violet to head back to the master bedroom and change.

She put on jeans and a tee, stubbornly not dressing herself up except for a smattering of eyeshadow. With her hair up in a ponytail, she was herself, not the beauty queen Lucia had tried to make her.

He hadn't seen a more beautiful sight in his life. It also exposed her graceful neck, which he took the opportunity to kiss as she inspected herself in the mirror. "Do I look ready for war?" she asked, pressing against his muscled front.

"Armed and ready." He teased his lips over her pulse, wishing they didn't have more pressing business. "I've gotten spoiled from our camping trip."

"Constant darkness and humidity?" she deadpanned.

"No. Constant you and me time," he said with a wink. "I intend to have more of that as soon as this meeting is over."

Her coy smile said that was just what she was thinking as

well. She turned, taking his hands in hers. "Thank you for saving me."

"No. Thank *you*." He rested her palm over his heart, in perfect sync with hers because of their bond. "You could still be a safe, ordinary mortal right now if it wasn't for me."

"Yeah, well, normal is boring." Her eyes sparkled like coins as she smiled up at him in adoration.

"Isn't that the truth?" He was laughing as their lips met, mutual love sparkling over their bond. Alex would rather be nowhere else than in her arms.

Chapter 45
Alex

THEY ARRIVED AT ALEX'S BOARD ROOM, A FORMAL PLACE FOR business affairs with enough seating for twenty comfortably, to find Adrius at the head of the table chatting casually with Gwendolyn, the two of them sipping from a set of champagne flutes. Neala, only notable from her mental voice and flame-red eyes, was wearing a different woman's glamor, complete with a curved figure and a dress she kept plucking at uncomfortably. She was mid-story to Korin and Sirius, gesturing animatedly and drawing a laugh from them both. Jaromir was on his feet, playing waiter with a bottle on ice and more full glasses on the side-table.

Alex and Violet paused at the door to take in this scene, exchanging an incredulous glance. "They're not fighting," she whispered.

"Gwendolyn and Neala are all right, too," he whispered back.

They were also all wearing modern clothing, looking less like something out of the pages of a storybook and more like they belonged. Adrius picked at his short sleeves, the edges pressing into his muscled biceps, but otherwise, he was smiling and relaxed. He was the first to notice them. "Please, sit," he said.

"This is a war council, hmm?" Alex asked, sitting at the other table end with Violet to his right. Jaromir passed them both champagne flutes.

"We knew it'd take you a while to arrive. The other guests

should be joining us shortly as well," he said, toasting them and drinking down his own alcohol. "Another!" he called to Jaromir, who refilled his glass.

"Who brought the champagne?" Violet asked, sipping hers slowly.

"I did, dear. Enough for everyone," Gwendolyn said, smiling over at her. "We have a cause for celebration even as we plan for the future."

"What's the...?" she drifted off as three strangers walked into the room, her mouth hanging open. She nudged Alex, jerking her head toward them.

He drew to his feet to greet them properly, and she followed suit. "Welcome to my coven's headquarters. And you are?" he asked, taking in the group. They had no auras to speak of but wore otherworldly beauty like a shroud of grace.

The shorter of the two women strode forward first, wearing a big smile over delicate features and a waterfall of blonde hair. Her blue eyes seemed to twinkle as she stuck out a hand. "Thank you for your hospitality. I'm Sorsha—and this is Keegan and our good friend, Ash."

She wore an unfamiliar style of dress, a scarlet gown hugging her curves, embroidered with filigree that was purple until she moved. It shifted colors to green and gold, showing flowers and gilt insect wings. She'd thrown a velvet, hip-length cape over her shoulders that shimmered between the earthy colors of her gown's embroidery.

The only man of the group was straight from a renaissance fair, a sword at his side and a similar cape flowing over his left shoulder. He wore dark gloves and a no-nonsense expression so reminiscent of Julian that Alex felt a pang of regret that his friend wasn't here to see all this for himself.

It was the last woman, tall and curvy, wearing a full set of dark leather armor that held hints of hidden weapons that convinced him he knew why Violet was still gaping next to him. "You're fae, aren't you?"

Sorsha bowed and flashed a wink that made her eyes literally sparkle as if filled with star shine. "You're so *pretty*," Violet blurted.

"Aww, thank you, sweetheart," Sorsha said with a brief giggle. "I see which virtue you have. Catch me after this meeting, okay? My mother shared you need a new occultarus." She gestured down the table to where Neala was watching them interact intently. "If you'd excuse me actually…"

She went over and hugged Neala's side, leaving the other two fae standing there. Keegan wavered uncertainly, and Alex remembered that Neala had adopted both him and Sorsha alike when they were merely babies. "Did you come over after the Eye of Worlds exploded?" Violet asked them.

He turned to her, a frown tugging at his lips. "Yes."

"And you helped Gwendolyn and Neala wake up from the languor dust?"

"Sorsha did." He patted the sword at his side. "She does magic. I just hit things."

"He's terrible at it." If Sorsha's voice was a bright chirp, Ash's was smoky and low. She smirked when he turned to glare at her.

"Don't mind her. She doesn't mean it," he said.

"I do. I mean it," she insisted, her smirk sparking to a full smile. "You probably haven't noticed I'm different from those two." She gestured between the other two fae.

Violet's brows furrowed in confusion while Alex kept his mouth shut. Their glamor made them all seem like average people to him. "First lesson in fae. Seelie like Sorsha and I only tell the truth," Keegan said for Ash when she glanced to him. "Unseelie like Ash can only tell lies unless you catch them on a good day. She's *very* fluent in sarcasm."

"Oh, guess we'll get along then," Alex said dryly.

"Guess we will," she responded, equally dry.

Alex turned as he heard more footsteps approaching. *More guests?* He wondered just how many people his new guests had sought fit to invite. The fae, he wanted to pick their brains. But he couldn't see who else they'd want to invite…until Cossette walked in, her hair done up in a messy bun trimmed off by a length of red ribbon the same shade as Sorsha's dress.

"Good evening, Mister Rehnquist," she said cheerfully. Arriving behind her was another surprise. One by one, every coven master except for Rockefeller and Collins lined up behind her, wearing expressions that ran the gamut from nervous to be in the presence of so many Ancients to gazing at Alex and the rest hopefully.

"I heard we were having a war council meeting," Cossette continued, gesturing to the men and women behind her. "I brought my alliance to join you."

Between them, they held most of New York's land, lacking only Coven Rockefeller's district and the abandoned subway tunnels Haven liked to skulk in. No great loss compared to the fighting force these coven masters represented.

If only Julian could see the power in this room, coming together for a common goal: taking down Lucia.

Something told him that Julian's solo task concerned the fallen vampire queen. For him, revenge was a personal affair. Alex felt a flicker of nerves in his heart. "Good to have you all. Have a seat. Make yourself comfortable. We've got a lot of planning to do."

Want more Blood Legacy? The story continues with Julian and his lifemate in...
The Winter Key: Blood Legacy Series Book 2

Also by Elise Hennessy
Altare World

Are you ready for a high-flying adventure on gryphon-back? Join Sivana as she becomes the first female cadet at the highly competitive Gryphon Rider Academy after the blind gryphon Arimus chooses her as his new rider.

Dragon Riders of Pern meets Song of the Lioness in this YA fantasy series in which a pair of underdogs rewrite what's possible in a formerly all-boys military academy.

- See Gryphon Rider Academy on Amazon -

Also by Elise Hennessy

Join an unlikely crew of five misfits and a mouse as they strive to become one of Altare's newest elite spy teams. Heists and adventures await!

The Gilded Wolves meets Six of Crows in this YA fantasy series in which a former thief uses her skills to become a spy. If you like clever heroines, strong friendships, and found family, then you'll love Royal Spy Institute!

- See Royal Spy Institute on Amazon -

About the Author

Elise Hennessy is an author of young adult fantasy full of adventure and found family. She holds a master's degree in journalism and enjoys crafting unique stories. When Elise is not busy writing, she's trying to reduce her prodigious TBR list. She lives in Texas with her family and is owned by two cats.

Find out more about her books at: www.elisehennessy.com

Glossary

Blood Prince: A title given to the few Fell Hunters that survived the Fell Crisis. They are the first vampires and each started their own unique bloodlines.

Coven: A group of three or more vampires, assembled for the protection of its members. Large covens establish territory where they can hunt with reasonable assurance that they are safe. Coven members are sheltered by their coven master, the oldest and strongest vampire in the group. A vampire without a coven is considered a rogue and often live short lives due to vampires' natural territorial tendencies.

The Crossing: Seelie fae can cross The Veil and travel between Earth and Faerie or vice versa during midsummer in a magical process called The Crossing. The only way to otherwise cross between the two worlds is through one of a handful of well-hidden portals.

Deveaux Accords: A set of laws created by the major covens of New York City and enforced by Ancient vampiress Cossette Deveaux. Covens are required to police their members to keep mortals safe.

Eyes of Worlds: A pair of giant tools that anchor The Veil into place. One was created by the willing sacrifice of an Archangel—it is the Light Eye located in Faerie. The other was created from an unwilling greater demon—it is located on Nyixa Island on Earth.

Faerie: A separate world magically linked to Earth. The place of origin for all magic and mythical creatures.

Fell: A fae afflicted with a curse of eternal hunger. The curse was spread from Fell to fae via a bite and was considered incurable. Fell are twisted creatures known for squat, frog-like legs, sharp and interconnected teeth like a bear trap, black veins, and pitch-black eyes. All Fell were banished from Faerie to The Fell Lands. The Fell Crisis or Fell War occurred when the Fell learned they could create portals to Earth during the Dark Ages and began consuming man and beast alike like a black tide of locusts. After their defeat, all records of the Fell were expunged from mortal record to hide the existence of vampires.

Fell Hunter: The first vampires. Soldiers exposed to Fell blood became strong and fast enough to fight Fell in the service to humanity. Though the first Fell Hunters were turned by accident, many were turned on purpose after the phenomenon was studied. In those days, being a vampire was considered a sacrifice for the greater good. Most Fell Hunters died fighting monsters.

Fell Keys: Thirteen in total, referring to a set of rings with gemstones of pure magic. Each one represents one of the schools of fae magic and grants the wearer great power.

Fell Madness: The boogeyman of vampirism. First manifested in Fell Hunters when they consumed too much Fell blood. Fell Madness gives vampires black veins, a mouthful of sharp teeth, and endless hunger for blood. Very little is known about the affliction because those that manifested it were swiftly executed. In modern day, the affliction can be cured by an Alchemyst's potion.

The Gift: Some vampires manifest the Gift rather than the abilities of their bloodline. They are capable of healing others from even the worst of mortal wounds. The Gift leaves if a vampire uses it to harm or kill others.

Lifemate: A perfect match to a vampire. It is possible to identify a lifemate on sight and many vampires describe the sensation as being as subtle as a punch to the gut. A lifemate is usually a vampire's perfect opposite. It is possible for a vampire to have more than one lifemate, but the phenomenon is exceedingly rare as most vampires don't survive to an advanced age if they lose their first lifemate.

Nephilim: A person with angel parentage, who is capable of wielding light magic.

Nyixa Island: A chunk of The Fell Lands that the Fell managed to drag to Earth. It is a relatively large island with the Dark Eye at its center. After the Fell were defeated, vampires made it their seat of power before it was sunk to the bottom of the ocean in a bid to eradicate Fell Madness. It has only resurfaced recently in modern times and is considered inhabitable.

Occultarus: A tool used by Sorcerers to concentrate their magic. Instead of using complicated gestures to summon magic, a Sorcerer can hold an occultarus and cast spells more quickly. An occultarus is a sphere of glass forged by dragon fire and contains concentrated magic within. The Eyes of Worlds were modeled after occultari and are giant versions of them.

Sorcerer: Originally a distinction for the rare fae who can control all thirteen schools of magic, this title is also awarded to the sub-class of vampire that has silver blood and the ability to control every school of fae magic. Sorcerers are highly trained and often manifest extra rare abilities called virtues. The five virtues are: true sight, future sight, empathy, druidism, and mediumship.

Vampire: Descendants of the original Fell Hunters, spread by their cursed blood. The existence of vampires has become a myth to modern mortals as the purpose of vampires has tarnished from war heroes into former mortals trying to avoid their mortal coil. Contrary to popular myth, vampires are not walking corpses; they eat, breathe, and reproduce, though the chance of conception narrows as a vampire ages. Young vampires act a lot like humans with a taste for blood, though as they age they grow more powerful and inhuman. Vampires manifest an aura, which communicate to each other how old and powerful they are.

Cast of Characters

Modern Day Vampires
Residents of New York City's covens.

Alexander Rehnquist

A vampire nearing his five hundredth year. Master of Coven Rehnquist and skilled shapeshifter. He is bitter rivals with Bryant Collins and lost his first lifemate due to the conflict between their covens. Fate crossed him one night and he ended up partnered with a second lifemate, Violet Reynolds.

Violet Reynolds

Formerly a mortal zookeeper, Violet was exposed to vampirism after Lucia secretly turned her into a kind of vampire that hadn't been seen in a thousand years.

Julian Fairfax

One of the officers of Coven Rehnquist. The only vampire who mysteriously manifests an icy cold aura. He searched for his life-mate for hundreds of years until they were united via Lucia's machinations. He was viciously hunted by Lucia due to him killing her obsession.

Armando Nizzola

Julian's cousin and a member of the supernatural police.

Bryant Collins

A bitter rival to Alex and Coven Rehnquist. He owns the telecommunications company Haven and thus members of his coven are referred to as Haveners. He is an Ancient a religious zealot, and one of Lucia's allies.

Kim Cox

Bryant Collins's wife, known for her sadistic personality and enjoyment of torturing others.

Cossette Deveaux

The Ancient leader of the most powerful coven in New York City. She is an albino and a rare vampire who possesses future sight. She is stuck in the body of a little girl due to the twisted ideals of her vampire master. Due to her unique circumstances, her mind is damaged. She usually acts like a cheerful and sweet girl, but sometimes shows hints of her age as she delivers prophecies of the future.

Ancients

Surviving Fell Hunters whose bloodlines have shaped the vampire world in their absence.

Adrius

King of Vampires

Strongest Fell Hunter and owner of the Shield Key. He fell into a deep pit of depression to be separated from his lifemate, Nyah. Possesses every vampiric ability.

Lucia

The first vampire Sorceress and briefly Queen of Vampires in *Blood Curse* while struggling with the titular curse. Nyixa was sunk partially to contain her evil.

Gwendolyn Firetree

A nephilim who represents the grace of duty. Conspired to sink Nyixa in *Blood Curse* to contain Fell Madness and Lucia. She has committed her immortal existence to curbing the damage of old vampires on the brink of Fell Madness by making them mysteriously "disappear."

Sirius
Blood Prince Sirius, the Dawn
Adrius's second-in-command and brother. Was once a kind and giving man, but emerged from his thousand-year rest bitter, angry, and unable to fully control the whims of his inner beast. He is a shapeshifter and possesses the ability to walk in daylight without harm.

Korin
Blood Prince Korin, the Bane
The gentle giant of the Ancients, a steady and quiet personality. He is a blood tracker.

Neala
Blood Princess Neala, the Wraith
A mute orphan raised by Gabriel and Gwendolyn. She defied the odds and survived the Fell Crisis, though she sustained several terrible wounds that scarred her face and chest. Despite being an illusionist, she refuses to hide her scars or make herself more attractive and feminine. Loved and lost her first mate, Marcus Hartson, to Lucia's machinations.

Elandros
Blood Prince Elandros, the Legion
Possesses the ability to make minor illnesses and blights. Lucia is blackmailing him for a crime unknown, commanding his unwavering loyalty.

Jaromir
Blood Prince Jaromir, the Mender

The doctor of the surviving Ancients. He is in possession of the Gift.

Qin

Blood Prince Qin, the Ascended

He is considered a greedy coward by his peers, as he took a payment from Lucia and went into hiding, never to be seen again.

Taryn

Blood Prince Taryn, the Blade

Lucia's bodyguard due to taking a stage three love potion and being enslaved by his emotions.

Marcus Hartson

A close friend to the Ancients and Neala's former mate. After his mating bond was severed by Lucia, he was poisoned by her cursed blood and grew increasingly insane as the years passed. Died in an honorable duel with his son Julian after he drove the family to the brink of ruin from countless wars with other vampires. Deceased as of *Blood Curse.*